MW01242716

Dave,
Thank you, always, for your friendship. Welcome home, and God Bless!

BLOOD
of
PATRIOTS

by

Daryl E.J. Simmons

Copyright © 2017 by Daryl E.J. Simmons

All rights reserved. This book or any portion thereof may not be reproduced, distributed, or transmitted by any means, including photocopying, recording, or other electronic or mechanical methods, without the prior written permission of the publisher except for the case brief quotations embodied in critical reviews and certain other noncommercial uses permitted by copyright law. For permission requests, write to the author at the address below.

Thinkery Group, LLC
P.O. Box 1138
Skiatook, OK 74070

Printed in the United States of America

First Edition, 2017

ISBN: 978-1974179893

Cover images taken from the public domain. Layout and design Copyright 2017 by Daryl E.J. Simmons

Printed by CreateSpace, an Amazon.com company.

Edited by Daryl E.J. Simmons

Author photograph by Cindy Kay Photography

The story and all names, characters, and incidents portrayed therein are fictitious. No identification with actual persons, places, buildings, programs, or products is intended or should be inferred. Any similarity or resemblance between the contents of this story and any locations, events, objects, or persons - living or dead - is purely coincidental.

This story is a work of fiction created purely for the purpose of entertainment. It is entirely contrived by the author's imagination, with absolutely no involvement of the United States Government, its officers, offices, or subsidiaries. In accordance with the Information Security Oversight Office, Executive Order 13292, 13526, 13556, 13587, *ad nauseam*, as well as any and all applicable Department of Defense directives and instructions, no privileged or classified material is contained herein, nor was used in the creation of this story. This story is not authorized or endorsed by the United States Government, any of its branches, divisions, or subsidiaries. Any similarity between any portion of this story and any real government activities, offices, or programs is purely coincidental, and not based on any forethought, foresight, or foreknowledge the author may or may not possess.

DEDICATION

First, foremost, and always: I thank Jesus Christ my Savior, who carried me through the valley of the shadow of death. Several times.

This book - every word, every letter - is dedicated to the brave men and women, past and present, who serve our country in uniform: my brothers and sisters in the military and law enforcement. We are the one-half of one percent. Nobody who hasn't been there can truly understand what it feels like to sacrifice your time, your livelihood, your family, or the promise of a future in order to secure the Blessings of Liberty for millions of strangers. Remember that the promise we made had a purpose. Stay strong for each other. We are the real Americans.

My continued thanks and love to my wife, who makes me want to be a better man.

To Robert Jordan, who taught us to "have character; don't be one." And to Jeff Stokes, whose love for his country is exceeded only by his love for God. It is no coincidence that the two finest officers I ever had the privilege of knowing earned their salutes through excellence instead of being handed them with diplomas. Your selfless service and example are truly inspirational.

To the memory of Chief "Ryan" Owens, a good man who gave his life for people who are all too often unworthy of such sacrifice. And the family and friends who lay their beloved on the Altar of Freedom.

And finally, my most sincere thanks to every one of my readers. I hope that you've enjoyed the journey, and that I continue to write things that you read on purpose.

PROLOGUE

The pigs still left alive were panicking. The Patriot had already done more to fix his country than anyone in the last century, but his work had barely begun. People were taking notice, but there was still a long way to go before the thorns corrupting the Tree of Liberty were completely eradicated.

And it was time for the gardener to get back to pruning.

The Patriot did nothing to hide his anger as he walked down the metro street. He did not need to; not under the cover of darkness; not while wearing a hooded sweatshirt like a cowl.

In an area like this, most people were too afraid of each other to look one another in the eye. *Too bad,* the Patriot thought to himself. *You can tell what folks are thinking just by staring into their eyes.* People in Washington were always rude at best, and usually upset. The indignation he felt was written all over his face, but it was considered politically incorrect for anyone else to acknowledge it.

Camouflage, the Patriot remembered, *was never about wearing colors or patterns. It is about going unnoticed.* Physically blending into your surroundings was one way to be unseen, but a man could hide just as easily by standing in the open and surrounded by a million people if they refused to look at him. Or could not remember him. Or if the idea of accusing him came with a certain social stigma attached.

And so the wolf wore a blanket of political correctness like a sheepskin as he boldly strode down the Washington, D.C. streets. He stalked his prey, protected from prying eyes by the blinders that his own targets forced upon themselves. He was a hunter in an urban jungle - a veritable game preserve stocked with weak, fat pigs ready for the slaughter, but too afraid of what others in the herd might say about them if they called a killer a killer.

CHAPTER 1

DANNY LEANED INTO the turn. His armored left knee dragged along the black top, barely an inch away from another bike's drive wheel. He hugged himself tightly against his bike, then twisted hard on the throttle at the curve's apogee - the furthest point along its arc - to slingshot around the bend and into the straightaway. A quick glance to the sideline updated his progress.

His split time for this lap was faster than his first, but he felt like he could still shave a little bit more off of it. *Twelve hundredths slower than my personal best.* This morning's volunteer official frantically waved a white flag to indicate the start of his final lap.

He leaned forward and opened his throttle wide. His red-and-white Honda CBR1000rr threatened to lift up off the racetrack from the surge of acceleration, but Danny held the front wheel down and picked up speed. He commanded the beefy bike as if it was a thoroughbred mount and willed more speed from its one-liter engine. *Let's giddy-up and see what all these horses can do.*

The first turn on the track was a soft left. Danny started wide and feathered his throttle to maintain speed through the curve. Dashed sidelines flew by underneath him, their black and white stripes blurred. Almost immediately the track doubled back in a harder turn to the right. Danny kept his front tire married to the sideline and leaned inward.

He had the track all to himself. Most people were at work at ten o'clock on a Thursday. It was the perfect chance for a guy with some time on his hands to run trial laps. Newly cleaned fuel injectors helped bring the red rice rocket's tuned engine to an adrenaline-inciting scream.

Danny grew bold and decided to unleash all of the power between his legs. He snapped his bike up a fraction of a second earlier than he had during his previous lap and wrenched his right hand like he was trying to rip the throttle clean off. Most riders would not risk launching themselves out of a curve early like this for fear of tripping up another rider or flinging themselves off the outer bank. But today he had nobody else to worry about and something to prove to himself.

The aggressive maneuver made the bike jump out of the curve. Keeping both tires on the ground and underneath him was like balancing atop a 500lb. soap bubble while trying to hold it down on the ground… all while it tried to fly off the deck like a jet fighter from a catapult. A two-count of straight track was followed by another left-right S-turn, which he managed with quick shifts of his hips. Then a wide left that marked the rough midpoint of the lap put Danny right on top of the inner line again.

His engine howled and the world around him evaporated. He was in the zone. Danny might as well have been a dancer lost in an aerial, or a horse galloping through the open country. The roar of his bike totally disappeared. He came into the track's third straightaway like a crimson comet. A part of his own mind interrupted his flow with a reminder that the next and final section of the track started with a hard, deep curve to the right followed immediately by the sharp left that led into the final straightaway.

Time lost all meaning. He had been on the bike for years - or a few seconds. He had always ridden this bike, ever since the universe was first breathed into existence, and he would ride it for all of eternity. Yet this lap had only started a heartbeat ago. And then there was no motorcycle at all. There was only himself, flying inches off the ground, propelled across the streaking pavement by force of his own will.

This is the freedom you want. Now, earn it. Make yourself worthy of it.

To the trackside observer - if there was one - the red Honda ripped down the final stretch of track. If Danny's bike had been a little higher off the ground, local RADAR might have tracked him as a suspected cruise missile cutting though Virginia airspace. Danny visualized himself as a superhero flying toward justice. Long past the finish line, flashing green numbers from the track's lighted signboard snapped him out of his reverie.

Point one five seconds faster than that last lap. It was Danny's new personal best time for this track. He rose up from his crouched position and coasted to gently bleed off speed and let the CBR's engine cool down from its high output run before shutdown.

Back in the pit, Danny stood on aching legs. Acid buildup in his thigh muscles threatened to cramp him up, but he shook his feet to walk off the stiffness. He hydrated and considered another run, but the phone in his duffle bag was lit, indicating a missed call. Since the track was otherwise unoccupied, he listened to the message left on his voicemail.

"Hey, Danny" the familiar voice said, "it's Jonas Wiley. I hope you didn't leave town, son, 'cause we need you to come in this afternoon. The board just came to a decision regarding your suspension. Everybody's out for lunch right now, but afterward they'll make it official with a formal announcement. Two o'clock in the conference room. Be there."

* * *

"Special Agent Wakefield," an unfriendly black woman Danny did not know peered down through angular reading glasses perched upon the tip of her beak as she read the report in her hands. "After a preliminary review of the events leading to and during the attack against this facility, this panel has determined that there is sufficient grounds to merit a more in-depth inquiry into your conduct on the date in question. Over the last two weeks, we have heard testimony by a number of your peers and superiors containing allegations that you flagrantly, knowingly, and repeatedly violated standard operating procedures and policies put forth by the Department of Homeland Security. This, combined with allegations that you ignored orders from your superiors during a crisis, calls to question your fitness as an officer of this department." The harsh woman looked up from the paper and glared daggers into

Danny's soul. "Until such time that these questions have been answered to this panel's satisfaction, we feel that it would be inappropriate for you to remain in a duty status of any kind. You are therefore placed upon an indefinite administrative leave of absence effective immediately and to remain in effect until the Professional Review Board has made its determination." Danny maintained a rigid posture of attention while she continued. "While you will continue to receive your regular pay and benefits during this inquiry, your building access and other privileges are suspended. You are also prohibited from meeting with department personnel or discussing official business with anyone, including personnel, employees, representatives, the press, or public."

Danny found Dr. Jonas Wiley - his department head and mentor from the Secret Service Analysis Division - with his eyes. The older man sat a few seats down from the speaker, whose name plate identified her as Assistant Director Maxine Flowers. *Well,* Danny inwardly mused, *that appointment didn't take long.*

Wakefield knew that in the aftermath of Phillips' attack on DHS Headquarters there would be personnel changes. Cynthia Dagenhart, the recently interred Secretary of Homeland Security, was the most publicly addressed casualty from the incident, but hers was hardly the only chair in DHS with a new occupant this week. Some folks were injured, others resigned, and a few - of most immediate concern to Danny, of course, was Wakefield himself - were being made into examples.

Jonas' eyes met Danny's gaze, then the older man looked down silently at his own notes as AD Flowers continued her scripted speech. "You will not be afforded any additional privileges of official travel and are advised not to leave the area of your regular duty station." She lowered her angular face to read from the bottom portion of the page in her hands. "You are not authorized to act on the behalf of or at the behest of the United States Government in any capacity until further notice. In accordance with all applicable directives, you are also specifically prohibited from discussing this investigation or any of the events pertinent to it with any outside agency, department, individuals or organizations until its resolution. Any violation of these orders shall constitute grounds for immediate termination and possible prosecution." At that, she dropped the page and plucked the reading glasses from her nose. "Do you have any questions regarding these orders?"

"Respectfully, Ma'am," Danny gave the shortest of nods, "I assume at some point that the board will want to depose and debrief me?"

"That determination has not been made at this time," she dryly answered.

Danny's ears began to ring. "Surely, if I am to be the subject of an investigation, at some point you'll actually want to hear my side of the story."

"We will contact you when and if we have any questions."

Danny consciously forced his jaw shut and stifled the desire to further protest the way his suspension was taking shape. Sitting under a professional review board was basically the same as having his career put on trial. And while he knew it was wrong to try somebody *in absentia,* Danny also knew that they internal workings of the federal government were not always concerned with the niceties or rules of law, morality, or by any other metric of propriety outside of the officials' own whims. Danny knew when he was beaten, and he knew that stirring the pot today would only make the rest of the process more difficult for him. *Don't make enemies on the board,* he stewed. *Not today.*

"Special Agent Wakefield has already surrendered his badge and weapon to me," Dr. Wiley added. "As his supervisor, I will escort him out once this meeting is adjourned and secure his access badge."

"Then, if there are no further questions?" Flowers glanced around the room so quickly that Wakefield was unsure if anyone had the time to ask a question if they had one - and he doubted that any of them wanted to bother. "Very well. Dismissed."

Jonas rose from the long table more slowly than the rest of the review board. By the time his ambling pace carried him around to Danny, everyone else had already cleared the conference room. "Bit of a sticky wicket you're in, Danny boy."

Wakefield gave the man a cynical look. "Well, Father, you're the one who suspended me."

"Not by choice, son. I had my orders."

Before Wiley was appointed the head of the Secret Service's Analysis branch, he rose to the rank of Captain in the United States Navy, where he served as an intelligence officer. And a lifetime before that, Jonas benefitted from a Jesuit education. Though the older man was more cerebral than Wakefield was, Danny usually saw his mentor as something of a kindred spirit. They were similar in many, many ways. And since Danny knew how obliged he felt to follow his own orders - even if he did sometimes reinterpret them along the way - he had a fair guess as to how the man he jokingly referred to as 'Father' felt, when he was similarly tasked.

Danny plucked the access badge from his suit jacket's breast pocket. "Any suggestions on what I should do with all of this time I've suddenly got on my hands?"

Wiley slowly walked him down the hallway toward the main exit. Clearly, he was in no hurry to see Wakefield drummed out of a job. "Think of it as a vacation."

"One where I can't go anywhere."

"Okay, a stay-cation, then. Just do whatever you normally do when you're not at work."

"Sleep?"

Jonas chuckled. "Pursue your hobbies. Relax with your friends."

Danny nodded. "I've taken the bike to the track four times in the last week. And all of my friends are feds."

"Just don't talk about work," the old Jesuit reminded him. "Other than that, nobody cares. Just do me a favor."

"Name it."

"Make good decisions," Jonas warned. "This suspension is a tough rap, but it's beatable."

Danny considered his mentor's advice for a few silent steps. Then they reached the door to the antechamber between the hallway and the parking lot. A pair of armed security guards made a show of not watching him as he departed. "Thanks," he extended his right hand, "for everything."

Dr. Wiley took Danny's hand into his own warm grip and smiled. "Take care of yourself, Danny boy." He winked, "And say 'hi' to that lady friend of yours for me."

CHAPTER 2

MALIQ ABDUL SHIBAAB was an angry black man - probably the angriest black man of his day. As the leader of the New Black Panther Party, he was always upset about something. And his indignation was never more fervent than when there were cameras to capture the melodrama that accompanied him as faithfully as any other member of his entourage.

Tonight, though, there were no cameras. Shibaab's personal security detail - rough men hand picked from within the New Black Panther Party's ranks - made sure those who attended the late night private meeting at Shibaab's office surrendered any electronic device capable of recording the proceedings. Such recordings had a way of surfacing at inconvenient times, and discretion required a certain level of deniability.

The violent and brutal murder of so many national figures put the Capital Police on high alert.

Overtime was stretched as far as the department could afford. Despite the extra shifts, many officers were earning money on the side by hiring themselves out as armed security escorts and guards to congressmen and other high profile individuals in the D.C. Metro area. The city's strict gun laws prohibited virtually anyone but the police from owning and possessing firearms. As a solution, a number of Washington's more affluent persons simply hired cops to protect them.

In the months that the Constitutional Killer had been active, enough officials were killed - either at his hands or his followers' - that paid protective services had gotten hard to come by in D.C. The laws of supply and demand applied. Increased demand resulted in increased cost for services rendered and fewer persons available for hire to new clients. Unofficially, some officials had started to find creative solutions to their security problems.

The Benning Park Community Center was not a priority for D.C. Metro patrols. Located in the Capitol Heights area on the Maryland side of town, most Metro cops would think twice about responding to a call for service to that particular building. And when the police did go into the area, it was rarely without backup. The rough neighborhood was a breeding ground for inner city gangs and related violence and drug use. Many of the residents had either spent some time in jail or narrowly avoided it. This fact was especially true of black males between seventeen and thirty five years of age.

That was the exact demographic the New Black Panther Party targeted in its recruitment efforts. And, as a result, the exact description of the large men that always accompanied Maliq Shibaab, and the other security goons he had stationed outside each of the doors to the community center while he conducted a discreet, late night visit. Large, unhappy, violent-looking black men. Six outside, paired to stand watch at the building's main entrance, rear, and emergency exit and two more as his personal bodyguards.

The Patriot had circled the building just once, so as to avoid being seen twice by any of the sentries. He had counted a half dozen 'brotha's' spread amongst the building's doorways. The enforcers did not display firearms, but he knew they were armed - no matter what the city's gun control laws said. Raising suspicion during the recon phase would surely ruin his chances of catching the gorillas by surprise, and he did not want to blow the operation tonight.

Discretion and thoroughness had kept the Patriot three steps ahead of his enemies his entire career. This professional focus had certainly helped him stymie his latest adversaries. Law enforcement officials cluelessly ran in circles in a vain effort to find him. In that spirit, the Patriot had initially planned for an evening spent gathering intelligence and collecting pattern of life data on his next target.

Just two days ago, he tagged the target's vehicle with a radio frequency identification beacon - purchased online using a prepaid, disposable credit card which was in turn paid for in cash from a common retailer. The RFID tag was paired with a burner phone he bought with cash from a mall kiosk, so the phone gave the Patriot the beacon's exact location - and, therefore, the vehicle's.

The Patriot and his 'mates had done this kind of human targeting during the war. He knew how the game was played. Two days of observation rarely provided sufficient data to understand a target's pattern of life - to understand their network of contacts with enough fidelity to fix him or her and forecast their activities with any degree of reliability. Especially without a dedicated intelligence asset doing the majority of the surveillance and analysis like he had back with the team.

As the Patriot had begun following the target vehicle this evening, it had gone into a rather rough D.C. neighborhood. Nestled in the shadow of one of the wealthiest cities on Earth, this ghetto reeked of street violence. It was a stark contrast with the target's expensive home in upscale Alexandria. The Patriot played a hunch that his target, being a slime ball by nature, was up to something they did not want publicly known. And one of the interesting things about bad people's dirty dealings was that they often provided an opportunity for bad things to happen.

Maliq Shibaab sat in the community center's great room like a potentate in his own palace. He perched upon the cheap, metal folding chair as if it was the supple leather wingback in his own posh office. His hands rested upon a cheap, metal and plastic folding table with the same authority as they would have his rich mahogany desk. Slums like this were not his normal venue; Maliq rarely visited such indignant places, and only when he needed publicity. But tonight, despite the lack of cameras, the charismatic, militant black leader still showed his small audience that he was the king of all he surveyed.

"Please," the black woman pled, "You've got to help me."

"The New Black Panther Party hears the cries of all negroes oppressed in the United Snakes of America," Shibaab smugly replied. "What are you asking from Maliq Shibaab?"

"Look, Maliq -"

"*Brother* Shibaab," one of the big black brutes grumbled an interruption.

The black woman, dressed in an expensive pant suit designed to convey the authority with which she herself had grown accustomed, shot the thug a reproving glare. Then she sighed in defeat, "Brother Shibaab," she corrected herself, "I'm scared. There are no leads. This man is out offing folks left and right, an' they ain't got nuttin'! This cat is crazy, an' I need you to give me some heat. You know, some muscle to keep me safe."

The Patriot glanced down at his burner phone. If anyone observed him, it would have looked like he was checking a text. The cell phone confirmed that the black BMW 335i parked at the derelict community center was the same car which carried the targeting beacon. At this late hour, he expected the community center to be unoccupied. Surely, the normal staff were home. The Patriot doubted that the other vehicles in the lot - a Mercedes E6 and two Lincoln Navigators, all black - belonged to volunteers and youth councilors.

"Why, Congresswoman Jefferson," Shibaab grinned, "where is your army of cracker feds? Does the Injustice Department refuse to protect you?"

"Nobody knows where this asshole is," the Democrat from Austin replied in dismay. "Or who he'll hit next. He just disappeared. They're sayin' there's not enough manpower to put us all into protective custody."

"There will be," Shibaab sneered, "if this goes on much longer. Because once there are fewer rich white folk to protect, there'll be enough vanilla slaves to protect whoever's left."

"You saw the video online," the Jefferson pointed.

"Maliq Shibaab does not make it a habit to waste time partaking of the vulgarities of the white man's internet." A brief pause. "But, yes. And the ravings of some dark knight out to butcher white folk are of little concern to Maliq Shibaab. As a matter of fact, it really should come as no surprise to you, dear sister, that the New Black Panther Party is pleased to see whitey get his."

"It's only been white folk so far," LaDasha could not stop herself from trembling, "but this psycho wants to kill everyone in the government. How long do I have before he or one of his disciples comes after me?"

The Patriot had no idea about the community center's interior layout. He lacked the normal resources to assault and neutralize a target. Unequipped and uninformed, his preferred course of action under these circumstances would usually have been to exercise a little tactical discretion and fight another day. But his gut told him he was looking at a rare opportunity. Two high profile targets at the same place and time, and oh so close to him. *No,* he decided, *this is too good to pass up.* Fortune favored the bold. The Patriot walked right up to the community center's front door like he owned the place.

Maliq Shibaab was grandiose, self righteous, and a show boater. Pompous beyond almost any measure. But he was not stupid. He knew that Congresswoman Jefferson's security concerns were at the center of why she requested a meeting with him. He had already prepared his answer the moment his assistant relayed the request to him, hours ago when LaDasha had called his office. Still, he paused for a few seconds and pretended to consider his response.

"The New Black Panther Party cannot ignore the needs of such a - *dignified* - sister as yourself, Ms. Jefferson. It is clear to Maliq Shibaab that the white devil does not value the safety of a powerful black woman. Crackers would rather see a black woman dead than see her in Congress fighting for the black community. Maliq Shibaab will therefore allow you the temporary use of two of our brave black brothers to protect you where whitey obviously will not."

LaDasha let out a sigh of relief. "Thank you, Brother Shibaab."

"For a price, of course."

"I -" Jefferson's heart stopped dead for a moment. "Say what?"

The older black man sauntered up to the community center completely unfazed by the two behemoths standing on either side of the door. The stubble on his face and worn street clothes showed that he had seen better days, but his strut told the guards he still felt some fire in his belly. One pace away from the biggest brute, the one standing on the older man's left, the older man stopped and threw his head back in the common urban salute. "S'up, brotha?"

A low voice rumbled from deep within the larger man, who barely moved. "Can I help you, pops?"

Easily a decade older than the gorilla, the smaller man hissed in laughter. "Yeah, yeah. Say, listen, homes," the smaller man leaned in close and whispered, "I'mma got sum'tin for you, ah'ite? But you gotta gimme a li'l sum'tin sum'tin. How 'bout a hun'red?"

The ogre was not amused. "For what?"

"'Cuz I got just what you want, homes."

The brute pushed the older man backward, an easy task that barely required him to move his massive hands. "Burn out, pops. We're clean brothers."

Pops laughed and crept back in, still whispering. "Naw, naw… it ain't drugs, homes. That's cool and all, you bein' clean an' all, but I got sum'tin you *really* want. I got the dee-el on some cracker ass dude creepin' round the block." Anyone with more than two minutes of street time referred to discreet information as the DL, or 'down low.' "Look like he up to sum'tin. Like he a poh-poh or sum'tin." Hood rats rarely said the word *police* out loud. The first syllable alone was usually enough to make them scatter into the night.

The grumpy black giant raised an eyebrow ever so slightly as his dark eyes bore into the back of the older man's brain. The diminutive informant knew that he had the gorilla's attention. He could read the meat head's simple thoughts in real time as they were born: *Even a cop should know to avoid a neighborhood like this one so late at night.* "Where?"

"Homes," the scraggly little man hissed in a whispered yell, "I know you gotta be rollin,' what with them nice wheels and that Gucci gear you be wearin.' Jus' one Benjamin, and I bird dog that cracker ass fo' shizzle."

Chocolate Shrek opened his outer shirt just enough to reveal the grip of a Glock 9mm tucked into the front of his pants. "Tell me now, street nigga, or when I find him I'll make sure you join Casper."

The older man hissed wide-eyed. "Ah'ite. Imma let you get me later. Cracker's ducked down by the Merc." He pointed quickly with his left hand to the black Mercedes E6 sedan parked between the matched Navigators. "Messin' wit sum'tin…"

Both doormen's eyes shot to the cars -

- Which was when the older man snatched the giant's pistol out of its owner's waistband with his right hand and double-tapped the other guard. To his credit, the talkative brute overcame his own surprise fast enough to make a grab for the smaller man. Unfortunately for him, all he caught was air as the older brother had already fallen backward to the concrete. Supine, the older man loosed three rapid shots, stitching the giant in the groin, center mass and head, respectively.

From the snatch to the Patriot's fifth shot, maybe a total of three seconds had elapsed. Maybe a little less.

The older man quickly scanned the area and returned to his feet. He hastily held the Glock 17 in his left arm pit and donned a set of black rubber gloves. Then, pistol back in hand, he checked both men on the ground for other useful items. His search produced a pair of cellular phones, two wallets, a small wad of cash, a set of car keys, and another semiautomatic pistol - a subcompact Springfield - which he tucked into his own waistband at the small of his back.

The hooded black man held the commandeered Glock at the ready and scanned again. There were no new arrivals to the scene, so he made for the nearby doorway. The double doors were locked. They were mostly glass and opened from within by pushing on a wide metal release bar. The thin metal wire woven within the panes indicated the glass was reinforced. This kind of safety glass was commonly employed in inner city buildings to protect them against casual break-ins and petty vandalism.

Three more quick shots from the Glock, spread perfectly near the inside edge of the safety glass, made for less-than-petty vandalism. In addition to a trio of holes, the shots created a spider web of frosted glass. Listening for sounds of response to his announced presence, the Patriot kicked into the grouped bullet holes. The glass pushed inward and expanded the damaged areas. He kicked again, a powerful front snap kick that stamped the damaged sheet inward even deeper. A third kick pushed the shattered area even wider and deeper, which pulled on the sheet of mesh-filled glass and separated it from the metal door frame at the seam.

There was just enough of a gap for the savvy black man to reach through the damaged door with a sleeved hand and pull the door's release bar. He entered the building both delighted and dismayed by the fact that all of his gunfire did not seem to merit a response from the Washington D.C. Metro Police. *Yet another symptom of the disease corrupting our nation. Shots fired near a residential area and nobody cares enough to call it in.*

And so the Patriot stormed the community center to administer a dose of cure.

"Maliq Shibaab does not order black men around," the suited man explained to Congresswoman Jefferson. "Such is the distasteful practice of a white master with his slaves. Were Maliq Shibaab to engage in such disrespect, Maliq Shibaab would be no better than the white devil against which we have fought for hundreds of years."

"Do you really have to talk like that?" Congresswoman Jefferson winced. "There are no cameras to play up to. It's just you and me here."

"Maliq Shibaab is who Maliq Shibaab is."

"Fine," she sighed. "But what about the men you brought tonight?" LaDasha asked. "Surely they follow your orders."

"These gentlemen are hired advisors. Staff members of the New Black Panther Party," he explained. "The New Black Panther Party periodically hires such men, liberated from their white oppressors. We provide them with vocational training and rehabilitation."

"I don't care what prison you 'liberated' them from," LaDasha snipped, "A million dollars a week is too much."

"The New Black Panther Party is not greedy, but we must make our payroll. And Maliq Shibaab is not without compassion, Congresswoman." He held up a finger thoughtfully, as if the solution had just occurred to him spontaneously, and smiled. "Surely, a sister as esteemed as yourself would have no problem arranging for a series of charitable donations. Perhaps spread out over time - say, a year or two. The New Black Panther Party does not require all of the money to come directly from *your* purse, and not necessarily all at once."

LaDasha thought over the proposition. She could dip into resources like her Congressional budget, donors and supporters back in Texas, even campaign funds if need be. Shibaab did not expect a duffle bag filled with cash tonight. Which was good, because she was only able to put fifty thousand dollars in cash together so far, and she had left that money locked in the trunk of her car.

Another idea struck the Congresswoman. "What if I were to offset some of the bill," she smiled slyly, "with a, um, *personal* favor?"

"My dear, sweet sister," the slimy lawyer smiled, "Maliq Shibaab has little need of personal favors. And what needs Maliq Shibaab does have can be quite... *specific*."

Jefferson pulled back coldly. "I mean of the legislative variety." She drew a breath as the idea matured. "I do sit on the Committee on Homeland Security. I can make sure that the Panthers avoid certain, *attentions*, from its partner departments."

"Such as the FBI, NSA, and IRS?"

"Indeed, Brother Shibaab."

"And," Maliq leaned forward, "would this courtesy extend to the leadership of the New Black Panther Party? Personally?"

LaDasha Jefferson had Shibaab completely hooked. For all of his showmanship, fancy trinkets, and his army of thugs, the leader of the Panthers was, at the end of the day, still a man. And like so many men, Maliq was attracted to a free pass in the light of a federal investigation into his business, associations, money or person.

"Of course," she nodded.

"Well then, Congresswoman Jefferson, we appear to have a -" Shibaab's voice trailed off and attention wavered at the sound of gunfire from outside.

"Oh, my God…" LaDasha trembled in her seat so fitfully that it resembled an epileptic seizure.

Both of Shibaab's guards drew pistols. "Front door," one of the muscular men said, easily identifying the direction from which the sound had come. He pulled his phone, dialed, barked orders, then hung up. "Sir," he said to Brother Shibaab, "get down."

The Benning Park Community Center did not have a complicated layout. Inside the compromised front door was a basic reception area, then an open great room. The Patriot moved down a hallway leading into the rear of the building, which was where offices and ancillary rooms were located.

Phillips assumed his targets were in one of those back rooms. He also knew he did not have time to search each one thoroughly. Even in this rough D.C. neighborhood, eventually someone would respond to the gunfire. The longer he spent on the scene, the greater his chances of getting caught - and the more opportunities his target had to escape.

The Patriot moved silently down the hall. His eyes easily adjusted to the soft glow of emergency lights and illuminated vending machines. People, by their very nature, liked light. The Patriot lived in a world of darkness. He was a predator, and as such he preferred shadows. Scanning the bottom lip of each door, he looked for a ribbon of light that would show which room was occupied. Then a woman's shriek made the process that much easier.

"Put your phone down, woman!" Shibaab barked.

LaDasha Jefferson's panic level had reached a peak. "We've got to call the cops!"

Maliq stabbed a finger at the congresswoman. "We cannot be seen together!"

"They're gonna find us *dead* together!" she cried.

The conference room had only one windowless door. Both of the guards that had accompanied Shibaab into the building stood facing it, guns drawn. The one on the left held a Glock 17; the one on the right wielded a Taurus 9mm, all stainless steel with pearl handles. Something hit the door with a thud. Jefferson squeaked. The guards looked at each other in confusion.

"Well," Maliq insisted as he flapped his hand in a shooing motion, "don't just stand there. Check it out."

Shibaab's goons seemed to work the situation out with a quick exchange of simple eye expressions. Then, the one on the right, being closer to the door, stepped cautiously forward. He reached out with his left hand and grasped the door's cool metal latch, while his right still held his pistol firmly. He pressed the latch down, but the door resisted a bit as he pushed it open. Something seemed to be leaning against the portal. Whatever it was, though, it was not heavy enough to keep the door closed. But it did drag on the ground and forced him to push a little harder than normal.

"What you see, Tayron?" the guard behind him called in a hushed voice.

Tayron peered into the darkness from the lit side of the doorway. "Nut'in." He turned to his partner. "Maybe we should -"

A dark hand lurched from the darkness and through the half-opened doorway, grabbed Tayron's shiny pistol and pulled him violently into the shadows outside. The big man was too startled to react, but the congresswoman who witnessed the frightful sight let loose another startled scream -

- Which was just enough to elicit a sympathetic reflex from Tayron's edgy, steroid-enhanced partner. The first negligent discharge from his Glock splintered the door next to Tayron's shoulder, peppering the black brute with multi-density fibers and dust. The second shot, a panicked heartbeat later, struck Tayron square in the flank and punched clean through his left lung. The big black man howled in pain as his knees buckled under friendly fire.

The shooter's eyes went wide at the sight of what he had just done to his partner. Shock rippled through his nervous system. It caused his grip to slack and his muzzle to drop toward the ground. He was still trying to overcome his own disbelief and stammer an apology when Tayron's pistol poked out from the darkness again, this time held in another person's disembodied hand. The Taurus flashed once; a dark red spot erupted on the second black thug's forehead, and a crimson plume sprayed from the back of his skull. It painted the wall behind him with a splatter of gore and a sample of matter from between his ears.

LaDasha Jefferson's voice - commonly the vehicle for delivering diatribes about the virtues of social programs and the evils of gun ownership - erupted into a prolonged, blood curdling scream.

"Jesus, woman!" Maliq shouted as he pulled her face to face. Then he backhanded the congresswoman. "Get a grip on yo'self!"

The black phantom entered the room with his shiny pistol in a firm one-handed grip. He still held Tayron's right wrist with his left hand. He ignored the couple for a moment as his attention swept from corner to corner. A second later, he casually placed the Taurus' muzzle atop Tayron's crown and drove a round through the bulk of his brain at eleven hundred feet per second. The two hundred and sixty pound bruiser fell to the floor silent and slack.

Phillips' inner clock was ticking. It had been almost a full minute since he had fired his first shot at the front door. Four sentries were down. He strongly suspected there were more closing from the perimeter. The longer he stuck around, the worse it would be for him when he dealt with them - plus whatever police had to be responding by now from the inevitable 9-1-1 call that usually followed a dozen-odd shots fired in short order, no matter what neighborhood in which one found oneself.

Tonight, in the absence of preparation, speed was the Patriot's friend. Just like the sergeants had taught him at Ft. Benning: *A poor plan, executed with swift enthusiasm, beats a well-conceived one that comes too slowly.* The D.C. Metro police had an average response time of ten minutes to a priority emergency call. As he was properly paranoid, T.J. figured that time would be cut to no more than six minutes tonight, what with the Capital City cops on high alert after his actions at the DHS Headquarters. That meant he had no more than five minutes total time on target at his disposal, from first contact to completed exfiltration and disappearance into the night. Still, there was no need to waste a second. Time burned was risk gained and an invitation for something to go wrong.

"Well, well, son," Maliq looked at the armed black assassin with warm regard. "That was mighty impressive." A million-dollar smile spread across his face. "Mighty impressive indeed. I've always said that nothing on Allah's Earth can stop a motivated black man."

"Jerome! Tayron! What's going on? You guys okay?" a voice called from down the hallway.

Speechless, the Patriot raised the shiny handgun and traced a line of fire through Congresswoman Jefferson. A rapid staccato of bullets ripped through her expensive pantsuit: a double tap to the chest, then another to the pelvic region, a brief pause as she fell to her knees, then a single round downward into her skull from the top of her overpriced beehive. Her body laid silent and motionless as blood spilled onto the cheap tile floor.

"Brother Shibaab!" the voice shouted again.

"Now, son," Maliq held out his hand to calm the shooter as he continued, "you didn't come here tonight for Maliq Shibaab. But, any sec-" Shibaab's diatribe was abruptly cut short when the Patriot splattered the back of the Black Panther Party leader's brain across the wall with a single shot placed between the eyebrows.

About two minutes, Phillips counted in his head as he turned toward the door, and backed slowly until he felt a wall with his right foot. *And probably four more motivated gunmen coming in.*

As if conjured by his imagination, another gorilla rushed into the room, his pistol held high next to his right ear like the star of a poorly choreographed action movie. The Patriot, already aiming, projected a single 9mm bullet into the goon's face, which exploded like a crimson firework as the muscled buffoon fell. The enforcer behind him was blinded momentarily by gory backsplatter. The wannabe actually stopped in the doorway to wipe his buddy's blood out of his own eye; the Patriot punched a shot clean through Black-zilla's left hand, which blew pieces of flesh and bone through his eye. A mixture of lead, bone, and flesh ripped through the left half of his brain. In a microsecond, a confetti of bone, blood, brain matter and other ichor splashed onto the wall across the hall. He dropped to the floor like a sack of potatoes.

Another voice shouted expletives from the hallway.

Two and a quarter mikes, the Patriot calculated. *Probably two tangos left.*

Bullet holes opened up in the wall next to the door. The Patriot fell onto his right flank as the last two enforcers decided to forgo the direct path to their target. Instead, they opted to spray random gunfire into the room through the walls. It was the wild, blind, desperate move common to street gangs and Islamic terrorists alike. *Spray and pray*, T.J.'s team had always called it.

A few dozen bullets passed through the room, fairly well stitching a path across a midline from wall to wall. Each of those shots passed a solid three feet above the supine Patriot while he quickly ejected the magazine from the Taurus, confirmed his latest acquisition's remaining ammo, then slipped the mag back into the pistol grip. After a handful of seconds, the gunfire stopped.

Two and a half minutes, the Patriot counted as he sprung up and sprinted to the doorway.

During the split second it took for the veteran to reach and clear the doorway, he remembered some interesting facts about most citizens and gunplay. Civilians were wrought with shortcomings - not the least of which were abhorrent marksmanship and an utter lack of discipline. Especially fire discipline. In a gunfight, civilians rarely aimed and almost always shot - wildly and all too rapidly - until they emptied the firearm. And when they did aim at all, civvies rarely hit their target anyway.

The Patriot stepped over the dead goon's bodies as he cleared the doorway. He entered the hallway at a dead run, saw the two remaining thugs - both holding handguns whose slides were locked back and betrayed their now-unloaded status. One of the wannabes startled in wide-eyed disbelief, then went into complete vapor lock. He froze in place like a statue. The other snapped his impotent gun up and aimed it at the Patriot's face.

The shootist let the second homeboy's finger twitch spastically on the trigger and shot the first with a well practiced, modified failure drill: a double tap to the groin followed by a quick single shot to the throat. Having seen his homeboy get his testicles blown off, the last remaining thug started to involuntarily wretch and hurl. The Patriot took aim and dropped the tango while he was dry heaving with a clean, meaty headshot.

Almost three minutes. The Patriot's ears rang too loudly to tell if there were sirens approaching, but he had to assume his time was running short. Forced hyperventilation flooded his blood with a fresh dose of oxygen to help keep his mind clear and stave off the effects of adrenaline for a moment longer.

The coast looked clear. There were no observers massing on the perimeter. There was no strobe of red and blue lights reflecting off any of the neighboring buildings. Scraps of trash in the parking lot remained motionless, unstirred by the rotor wash of the helicopter that should normally be dispatched over a major crime scene for recon, command and control.

Four and a half minutes. Phillips liberated each of the downed targets of their pocket litter and evacuated the building. He was careful to avoid stepping in or tracking any blood.

Out in the parking lot, the Patriot produced the keys he seized from the first duet and punched a button on the fob. One of the Navigators obediently flashed its lights. Phillips faintly heard the truck chirp through whistle that rang in his unprotected ears. He started the truck, pulled his tracking beacon from Jefferson's back bumper, and made a quick check of the other vehicles for other useful loot.

Phillips was four blocks away from the community center when he pulled the black Lincoln Navigator closer to the shoulder and yielded to a pair of D.C. Metro squad cars that sped past him in the opposite direction, no doubt headed to the community center. He made an immediate right turn to break line of sight with the police then checked the clock on the Lincoln's radio. *Seven minutes,* he nodded. *Not bad...*

CHAPTER 3

"YOU'VE GOTTA BE friggin' kidding me." Danny rubbed the sleep out of his eyes as he reached for the phone on his bedside table. He pried an eye open long enough to find the virtual button that accepted the call, then shut his eyes against the morning sun and grumbled. "Go for Wakefield."

The voice on the other end of the conversation brought news that livened the former Marine. His head perked up off his pillow. His voice became more clear. His mind sped to alertness. "I'll be there aye-ess-aye-pee." Danny deactivated the phone and returned it to the charging plate.

"You said we'd sleep in this morning," Sandra's still-sleepy voice mumbled as she burrowed her head into Danny's chest and snuggled more tightly under the heavy down comforter. "Just once…"

When it came to his home life, Wakefield was a man of habit who managed to keep things just on the sane side of compulsion. Years in the Marine Corps had instilled in him the habit of waking each day at exactly oh-five-thirty. This customary behavior was so deeply ingrained in him that he did so even on the rare occasion when he forgot to set an alarm - or, as was the case this morning, if he felt particularly inclined to stay between the sheets just a little longer than normal.

"That was Derek," he rubbed his partner's shoulder. *Former partner on the job,* he mused, *now partner of a different sort.* Special Agents Wakefield and Elbee first met when the former was assigned to assist the latter while she investigated the murder of a Louisiana senator who was assassinated in a bayou brothel. It turned out that Senator Evans was only the first name on a laundry list of American politicians who were either personally corrupt or whose political ideals ran contrary to traditional interpretations of the Constitution that seemed to be embraced by their assassin.

Sandra's blue eyes popped open. "Phillips?"

"Looks like it." The crime fighting duo's investigation led them to Thomas Phillips, a former Ranger and retired Army Master Sergeant with an illustrious career at the Joint Special Operations Command. The perfect soldier, turned for his own reasons into the perfect serial killer. And his repeated success led to not only a high body count, but also Sandra's removal as the lead investigator from the case and Danny's own career troubles.

At the beginning of November, Phillips staged an attack the Department of Homeland Security's own headquarters building. What was assumed to be a lone-wolf operation eventually culminated as an armed protest conducted by thousands of civilians angry with their government in cities all across America. The incident also ended with a dramatic escape by Phillips. And ever since then, the number of credible reports of the killer's location or activities could be counted on zero fingers - with hairs to spare.

"How's he know for sure?" she squinted through sleepy slits. "I thought he was reassigned."

Danny sniffed. "Looks like we still have friends on the task force. Little D said he got the word."

"Friends?" Sandra rolled over far enough to look at him with half-wakened eyes. "You mean Stevenson." She reached up with her right hand and played with his disheveled brown hair. Special Agent Dianne Stevenson was one of the original members of their team. She was still junior by rank and grade, but her consistent performance and dedicated efforts had helped her ride out the Task Force's unnaturally high turnover. Five months of shuffling temporarily assigned volunteers - with all manner of force reductions and increases, as well as various shifting priorities and funding issues - into and out of the task force left very few familiar faces on the case. And the administrative fallout from Phillips' attack on DHS Headquarters a few weeks ago did not exactly help improve staff stability.

"I dunno who," he scooped up her hand into his own and kissed it, "but I'll take whatever help I can get."

"You're not supposed to be anywhere near this case," she warned. "You know that."

"This case started off as ours. Yours, really," he corrected himself. "Doesn't it bother you that some other joker's out there fumbling around on it?"

"Get over it, Daniel," she warned, "for your own good. You and I aren't the only competent people in the Department."

"Don't you want to see it through, though?"

"Of course," Sandra's eyebrows furrowed. "Which is why I'm staying out of the way of the agents who are handling it now. Like I was ordered to do." She closed her eyes and settled into her downy pillow. "Like you should, too."

"Sorry, Elbee," Danny threw back the covers and set forth to cleaning himself up for work. "I can't do that. I can't give up."

Sandra huffed and laid in the bed. "You're gonna get fired," she warned. "Or worse."

"Not if I'm the one who catches him."

Elbee and Wakefield had only been together for a couple of weeks - romantically, anyway. Their partnership as colleagues involuntarily assigned to work together unintentionally grew into something more personal. Each was actually involved with someone else - her with an up and coming musician; him with their now-former forensics lead - when Sandra and Danny finally broke down and became honest with each other about their feelings. The transition was not always smooth, but Danny assumed that Sandra knew him well enough by now that she understood. Once his mind was set on something, no force on Earth could stop him.

"Fine, Daniel. I'll get the coffee pot going."

Cool air hit Danny like a wave as he padded to the bathroom attached to the apartment's master bedroom. "Did you fiddle with the thermostat?" he called as he reminded himself once more which toothbrush was his own. "I swear it feels colder in here."

"Well, it *is* in the twenties outside," Sandra noted from the kitchen.

"Temperature outside doesn't matter when it's seventy-two inside," he reminded her. *I haven't changed the thermostat since I moved in here two years ago,* his tired mind grumbled, *but now all of a sudden, I turn around and it's either sixty-eight or eighty or something.*

"A lower temperature at night saves money on your energy bill."

"I'll happily pay for the comfort," he quipped before he set to cleaning his teeth. As his mind and body adjusted to a new day, Danny looked across the bathroom vanity and all of its new amenities. His Spartan supply of hygiene products had somehow multiplied - and the growth rate was logarithmic. A few days ago, his bathroom sink was home to a toothbrush, razor, and a bar of hand soap. Now it included a collage of scented lotions, three giant bottles of various hair care products, a pink can of shaving gel, two different soaps he had never heard of - *probably wasn't enough room in the shower to fit all of this stuff,* he mused - plus a collection of cotton pads and products in all manner of shapes and sizes, and an electric toothbrush whose operation he could barely discern. Out of habit, Danny opened the drawer that used to hold his hair clippers, only to be reminded that it had become the temporary resting place for a pair of brightly colored bags, each stuffed to the point of overflow with make-up, but neither of which, Sandra assured him the other night, contained the same type of make-up as the other.

"You know," Danny called out to the kitchen through the open door, "we really need to talk about this." He knew that it only took a touch of vocal projection for his voice to reach that far.

He heard the door frame creak as Sandra leaned into the bedroom from the apartment's main living area. "I'm not coming with you," she flatly announced.

"No," he splashed hot water on his face. "I mean the living situation." He rubbed shaving oil on his face and waited for her to say something, but when she did not he continued. "All of the stuff you brought here from New Orleans is either stuffed in your car or sitting in my spare room."

"You said it was okay," Sandra shrugged. "But if you've changed your mind, I'll take it all back to my hotel room -"

"That's not what I meant." Danny whipped up some shaving foam on a bristle brush. "What I mean is, you know, if you want, that there's an alternative to camping out at the Marriott indefinitely."

"Can't very well stay at Hudson's aunt's condo anymore," she challenged, "can I?" Amanda Hudson was the lead FBI forensics technician on the Phillips case assigned under Elbee from the beginning. When the FBI temporarily assigned Sandra DHS Headquarters so that she could run the task force, Hudson lent her a relative's condo in the Washington D.C. Metro. But Amanda and Danny had also shared a brief dalliance at around the same time, and when Wakefield and Elbee escalated the nature of their relationship, Sandra lost both her technician and her convenient lodgings.

"No," he said dryly as he looked at her reflection in the mirror. Then he painted his face with white foam. "I mean, you could stay here. If you want."

Sandra stood silently and started back at him in the mirror. "Are you sure?" she managed with neither commitment nor enthusiasm.

Danny rinsed his brush and traded it for his razor. It was not the kind of high-speed, low-drag, high-tech, multi-bladed, plastic toy used by so many guys. No, Wakefield used an old-fashioned safety razor - the kind with a double-edged, thin, metal blade fitted within a stainless steel trap that rode atop a bulky, ribbed handle. "Wouldn't've offered if I didn't mean it." He angled his head and started to scrape his skin with long, smooth strokes. "I mean," he continued through clenched teeth to avoid nicks, "you're here more nights than not anyway."

Sandra shook her head. "The Bureau won't pay me housing for temporary orders, Daniel. And the travel office won't reimburse me for a lease."

Danny rinsed his blade. "I don't need you on the lease," he contorted his head so that he could work the other side of his face. "Don't know if you noticed this or not, but I paid for this place just fine on my own before I met you." He rinsed the blade, then pointed his chin skyward and set to work on his throat. "Look, you told me the other night that you put in for a permanent transfer to a narcotics gig here in D.C., so you're obviously not keen on heading back to New Orleans. We'll make some room so that you can settle in properly. You can stop living out of a suitcase for a while."

Sandra crossed her arms in consideration. "I'll think about it."

"So," Danny inspected his handiwork. Satisfied, he rinsed his razor again, returned it to its stand, then reached into the shower and fired up a cascade of hot water. "You sure I can't talk you into coming with me?"

"Into the shower?"

"Not what I meant," he smiled, "though you're more than welcome."

Sandra shook her head. "I don't think that's a good idea. I'm not on the case anymore, Daniel. For either of us. And neither are you."

"Don't you wanna know what's going on?"

"What I want," she un-crossed her arms and shifted her position so that she could maintain visual contact as Wakefield shed his lightweight sleep shorts, "is to keep my job. Flowers isn't just the new Aye-Dee. She's also the new head of the task force. Yep, that's right. After what happened with you and I, some higher-ups decided that the situation merited leadership from more senior personnel."

Naked, Danny made a face and shook his head. "So they turned a perfectly functional team into a complete dog-and-pony show."

"Flowers has a reputation at the Bureau, and it's not for her sense of humor."

Danny slipped past the walk-in shower's glass door - which was fogged by steam from the inside. "You think she'd get pissed if she saw me there? Just watching? Or that she'd even notice one more white guy in a crowd full of crackers?"

"I don't believe she's big on spending time in the field herself," Sandra answered matter-of-factly. "But if she found out you were there, I think she'd throw the book at you. Including charges of interfering with a federal investigation."

Before Phillips attacked DHS Headquarters, there had already been talk about handing the Constitutional Killer manhunt to someone higher up in Homeland Security's chain-of-command. After the whole world got to watch Secretary Dagenhart's bloody murder live on the news, Undersecretary Lehman increased his visibility as not just a manager, but *the* administrator of the Department. He shuffled personnel, issued a never-ending stream of orders - including Wakefield's administrative review - and appointed a politically attractive and career-minded Beltway insider to take over the most visible criminal investigation in the country.

The word around D.C. was that in the wake of his boss' assassination, Undersecretary Lehman was virtually guaranteed a presidential appointment to officially lead the DHS. He certainly made every effort to be seen acting in that capacity until anyone else got around to actually governing.

"I'm not interfering," Danny explained as he lathered himself under a steamy cascade. "I'm just going down to a public street on a lovely Saturday afternoon."

"A street that just happens to be the home of a murder scene? On the other side of town?" Though his eyes were closed tight to keep the shampoo out, Danny could tell by the tone of Sandra's voice that she did not buy into his excuse. Not for one second.

"Just another friggin' observer." He blew raspberries to keep sudsy water from running into his mouth while he rinsed his head and face. A pair of cold hands grabbed his warm, wet chest from behind, prompting him to turn suddenly. His reward was to see Sandra, disrobed, sharing the shower with him.

"Just be careful." She held him tightly, but Sandra's face carried an expression of deep concern. "If the wrong people catch wind of what you're doing, you could be facing more than a suspension and review."

CHAPTER 4

"IF GUN CONTROL laws worked," Derek mused aloud, "D.C. and Chicago would be the safest cities on Earth."

Danny hummed his agreement and stood shoulder to shoulder with his friend outside of the Benning Park Community Center. A solid line of yellow tape and an intermittent line of blue uniforms held the curious crowd at bay. "Speaking of other cities, how did you ever convince them to let you stay here in Washington?"

Derek hissed a long, loud breath from his nose. "I kissed a lot of ass," he admitted while shaking his head. His face twisted like he just ate a lemon. Derek Martin was Wakefield's best friend and a teammate from the Secret Service's Analysis Division. Little D, as he was affectionately known, was part of Danny's support team on the Constitutional Killer task force. Up to and during the attack on DHS Headquarters, Derek stood by Danny's side with unwavering support. In the wake of Secretary Dagenhart's murder, his steadfast dedication to Wakefield nearly cost him his position. "Aliyah needs to stay here in the Metro more than I need any self respect."

"I'm sorry, Little D."

"Don't sweat it, brother." Derek sniffed again in the cold D.C. air. "I mean, I need an industrial-sized bottle of salve for my butthole, but I should be okay in the long run."

"You know it's only going to get worse in the Spring when Nick's in charge."

"Maybe Father won't leave," Derek mused. "I mean, some people stick it out after they're retirement eligible."

Danny shook his head. "You know he's already pulling one retirement pension from the Navy, right? Can't imagine he'd want to hang around if he can walk away with a second one."

"Yeah, well, whatever." Little D perked up. "Alright, there's Stevenson. She sent me the text about this place."

A familiar brunette in a stereotypical trench coat broke away from the collection of identical tan jackets and made her way to the point on the perimeter nearest to Danny and Derek. Danny knew that the action past the flashing lights and badges was composed of federal agents assessing the scene of a gruesome multiple murder. While most of the city cops were preoccupied with controlling access to the property, the feds were busy evaluating whether or not the previous night's carnage was T.J. Phillips' handiwork.

Known to the public as the Constitutional Killer, Phillips was the most wanted fugitive in America. He was a Special Forces Ranger, a hardened combat veteran on a personal crusade to eliminate anyone in American government that he judged corrupt or traitorous. He was also the person who killed Danny's now-late-boss in a savage attack that Danny failed to stop.

"This is bullshit, man." Derek looked left and right at the sea of faces that surrounded them. "We're acting like a couple of voyeurs looking at a crash on the side of the road."

"Wait for it," Danny chided as he watched. The woman ushered them closer. He answered her call. "Hey, Stevenson. Whaddaya know?"

"Wakefield," Dianne extended her hand in greeting. "Hey, Martin. You got my text?"

"That's why we're here," Danny nodded. "So, what'cha got?"

"Three years on the FBI's gang task force before I got put on the Phillips case," Stevenson looked back over her shoulder at the darkened doorway that led into the community center, "and I've never seen anything quite like this place."

"It's a rough neighborhood," Derek chimed.

"Which is probably why at least one of the vee-eye-pees brought their own personal security detachment." Dianne blew out a breath that turned into a cloud as soon as it cleared her lips. "Not that it did them any good."

"On the news they're saying that it was LaDasha Jefferson."

Stevenson nodded in affirmation. "The Democratic congresswoman from Austin. Whe was meeting with Maliq Shabaab. Pretty sure the goons were his."

"Texas' most famous Liberal politician and the head of the Black Panthers?" Danny sniffed. "That's some pretty high rollers for a joint like this,"

"Especially one on the Maryland side of town."

"Little D's got a point. You'd think if they were having a rendezvous, it'd be in DuPont Circle or something. You know? Someplace less ghetto?"

"Might not have been that kind of rendezvous," Stevenson shrugged. "In some circles, 'ghetto' adds to credibility."

"So," Danny leaned in and adopted a more conspiratorial tone. "You gonna let us in?"

"*Pfsh,*" Dianne huffed. "Not a chance. I like my job."

"So, if you're not gonna let us dance, why invite us to the party?"

"I wanted you to see that we're doing everything we can," she replied. "You're a great investigator, Wakefield. And I wish we still had you on the team. But there are good people working on this. We'll get it." Stevenson checked over both of her shoulders to make sure nobody was watching, shifted her body so that her shoulder brushed Derek's, and slipped a gloved hand into his coat pocket.

Danny observed the drop easily, but kept his comments to himself as he scanned the area for any indication that they were compromised. Stevenson's effort was amateurish, but low key enough that he doubted it was noticed by the other feds or anyone in the crowd. "So, you're convinced this was Phillips?"

"Personally? Yes."

"Personally?" Little D regarded her for a split second. "How about evidence? I assume there's something that draws you to that conclusion?"

"At this point, it's just my gut. It fits his profile, if not his grandiose style. But Jefferson wasn't exactly popular. Sure, she carried her district, but there are plenty of people in her state and around the country who absolutely hated her. There'll be a lot of cheers in Texas today, I bet. But it was dark," Dianne fumed at the droll list of hurdles familiar to any criminal inquiry, "there's only one or two cheap cameras in there covering entrances, and the picture's not great, and everything's happening so fast… It's hard to get a positive eye-dee on the suspect." She rolled her eyes. "And if I hear one more guy say, 'they all look the same,' I swear I'm gonna lose it."

"Well, then," he sniffed a nose full of bitter air, "I guess we'll just move on."

"Yeah," Dianne suddenly seemed interested in something being scrutinized by a cluster of agents near the community center's door. "I should probably get back to it. Keep your nose clean, Wakefield," she warned. "Nice seeing you, Little D."

The two ostracized agents silently shuffled through the crowd around the community center and hoofed their way back up 53rd Street Southeast to where Danny left his Jeep parked. Safely out of sight from the crowd, the former Marine perked up. "So, Little D, what's she give you?"

Derek pulled his hand out of this wool peacoat and held his price aloft. "Jump drive."

"I've got my Toughbook in the back seat," Danny keyed his fob. "Let's grab a cup of coffee somewhere and see what's on it."

Derek shivered as he flopped into the red utility vehicle's passenger seat. "Sounds good. But let's make it someplace nice. And in a better neighborhood than this dump."

*　　　*　　　*

T.J. settled into the black Sahara's passenger seat and signaled the driver to roll. "Thanks for the ride, Randy."

"It's nothing," the fellow veteran - Phillips' white brother and former teammate from his time as a Green Beret - pulled out of the southern Virginia junkyard and out onto I-95. "So, how much did you get?"

"Five hundred cash for the Navigator."

Randy shook his head. "That's robbery, bro. They'll get that back just on the stereo. Hell, we could'a hocked the seats on eBay for more than that. Those were real leather."

"Yeah," T.J. nodded, "but then we'd still have a hot car on our hands."

"I told you, man. I heard from a guy I know that they're running a chop shop outta that joint," Randy continued. "I bet they're swapping the VIN on that truck as we speak. Probably sell it for ten, fifteen grand to some shady auction house - who sells it again for twenty to some dealer out of state. A month from now, some dude'll find it on a lot for thirty-something, thinking he's just found a bargain."

"Be funny if the guy was a Colonel or something back at the unit," T.J. snickered. "A good guy getting a good deal on a good ride."

"It ain't right," Randy downshifted the Jeep so that he could gain speed as he drove up a hill. "Five hundred bucks for a thirty thousand dollar truck."

"That's the scrap rate, dude. I ain't doin' this for the money, Randy. That's five hundred bucks and me free of a dead guy's very flashy car. That's another day of freedom for me." He looked at his partner. "For us."

"Yeah," Randy hissed. "I guess you're right." He drummed his thumb on the steering wheel and shifted back into high gear. "Well, at least we pulled all of the kit outta the back of all the cars. Speaking of which," his countenance instantly improved, "I can't believe you found a duffle bag of cash in that bitch's trunk."

"Like the el-tee always said: *It pays to be thorough.*" T.J. gazed at the passing scenery just outside the Jeep's window while the wheels of his mind weighed various plans and options. "Speaking of which, I kinda figured a perfectly legitimate businessman such as yourself might be able to help me use that cash wisely to pick up some supplies."

"You know we can't just drop that in the deposit slot at the bank drive thru." Randy sniffed. "But, yeah. We can make something work. And you know that you can always pluck anything you need from the shelves at the gun shop."

"Yeah, well, your inventory ain't gonna replace itself." T.J. took a pull from his oversized soda. "Least I can do is cover the cost of restocking your inventory." The former Ranger tapped his fingers along the trim around the door's frame. "Thanks again, bro. For everything. I couldn't'a pulled the last couple of ops off without you."

"According to the news, you did just fine on your own last night."

"You know what I mean."

Randy sniffed again. "I know." Highway signs whipped by as they drove along the open road. "You know, the Beast is gonna need a new scope. That dive you took shattered the original one."

"Sorry, man. But I did what I had to do." Phillips glanced at the duffle bag in Randy's back seat. "Just pull a couple of bucks out and grab yourself a new one."

"Oh, I will," Randy smiled. "I'm just saying that I need to put the rifle on the bench, check it out, and make any repairs before you use it again."

"Don't suppose there's another gun tucked away somewhere that I could take off your hands?"

"Dude. Please. Who am I?"

CHAPTER 5

WINTER'S CHILL hung in Washington's atmosphere, but Danny's garage unit still smelled of sweat as he toiled at his workbench. A circular fan in the corner moved the air around a little bit, but there was only so much that could be done to keep things fresh in the tiny enclosed structure. The fan simply spread the modest amount of warm air put out from a small space heater in the corner, but it could not fully diffuse the chamber's musty odor. The small, private, one-car garage space that came with his apartment was really little more than a trio of enclosed cinder block walls, a ceiling, and an overhead door - and an extra few hundred dollars each month on the lease. It featured a single electrical outlet, but no dedicated heat or air conditioning of its own. Still, it was better than nothing, and the utilitarian space served its purposes.

The closed door kept casual eyes from glancing into Danny's urban cave. There was a full set of tools in the cabinet against the wall next to his motorbike. The weight rack on the opposite wall was reloaded with iron plates - tools of a different sort - after this afternoon's workout. The well-used punching bag near the corner had stopped swinging like a pendulum from its anchor set deep into one of the ceiling joists. Danny stood before the work station tucked into the mini-garage's rear right corner and regarded the finishing touches upon his latest masterpiece, securely hung in a jig within the vice's firm grasp.

He called her Vera, which meant "truth" in Latin. She was truly the sexiest thing that ever came off of his workbench. Light played off her bronze lines as they flowed smoothly from top to bottom. Her contours imbued his lovely lady with false shades. Parchment toned highlights traced her peaks and ridges. Sensual shadows the color of dark chocolate enriched crevices along her spine and sides.

Vera's sepia finish seemed to radiate heat into the cool December air. A viewer might imagine that her modest coverings had been blown back by the breeze her creator wished he felt while she was born - like Venus, fully formed and ready to please her master. Without moving, Vera stirred something primal in Danny. Despite the airs of political correctness that blew about the Metro, he questioned the manhood of any male who was not at least a little excited by the sight of her ample features. Her smooth form begged to be held. As he rubbed her polished finish, his hand passed to her rear. He nodded in approval at its curve. Some guys preferred the kind of skinny backside that all of the popular lightweights sported, and Danny certainly enjoyed those, too, from time to time. But he had decided early on that Vera needed something more robust. *A little cushion for the pushin,'* he chuckled. So he gave Vera the kind of firm foundation that dared a man to get behind her and prepare for not just playful pushback, but a powerful pounding.

Vera was more than just a great rifle. She was a piece of art, lovingly crafted and perfectly finished to deliver massive .458 SOCOM bullets with the highest degree of precision. The mere thought of pressing the gun's match grade trigger and sending that much kinetic energy downrange stirred up special feelings in the former Marine sniper. Excitement. Anticipation. A giddy smile crossed his face. *I'll have to take you out this week*, he mused. *Put you through the paces at the range.*

Danny's phone erupted on the bench. The cacophony broke his revery like a baby's cry during church service. His special moment was gone. He keyed the phone's speaker function so that he could take the call hands-free. "Go for Wakefield."

"Hey, Danny," a woman's voice responded, "it's Yvette."

Figures. "Yeah. S'up?"

"I saw the news, Danny. The attack. Are you okay?"

"How did you get this number?"

"You're not the only one with sources, Danny."

"What do you care, Yvette?"

"Look, Danny, can you just…" Static played over the phone as she huffed on the other end of the line. "You were right there. I saw it on the news, okay? So don't try to bullshit me about how you were back in Montana when it happened. I don't wanna hear some crap about how you're all fine and everything is all fine. Alright? Just, for once, can you please tell me the truth?"

Wakefield's jaw unconsciously set. "Oh, you wanna have a truth session, Yvette? Is that it? Tell you what: how 'bout we take turns? You first. The truth. What. Do. You. Want?"

"Goddammit, Danny! I called to see if you're okay. That's all."

"Yeah. I'm fine. I'm great. The last decade's been just tits, Yvette."

"Are we really gonna do this? Most guys move on a decade after their divorce, Danny."

"Most guys don't get a call from base telling them that their wife was shagging a JAG officer while I'm in Afghanistan. Speaking of which, how's Major Dick?"

"That's Colonel Richards now, Danny. And, we're actually stationed at the Pentagon, so if you needed someone to talk to -"

"Ooooohhhh, no-no-no-no-no. *He's* stationed at the Pentagon. You're just a resident. Dependents don't enjoy privilege of rank or position. Regardless of what your husband does for a living, you're just another civilian. Or didn't they teach you that at bed jumper school?"

"Ohmygawd, Danny, you are so unbelievable."

"Look, Yvette. I've got stuff to do. So, if it's all the same to you…"

"That psycho killed all of those people, Danny. I saw it on the news. He was there, and you were there, and then you looked him in the eye and let him walk away. I mean, what's going on, Danny?"

"He didn't just walk away, Yvette. He did a Greg Louganis off an overpass while using my boss as a human shield. He should'a been dead anyway from the fall."

"Why didn't you just shoot him, Danny? Isn't that what you do?"

Danny scooped up the phone and switched it to the more traditional handset mode. "Really?" He forced himself not to crush the phone in anger. "You're gonna start on me, too, Yvette? Is that what this is? I'm a federal agent, Yvette. We don't just shoot people. Especially when there's a good chance I might hit a hostage."

"You have before."

Danny blew heavily out of his nose. "That was different and you know it."

"What I know is that there's a guy running around the country killing people in the government, and my ex-husband, the ex-Marine sniper, let him go after he shot down a helicopter, set a car on fire, and shot a Cabinet member all in the same day."

"Wow. How embarrassing for you as a voter. How will you ever live this down?"

"You sonofabitch. That's not what I mean and you know it." There was a pause, then Yvette's voice returned. "Danny." She said more calmly, "Please."

"What, Yvette?" he spat. "What do you want?"

"Look. We're both in the Metro. At least meet me for coffee. We can talk." Her voice took on a coy tone. "You know, as a taxpayer, I'm your boss. I could make it an order."

Danny's teeth clenched as he sneered. "You left me for a superior officer, Yvette. And what's worse, a guy from the Army! I mean, he's not even a Marine! The only thing I want from you is alimony." Danny jabbed the screen hard enough that he was surprised his thumb did not drive a hole clean through his phone.

Every time his left the little box unit, Danny hung a dust cover up just inside the overhead door like a backdrop, obscuring the view of the rest of the unit's contents from opportunistic thieves who might have been casing the parking lot. With the power shut down and his curtain in place, Danny slung his rifle case over his shoulder and exited the little one-car garage, careful not to drop the fairly large box tucked under his arm. *Quick shower,* he checked the sky and saw the last traces of grayish light as the sun disappeared beneath the skyline, *then a bite to eat. Maybe grab a flick with Elbee.* He grabbed the mail on his way back up to his apartment and tried to put the conversation with his ex-wife out of his mind.

"Man," Danny dropped his bundled supplies just inside his apartment door and shivered, "Jack Frost is nipping out there tonight."

"And that's why I'm in here," Sandra held up her open book, "Hanging out with his brother, Robert."

"It's Saturday night. Did you check the movie listings?"

"Is that a new gun?" Sandra's voice sounded from the sofa before the apartment door was fully closed.

"Yep." Danny threw the deadbolt, "and the Christmas decorations, too," then the lock in the doorknob. "I know it's still a week before Thanksgiving, but I figure, *'Why wait until last minute?*" He set the chain, just for good measure.

"Don't you already have some guns?"

Wakefield shrugged. "Gosh, officer. Why do you ask?"

"How many guns do you need, Daniel?"

"I don't know," he turned to her and smiled. "How many were you thinking about buying for me?"

Sandra blew out a raspberry. "Yeah. That'll be the day."

Danny moved to the apartment's second bedroom, which served as a storage room as well as his makeshift office and armory. Elbee still had a few large bags half-filled and tucked around the room's edges. The desk butted up against the wall next to the door was covered with reloading equipment, supplies, and padded work mats with technical diagrams that were helpful for when Danny maintained some of his guns. Just past that, the main wall - shared with the master bathroom - sported a collection of rifles in various calibers and configurations hung on several rows of adjustable tracks. He placed his case on the desk and set to rearranging the guns at chest height.

"I'm just saying," he held one of his AR-15s - mostly black with some colored highlights, the one which he used during that ill-fated raid in West Virginia where he was forced to shoot a suspect in self defense - in his left hand while he reset the prongs that held it on the wall over toward the right a bit closer to the window. "You know, with Christmas coming up and all, if you ever needed any gift ideas then just ask." He placed the old rifle in its new position. "I mean, I've been working on the new one for a while now. But I'll point you at some toys that I like, if you want. I could always use some more mags or ammo. There's this company called Black Butterfly -"

"I'm not sure that's really appropriate," Sandra sounded like she was in motion and headed toward him.

"Look, Elbee," Danny opened a drawer in the file cabinet next to the window and plucked out a fresh set of prongs that fit into the track, "I'm not saying you owe me or anything," a smile played across his lips, "but after what I gave you in bed last night, a little something in the stocking wouldn't be totally out of place." He turned toward the door and saw her standing there with her arms crossed as she leaned up against the jamb. "Besides, I got you something."

Sandra baited him with a raised eyebrow. "A gun?"

Danny shook his head. "I don't know your size."

She did not appear amused. "I don't think that guns are an appropriate gift for Christmas, Daniel."

"Opinions vary," he shrugged as he placed the new prongs into the track near its middle. *Front and center. The perfect place for my masterpiece.* "When in doubt, gift cards are always a winner." He fetched his black rifle bag and unveiled his latest creation. "Or nothing. Whatever you choose." He hung the bronzed beauty up on the rack, then stood back to admire his handiwork. "Whaddaya think?"

"It's…" Sandra frowned as she gazed upon the gun, "shiny."

"I wanted something different."

"It looks just like the other one."

Danny let the offense show on his face. "It's nothing like the other one."

"Well, the other one has more stuff on it."

"I don't think I'm gonna put a fore grip on this one. And the optics I ordered online should get here any day. I'm gonna keep it simple, though. Basic scope, offset iron sights for back ups."

"Still looks the same to me."

Danny plucked a cartridge from a cardboard box about the size of a pack of playing cards on the room's desk. "See this?" he held it up for her review. "This is a two-two-three Remington round. It's the standard, fifty-five grain bullet used by most shooters." He pointed to the black rifle with green and tan accoutrements. "That gun over there shoots it. Same as everyone else's rifle. It's the most prolific centerfire rifle round in the western world."

"Okay." Sandra was clearly unimpressed.

He retrieved a different round from a much larger plastic box. "This," he held the prized ammunition aloft, "is what the bronze gun shoots. It's called the Buzzsaw. Five hundred grain subsonic hollow point. That's almost the same mass as two shotgun slugs. It hits the target with about the same force as a car going thirty-five without stopping."

"Jeez, Daniel," Sandra took the beefy cartridge into her hand. It was approximately the same size as her lipstick. "What do you need a bullet that big for?"

"Knock down power," he explained. "When the troopers from Task Force Ranger got back from Somalia, they complained that it took too many rounds to drop Starvin' Marvin and his Skinny friends during the Battle of Mogadishu. According to urban legend, some of the Pipe Hitters and gunners got together and redesigned the ammo used for big game safari hunts into something that could be used by those of us who were tasked with hunting the most dangerous game of all."

"You mean man."

"And, *voila!* Born unto us that day was this lovely piece of munitions. The .458 SOCOM." He placed the cartridge back into its box. "Specifically designed to help soldiers do what soldiers do with the gun soldiers already do it with. Take your standard mil-spec rifle already in service, swap two parts - the bolt and the barrel - and you're in business. Total conversion costs less than a cheap handgun. Unfortunately, the Defense Department never bought into it, so it never really caught on. Lack of demand means lack of production volume, so the bullets are few and far between… and pricey. Most of the folks who use it today are pig hunters and the like. I hear that some of the top-shelf security contractors dig it, too. They can afford the ammo."

"So why do you have it, Daniel? Are you going on a pig hunt?"

"I might." He cozied up closer to the beautiful blonde and took her arms in his hands, "Mostly, I have it because I *can.* Because it's neat." He kissed her on the cheek. "And because a free man doesn't ask permission to bear arms. Nor does a grown man doesn't need permission to have a hobby."

Sandra pushed him back. "Yeah, well, a grown man needs to take a shower, because you stink."

"While I'm doing that -"

"I swear, if you ask me to make you a sandwich, I'll punch you in the balls again."

Danny frowned as he remembered the incident at the elevator in Richmond a few weeks ago. *In retrospect, I think I had that one coming*. "I was gonna ask if you wanted to nominate some movie choices."

"Nice save," Sandra smiled and pecked him on the lips. Danny was halfway to the bedroom and half out of his workout clothes when he heard her call after him. It was something about towels. He did not care.

CHAPTER 6

"I'M LESS CONCERNED about the legality of the issue and more concerned about its feasibility," Earl Warner, the Secretary of Defense, declared.

"I've gone over the CONOP," Admiral Chet Boutwell, the Chief of Naval Operations and sitting head of the Joint Chiefs of Staff, responded. "Functionally speaking, there's nothing wrong with the plan. But that doesn't change the moral or legal questions that we should -"

"Those questions have been laid to rest," Secretary Warner announced.

"Maybe for you," Boutwell countered, "but I still have reservations."

"Well *I* don't." Warner glared at the decorated commander. "Listen, Chet, and listen good. If this was still open for discussion then we wouldn't be meeting on a Sunday morning. This is happening whether you like it or not. Tonight."

"And you listen to me," Boutwell growled. "Does the phrase 'Crossing the Rubicon' mean anything to you?" He looked around the table to his fellows, each of the heads of the Army, Marines, and Air Force; the Attorney General and the Director of National Intelligence; the Director of the FBI; the Speaker of the House and the Senate Majority Leader.

A long time ago, in a republic far, far, away, the High Protector of Rome had just finished his latest campaign to subdue the Gauls in the north when the senate ordered him to stand down the republic's army, return, and abdicate his office. Instead of heeding the wishes of the people he was sworn to protect, Consul Gaius Julius marched his Thirteenth Roman Legion back into his own country - the border of which was marked by the Rubicon River. Tradition demanded that the legion disarm on the far side of the river, as Rome was, by law, a demilitarized nation whose armies only projected force outside of her borders and never exercised it against their own people. The sight of Julius as he led the Thirteenth Legion across the Rubicon with weapons in hand told every Roman that the Consular and his men had reached the point of no return. Their actions, once taken, could not be undone.

Once Julius and the Thirteenth Legion crossed the Rubicon, Rome was at war with itself. Countrymen slew each other in droves over political principles and petty grievances. By the time the fires died down, the republic was shattered. Gaius Julius declared himself Caesar - emperor. And centuries of democratic governance were undone by a series of totalitarian rulers and brute force.

Admiral Boutwell continued. "Surely, I'm not the only one who gets a bad taste in his mouth when he hears people seriously talking about doing this."

Senator Chip MacDougal steepled his fingers. The flesh on his hands was still pink, raw from the burns he suffered during the Fourth of July attack that he barely survived. "Sometimes, Admiral, our duty requires us to take unpleasant actions." He leaned back in his chair. "Now, if that fact is too much of a burden for you to bear…" MacDougal's voice trailed off with his threat unfinished.

The admiral glared at the senator from above twin shoulder boards, each adorned with a quartet of shiny stars. If his eyes had been missile launchers, he would have shot Tomahawks across the table. "In thirty-two years I've been wearing this uniform, that'll be the first time anyone was ever fool enough to question my devotion to my duty."

Secretary Warner scribbled absently on his notepad. "I wouldn't worry yourself over it too much, Admiral. I mean, this is basically a ground game we're talking about here. Nothing for the Navy to worry about."

"With all due respect, Mr. Secretary, but regardless of the uniform they wear, each one of us is responsible for every man and woman who wears it. And it's not the Fleet I'm worried about," he grimaced. "It's the nation. It's the principles we're supposed to be defending."

"As legislators, it's Congress' job to defend our principles, Admiral Boutwell," Senator MacDougal charged, "and your job to defend the people. Right now, you'd best focus on defending a very specific group of people - the men and women who control your budget - so that they can continue to do exactly that. You wouldn't want to find yourself bouncing reenlistment checks next time we have to fight a war, now, would you?"

"When was the last time we *weren't* at war?" Boutwell grumbled. "Then again, when was the last time you did your job and actually *declared* one before you sent us off to fight it? No, wait, don't bother to answer, Senator." He returned his attention to the only person in the room who could actually count himself as the officer's superior. "You know what, Mr. Secretary, this has been a fascinating discussion, but we don't answer to you on this kind of matter. You have oversight on policy, but unless a whole bunch of people have been removed from the line of succession, I only take orders from the President."

"The President has given me full authority," Secretary Warner countered. "Under the provisions of the PATRIOT ACT. Effective the day before yesterday."

Hearing those words took the wind right out of the admiral's sails. "He's suspended the War Powers Act?"

"Indeed." The civilian head of the American armed forces - appointed to that position solely due to his political alignment and despite the fact that he never actually served in the military himself - flicked his pen rapidly between his pinched fingers like the world's most ineffective fan. "At least until such time as a new head of Homeland Security is chosen, I've absorbed all of the operational responsibilities that normally fall under that office's purview." The white haired man allowed himself a wicked smile. "Like I said, gentlemen, there is no longer a question of *if*, but *how* we shall proceed. Whatever exceptions or misgivings you may feel are noted, but irrelevant. Now," he turned to the Army's civilian leader, "Secretary James, let's go over the timetable again…"

* * *

"Why does everybody keep staring at me?" Elbee hissed.

"Look, we talked about this already. Work sometimes keeps me from coming here every Sunday, but the regulars are sure to notice that I'm in the company of a woman this time - and that's a rarity. Catholics gossip. By now, a lot of these folks've already invented at least three different stories about you that some of them will just never let go of no matter how many times we try to tell them the truth."

They paused long enough to shake a little old lady's hand. "Nice to see you make it today, Danny," the old lady smiled from under her bluish silver beehive. "And who is this darling you've brought?"

"Hi. I'm Sandra. I'm his partner."

"Oh, really?" The little old church lady pulled her chin in tightly and, though she was a half-foot shorter than Sandra, somehow managed to look down upon her. "Well, I suppose that explains why you didn't take communion, Deary."

"I mean, I'm-"

"She's Methodist," Danny interjected.

"Oh," the lady's face fell just a bit. "Well, nobody's perfect. Still, that is a lovely dress, Deary."

"Thank you," Sandra forced a sociable smile. It was, indeed a nice dress. Danny had not seen her wear this one - dark green and cut along conservative lines - before. Three steps further toward the church's exit, she hissed at her companion. "Tell me again why I let you talk me into this."

"Sunday is my day of rest," he explained. "I sleep in, go to Mass, and eat whatever I want. The only way I miss Mass is if something really big is actively going down."

"That explains why you're here, Daniel. Not why I had to come."

Before either of the agents could continue their argument, an older man in a frock appeared before them out of nowhere. "Father Crane," Danny nodded respectfully.

"Hello, Danny boy," the slender man smiled beneath white hair shot with dark streaks. "Nice to see you. All is well, I take it?"

"Father, this is Sandra Elbee."

"Ms. Elbee," the priest took her hand. "Welcome to St. Ann. And where are you visiting us from?"

"New Orleans," Sandra's strained smile became easier.

"Ah. I have an old friend who preaches out of a Parish down south. Father Thomas Ryan. Do you know him?"

"I'm sorry," she answered apologetically.

"Elbee's Methodist," Danny offered.

"I see," said the priest. "Well, then, God's hand on you too, dear. And it's perfectly alright that you're Methodist," he patted her gently in the shoulder and flashed a genuinely friendly smile. "It's as good a starting point as any." He turned back to Wakefield. "I presume you will be staying for lunch?"

"Yes, sir, Father."

"Great! See you in a few minutes."

They made it the rest of the way to Sandra's car with only a few more exchanged pleasantries. "Lunch? What lunch? You never said anything about a lunch!"

"Relax, Elbee," Danny forced an extra soothing voice. "Traditional Thanksgiving dinner. Well, except it's lunch, really. It's in the fellowship hall right around the back. It's already getting started, really. We just walk over, grab a plate of free food, then ten minutes later you tell me something's come up, and *pow!* we're outta here."

"But why are you taking me?"

"Because I don't want to go."

"Then why are you going?"

Danny looked at her incredulously. "Because it's my church's Thanksgiving dinner. And with the actual day later in the week, that means we're having it today."

"Why don't you just skip it?"

"Because I have to go."

"Why?"

"Don't you Methodists do Thanksgiving as a congregation?"

"I'm not Methodist! You made that up."

"You're not? I could've sworn you said you were. Huh. I mean, with your more Liberal leanings I guess I just assumed…" Danny stopped walking and faced her squarely. "Okay. I can see you just aren't getting it. Today is the Sunday before Thanksgiving. I'm Catholic. We dine together. I have to go. If I don't go, I'm gonna catch Hell - at least from the other parishioners, if not literally. But I don't want to go, because that means spending my God-given day off with a bunch of smelly old ladies and other people's kids. So I need you to come along and get me out of here as soon as we can leave with a respectable level of deniability."

"But why?"

"Because neither of us wants to be here when these folks start playing games. Don't ask."

Sandra growled. "Why me?"

"Because this is what partners are for: being able to count on each other."

"Couldn't you just have Oscar or somebody do it?" Elbee nearly swore, but evidently thought the better of it. Given that the couple stood on Holy ground, Danny did not blame her. "Why can't you just tell them yourself that you have to leave?"

"There's a very good chance at least one of these people - probably Father Crane - will want to talk with me. They'll be less likely to do that if I'm already talking with someone else. Besides, telling them that I have to leave when I really don't would be lying. I can't lie. Not at church. Especially not to a priest."

"What do you mean? You can too lie."

"Nope."

"Everybody lies, Daniel."

"I don't."

"I've seen you lie."

"Doesn't count when you're running an approach on a suspect." Danny shook his head. "No, you've seen me focus on the parts of the truth that I think are most important, but that's totally not the same thing as lying, *per se*."

Sandra fumed. "Well, even if you don't lie - which I think is a total crock - what makes you think that I can?" she accused.

"You're a woman. It's in your nature." He offered her a roguish grin. "Besides, you just did."

"I'm a -" she growled. "Wait. What do you mean, 'I just did?'"

"Just now. You lied to Father Crane about being Methodist. And he believed you." He beamed with pride. "Like I said: you're a natural."

"You're the one who told him that I'm a Methodist!"

"Okay. First off, I really thought you were one. So that makes it true enough, at least as far as I was concerned at the time. Secondly, you went along with it. That makes you complicit in the lie. You're an accessory. Arguably, you're even more culpable than I am. Because you knew the truth when I said it, whereas I was operating under the best information I had at the time."

"The best information at the time? You pulled that out of your -" being on church grounds made Sandra reconsider her phrasing. "You totally guessed! Wrongly, I might add."

"Honest mistake," he shrugged. "But you're the one who knowingly misled a priest." He offered her a sly grin. "That's no small thing, Elbee. If it wasn't such a horrible sin then you could be proud of it." They strolled toward the adjoining building and entered with the rest of the congregants.

"I can't believe you," Sandra grumbled as she shook her princess cut black coat and let in some of the fellowship hall's warmer air.

"Apparently," Danny countered quietly, "it's *me* who shouldn't believe *you*. Either you've got a serious gift or major issues."

They made it through the food line, then settled into a corner on the periphery of the gathering that allowed them to see almost everyone yet still stay out of the way. After a few minutes of peace and a small portion of old lady Flannery's white-wine-basted turkey, Elbee seemed less incensed.

"So," she probed over her half-eaten plate, "I'm guessing none of these people know you're with the Secret Service?"

Danny spared a carefully guarded look around their surroundings. They sat at the edge of the room near a corner at an otherwise vacant table. With his back to the wall, Danny faced the open assembly hall and maintained a clear view of each of the exits and every person's comings and goings. "They don't call it the 'Advertised Service' for a reason," he finished a bite of potato salad. "Most probably wouldn't really care, honestly. A few curious ones think that I'm a traffic engineer working for the city." He wiped his mouth with a paper napkin. "Which is as good a cover story as any, really. Close enough to the truth to matter to these folks."

"How is that even remotely true?"

"I'm a government employee with a boring job that nobody understands even though it impacts almost all of their lives."

"You spent most of this year hunting a high profile serial killer."

"Okay, fine. It's *usually* boring. At least, when we do it right. Boring enough that nobody cares, anyway. And it explains why I'm sometimes out on the weekends. It's for the best. It's not so much a lie as good operational security and all that jazz."

"Just what does the Secret Service do, anyway? I mean, other than the obvious."

Danny freshened his pallet with a sip of sweet tea, then answered in a quiet, dry voice. "Security for the First Family is a relatively minor portion of our mission. A modern one, too. Historically, we investigated financial crimes for the Department of Treasury. Counterfeit currency was a real problem in the beginning, around the time of the Civil War. Shoot, before 1901, we didn't even do personal protection servise. That didn't happen until after the McKinley assassination."

"How do money cops become bodyguards?"

"Well, you've gotta remember that a hundred years ago, the federal government was a lot smaller. More fluid. The secretive nature of what the Service was doing back then meant that they could be discreetly re-tasked. And since there were rumors at the time of shutting it down, the new mission reinvigorated the department. Gave us a new lease on life, you know? From a budgetary view, it made a lot more sense to just recycle an existing asset than to stand up a whole new department. So, just like that, the Service as you know it was born."

"But your legacy mission continues," Sandra noted.

"Yep. There are agents in every major city across the nation working with banks and other institutions to track fraud and other financial crimes. You see, Elbee, some folks might care about politicians, but everybody cares about money. Say what you will about political ideology, but when the economy gets punched in the nuts, everyone suffers. Fiscal security is national security."

"Father Crane seems to know the truth," she pointed. "The bigger truth, I mean."

"Lying to a priest is a bad habit," he replied with a mock accusation. "Seriously, though. He's my priest. I'd never tell him anything classified, but he does hear my confession." He offered a playful smile as he helped himself to a heaping forkful of Mrs. Abernathy's homemade potato salad.

"And what sins do you have to confess today, my son?" a third voice called from Danny's blind spot.

Danny almost choked on his food. "Nowffing, Fawwer Cwayng."

"I doubt that very much," the older Catholic man chuckled. "Ms. Elbee," the priest nodded to Sandra, still wearing a warm smile. He leaned in close to her ear and lowered his voice conspiratorially, "Or should I say, Special Agent Elbee?" He raised a hand to stall any protestation as he returned to his full height and a more modest distance. "Oh, don't worry, dear. I'm a priest. Privileged information is all just part of the job. I didn't mean to interrupt. Just making the rounds."

Danny finally cleared the food from his pallet. "Oh, no, sir. You're not interrupting."

"I know that work keeps you busy, son," the priest ribbed him, "but you know I'd like to see you in service on Wednesday nights, too."

"It was a lovely sermon, by the way," Sandra offered.

"Thank you, dear."

"Speaking of work…" Danny looked at Elbee meaningfully. His partner speared a broccoli sprig with her plastic fork. Then she looked at him and nodded, waiting for him to finish his statement. "Elbee?"

"Oh," her eyes perked a bit. "I'm not Catholic, so I don't have to confess anything."

"If it were only that easy," the priest smiled.

Danny cast her another look, trying to convey to her that this was her chance to bail him out of his commitment before the situation became too socially awkward. Realization dawned upon Sandra's face. "You know, I just remembered," she announced, "didn't I hear something about there being games here in a bit? When do those start up?"

Father Crane perked up even more, as if that was possible. "Certainly," he sang. "Of course, we'll kick things off with a round of Bunco in just a few minutes. I believe the seniors are gonna start some bingo up soon, but we've also got cards for gin, and some of the youngsters will probably be playing bean bag tic-tac-toe, if that's your sort of thing…" As the priest continued his outline of all of their recreational opportunities, Danny knew he was busted. He stared daggers at Elbee for her sudden yet inevitable betrayal. And all the while, Sandra just sat at her table and smiled while she sipped her tea and enjoyed the show that came with lunch.

CHAPTER 7

PHILLIPS LOOKED AT the collection of samples that were quickly cooling to room temperature in the plain, styrofoam take-out container. Fried strips of white-ish meat that were allegedly turkey tenders; a congealed, burgundy glob that still sported the cylindrical outline of the can it came from and claimed to be cranberry sauce; a scoop of dull, off-white substance that might have been the most bland and gritty potatoes ever; and a lumpy dollop of some orange and tan substance that T.J. could only guess was supposed to be sweet potato pie.

"Thanksgiving to go," Randy smiled as he cracked upon a beer and handed it to his guest with a bemused smile. "Happy holidays."

T.J. picked up a once-warm turkey strip, dipped it in a plastic cup of instant gravy, and embraced the suck with a hearty bite. *I've had worse,* he admitted as he thought back on holiday meals shared with battle buddies thousands of miles from home. The worst food in America was better than the best meal ever served in Afghanistan. "Thanks, man."

Randy dropped down in his own, ragged chair next to the beat up couch upon which T.J. sat. "Sorry, man. In case you haven't noticed by now, I don't do a lot of cooking here."

"Oh, no." the Army veteran dunked his mystery meat into the lukewarm gravy. "It's great, dude. Thanks for picking it up. Good lookin' out."

"Downside of clandestine operations. Can't go to a restaurant full of people and tear up the buffet."

"It's all good, brother." T.J. slammed the strip and plucked another from his tray. "So, where're we at?"

"Lance says that he and Heather are all set up to do another video. She's got an apartment over by campus. Did you know the GI Bill pays for housing?" T.J.'s mouth was full, so he shook his head in answer to Randy's question. "Yeah, dude. I need to sign up for classes. Just to offset the rent here at the shop. You know? Anyway. They set up one of the rooms at her place so that we can do it all there. Shoot it, edit it, then dump it onto the 'net. She used her computer ninja skills to set up some kind of magical 'net connection that can't be traced."

T.J. tried not to regret his life choices as he swallowed his potatoes. "You gotta get you one of those, dude."

"Maybe she can hook me up. Speaking of hookups… I think her and Lance are a thing now."

"Good for them. They're a cute couple."

"Yeah," Randy shoved his plastic spoon into his own potatoes and shoveled up a scoop, "anyway, once you're ready to spur the masses on, the kids are good to go."

"Dude," T.J. warned, "I don't think that's a good idea."

"What are you talking about? Those videos are viral. Every time the Constitutional Killer hits the 'net, folks all over the country respond. And you know it ain't all talk, either. Demonstrations, riots… Hell, dude, your celebrity is fueling a revolution."

"No, bro. I mean: Don't eat that. That stuff might self-identify as potatoes, but it ain't potatoes."

Randy looked down at the food as if it had betrayed him. He tossed the contaminated spoon aside and dropped the container onto his worn out coffee table. "Screw this. I can't do it, dude. Let's go get a pizza." Neither man hesitated to grab their coats on the way to the door. "But seriously, brother. You've gotta do another video. And soon, too, so the sheeple can see their hero has risen from the dead."

T.J. nodded. "I will. And, I've got the pizza this time."

"I'd say we're about even," Danny shook a steamy, peppery french fry toward his treacherous companion.

"Not quite," Sandra corrected with a chuckle. By the time they left St. Ann's it was time to eat again. They had settled on a Flanders', as it was along the way. "We're even on the Methodist thing. But not the rest. You used me, Daniel. You should feel ashamed of yourself, dragging me into a church under false pretenses and asking me to lie to a priest! Just so that you could duck out of a game of bunco! You'll owe me for a long time on that one, buster."

He pointed to her plate. "You trying to get me to pick up the check for that salmon?"

"It'll take more than dinner at some place where they staple a flea market onto the walls for decoration to settle that score, Daniel."

"I'll make it up to you later," he flirted.

"If you're lucky." She pointed her fork at him as if to cast a spell with the asparagus trapped on the tines. "You know, something your priest said today struck me."

"Was it good touch, or bad touch?"

She snickered. "No, I'm serious. He told me you've seen a lot of stuff, but that he believes God is watching out for you."

"When did he say that?"

"While you were losing your manhood to a sixty-five year old who knew how to throw bones."

Danny plucked another buffalo wing from his basket. "Yeah, well, dice games suck."

"Back to the point," she ordered. "What's your story, Daniel? Was he talking about Miami? The Marines? Something when you were growing up in Montana?"

"Nothing exciting ever happens in Montana," he smacked. "That's exactly why I joined the Corps. Well, that, and one other thing. But just about everywhere else I go trouble seems to find me easily enough."

"What do you mean?"

Danny finished his wing, licked the sauce from his fingers, then wiped his lips on a napkin. "Case in point: it's Thanksgiving time. What does Thanksgiving mean for most people?"

"I dunno," she searched, "turkey dinners and shopping for Christmas presents? Church, family, and that sort of thing, I guess."

"Right. That's what it is for most folks. Peace. Normalcy. But not for me." He saw she still did not understand his point. He consulted his whiskey, then came back inspired. "Take Thanksgiving of oh-three, for example. I was in Afghanistan. It was my first deployment after sniper school. Me and my sergeant were on a recon patrol. Just the two of us. He pulled the shooter spot, so I was his spotter for this one. Usually it'd've been the other way around. Best part of that arrangement was that I didn't have to carry the fifty cal. The worst part was that I didn't get to shoot it. It wasn't a super long hump, but it gets wicked cold there. So we figured we'd turn it into a bike ride. Make life easier on ourselves."

"A bike ride?"

"Yeah. Off-road motorcycles. Sometimes we rode these special dirt bikes on patrol. Move light but fast, cover more ground. Lower profile than a Humvee or Em-Rap. Anyway, we were young and naive, and maybe we got a little carried away with the fun factor of the ride. Either way, we're tearing around, just the two of us, riding cross country when we happen upon this huge ground force crossing into our Area of Operations from the other side of the border. This wasn't some little group of *Muj* coming back from spring break. We're talking about a huge movement of Taliban troops caravanning from Pakistan. On their way to Kandahar."

"Holy crap, Daniel."

"Yeah, right? Looked to us like they were trying to beat the big freeze. Once the hard ice sets in that area, the highlands become almost completely impassable." He refreshed his whistle with a little more whiskey. "So, we tracked them for a while, reporting back to the rear with updates as we go. You know, we do our job. Somewhere along the way, though, we stumble into this little village that we lost track of. Some hole called Hahtqul."

"Hot cool?"

"Hahtqul." His phonetics were more nuanced, but he doubted she truly appreciated the difference. "Anyway… We barely trip on the edge of this place, and a bunch of these towel heads change direction. Baker figured some village goat herder or something tipped 'em off. So, instead of a nice little column running parallel to us a couple of miles off in the distance - barely close enough to track with our optics - we had a few hundred mechanized *Muj* bearing down on our position."

"Oh, jeez…"

"Yep. I was the spotter, so I had the radio. I barely got the call in to request air support before we made contact. Direct contact. None of that over-the-horizon bullshit the Navy likes. Not even a nice little exchange of personal hate mail like we snipers prefer. And that's when things got right sporting."

Corporal Wakefield raked his rifle to the right in a steady, sweeping motion. Taliban troops swarmed up the embankment like ants. Every time his front sight post fell across a silhouette he pressed the trigger. *Smooth is fast. Just like they trained us.* He emptied his third magazine on the return stroke. A pair of H-60 gunships had just arrived to provide the Recon Marines with much-needed air support. Their rhythmic thumping and rotor wash drowned out the *clack* of the discarded aluminum magazine skittering across the rocky ground. One of the gunships whizzed by and stitched the enemy ranks with another strafing run. An air-to-ground rocket, then another, punctuated a steady stream of 30-caliber machine gun fire from the chopper's door gunners.

Wakefield slapped his bolt home and prepared to pour a fourth magazine through his M-4. "Running low," he announced. *Not that there's anything to do about it if I run out of ammo,* he left unsaid. It did not need to be said. He was a Marine - a Force Recon Marine. If he shot his rifle dry then he would switch to his sidearm. If he shot that dry then he would throw rocks. If he ran out of rocks, he would fix his Kabar into place for bayonet work and fertilize the ground with the blood of his enemies.

Beside him, the thunderous report of Baker fielding his fifty-caliber rifle sounded once more. "Get us the Hell outta here, Wakefield!" the sergeant called as he cycled the heavy rifle's long bolt. A snapshot sent another half-inch projectile into enemy ranks. A melon-sized hole erupted in the torso of the lead *Muj* running up the ridge at their eleven o'clock. The insurgent behind him dropped with little more than a stump where his head used to be. A few more *Hajjis* behind them fell to the ground as well.

Corporal Wakefield found his radio handset once more."Maestro-One-Four," he growled at the Joint Tactical Air Controller on the other end of the transmission, "this is Romeo-Three-Three. Request update on evac. Over."

"Romeo-Three-Three, Maestro-One-Four," the controller responded flatly, "Angel-Six-One and Six-Two engaged heavy contact approximately ten mikes from your location." *Ten minutes,* Wakefield drew a ring around himself on the imaginary map of the battlefield in his head. That pretend circle marked his best guess on how far a pair of H-60s could fly in ten minutes. And that was how far away his help was at the moment, in one direction or another. "Sending Viper-Zero-Eight and Zero-Niner to your location best speed. ETA on fast movers: two-and-a-half mikes. Over."

Wakefield resumed fire. "Baker! Fast movers incoming!"

"How long?"

"Be here in three or the next one's free."

"I hate this," *BANG!* "-ing country!" Baker spit the last of his chew. "Alright. Time for Plan D. Ratline over to the blind side of this ridge to our six and tell those jet jockeys to light this place up!" The sergeant matched action to words, swapping the big Barrett for his own M-4 as the enemy closed like a wave of ants setting upon an unattended sandwich. Baker fired indiscriminately at the swarm of *Mujahideen* scrambling up the hillside in front of them. Despite the covering fire coming their way, the local troops seemed unanimously eager to be the first one to kill an American Marine today.

Both Leathernecks stood and ran for the top of the ridge behind them. Baker shuffled backward with the Barrett slung over his shoulder. He sprayed 5.56mm lead at the enemy while Wakefield ran at a full sprint and barked into his radio.

"Viper flight, Romeo-Three-Three. Lay down heat on east face of ridge at my last grid! Danger close!" At the hill's crest, Wakefield ignored his radio, braced his rifle against his shoulder, and faced his enemy like a Marine. Baker, a step behind and still shuffling to the rear while firing, was caught unprepared for the change in slope. He tripped, stumbled, and fell backward - knocking his spotter back as well.

The duet tumbled backwards a few yards down the western side of the ridge before they were able to arrest their momentum. Wakefield managed to roll into some semblance of a prone shooting position just in time to drop a *Muj* cresting the ridge. His aim shifted to the next. In his peripheral vision, he saw several other *Hajjis* drop. A quick glance revealed Baker, sprawled on his back, knees apart, firing up the hillside from between his legs and screaming curses that managed to use the same profane word a noun, verb, and every other part of speech in the English language.

And then the opposite face of the ridge - the side they had just vacated - erupted like a volcano.

"That's a Hell of a story, Daniel."

"Yeah, well, it was a Hell of a time." He helped himself to a taste of whiskey from his glass, then cracked a smile. "You should'a seen Baker. Spitting lead and pissing brass. You know? That day alone he took out, like, twelve trucks with that Barrett. Just lined 'em all up at the bottom of that hill like a boss. Held all those *Muj* off our left flank, too. Between the fifty-cal and his carbine - shoot, there's a whole generation of Fuzzy Muzzies that were never born cause'a that guy. He was a real Marine. He was still in after I got out, just carrying on. Getting some. Sending *Muj* straight to Allah."

Sandra held her glass low and tried to ask the obvious question as gently as she knew how. "How many people did you guys kill that day, Daniel?"

"None." Danny said sharply. He spun his whiskey glass on the table. "Marines don't kill people, Elbee. We neutralize the enemy. What those barbarians did - long before we ever got there, may I add? - that ain't human. But the final count was just over two hundred enemies killed in action. No friendly casualties." Sandra was speechless. *What do you say to something like that? Does she see me as a mass murderer? The next T.J. Phillips just waiting to pop?* "But we can probably chalk most of that up to the ordinance dropped by the gunships and the F-18s."

As Danny finished his whiskey, he caught a look out of the corner of his eye like maybe his partner wanted to say something. After a moment of silence, Sandra's face changed a little. Danny signaled the waitress for a fresh round of drinks.

"So, it's true. You're a *bona fide* red-white-and-blue war hero."

"Nah," he waived dismissively. "I was just an idiot kid who started off thinkin' he could make a difference. I learned how to do some stuff, that's all. By the time I was done I was just another idiot tryin' not to get killed." Danny's voice dropped a bit. "Knew some heroes, though." His eyes fell. His finger tapped the table slowly. "Real deal heroes."

The waitress returned with a fresh whiskey, and none too soon. Sandra politely declined another glass of wine. "Do you miss it? Being a Marine?"

"Still am a Marine," he pointed. "Once a Marine, always a Marine."

"You know what I mean, Daniel."

His head bobbed a little from side-to-side. "I miss the guys. Some of them. I don't miss the war."

"I can imagine it's hard sometimes, isn't it? Watching friends die?"

"Well, you don't get used to it. That's for damn sure." Danny poured the caramel colored liquor down his gullet. "You know what they say, Elbee? They say, 'Marines never die.' Nope. We don't die. 'Marines,' they say, 'just get redeployed.'"

"I don't know what that means."

"Redeployed," he repeated. "It means 'sent home.'" Danny's stormy eyes locked onto her softer blue irises with full intensity. "You understand? Right? We get sent home."

Home? she thought almost audibly. "You mean, sent to Heaven?"

"Heaven? Heaven…" he considered. "I suppose a few might make it there." He shook his head. "But wherever it is, it must be a place with a helluva lot of fighting. 'Cause that's all we're really good for, isn't it? In everybody else's eyes, anyway."

"That's not true, Daniel."

"Isn't it?" His green eyes stabbed into hers. "Tell me something. Honestly. What do you think DHS would've done if I had shot Phillips last month?"

"I'm not sure. I guess it depends on the circumstances."

"You saw the circumstances. You think they'd've suspended me?"

"Probably not."

"How about a commendation? You think they'd've given me one of those instead?"

"Possibly. I guess it might depend on whether Secretary Dagenhart - well, I mean -"

Danny cut her off with the index finger from his whiskey glass. "Now, hold onto that thought for a second. What about Phoenix? If I'd've chased that bastard into a crowd of black protestors, there ain't no way they'd've just watched him an' I tussle. They'd've lynched my pale Irish ass."

"Probably," she conceded.

"And as soon as one of them got ahold of my gun, it'd be game over for me." He raised his eyebrows to add emphasis to his point. "A nice Fourth of July funeral for Special Agent Wakefield. Flag draped coffin, bagpipes, the whole works."

"I don't see your point."

"My point, Elbee, is that as far as my government and my countrymen are concerned, a trooper's only good for one thing: killing. Once we've served, that's all we are in their eyes." He cut off her protestations with a raised finger before she could speak. "If I'd've killed for my country they'd've given me a medal. If I died for my country then they'd give me a hero's send off. As long as the civvies - the real people, like Secretary Dagenhart or Senator McKissass - are safe. That's all that matters to our masters. But when I do my job - by the book, I might add - I get punished. Hell, Elbee, they still might fire me over it." He finished his whiskey and put the empty glass on the table. "You're not totally out of the woods, either. You know? And you didn't even do anything wrong."

Sandra shrugged. "Yeah, well, what can we do about it?"

"Well, I mean, if we're screwed either way, we might as well go out like champs."

Sandra leaned back in her chair with a deeply concerned look upon her face. "I'm not sure I like where this conversation is going, Daniel."

Wakefield remained firmly in place, his whiskey held before him. He turned the glass in his hand, took another sip of the caramel colored liquid, then set it down. "You're probably right," he nodded. *Don't push her limits,* he resigned. *If it comes down to it, you'll need her on your side.*

CHAPTER 8

HEADLIGHTS CUT through the dark predawn morning. Then more followed them. Four lights became four pairs, then four pairs of pairs, then dozens. All of them the same. Moving the same direction at the same speed. Coordinated. Uniform.

Most Americans were still snuggled up under their blankets, tucked into their beds as armored military vehicles rolled through the streets in the early morning hours. Most Americans were stealing the last bit of sleep from what was left of their weekend before life forced them back to work on a cruel Monday morning. They were blissfully unaware as those convoys split into teams, groups of armored trucks and personnel carriers that maneuvered into predetermined positions that would allow their operators to control critical access ways and lines of communication; positions that would allow their riders to secure key areas throughout cities across the country.

Most Americans woke up on a Monday morning to find uniforms that they usually only saw in brief snippets on the news or on nondenominational holiday commercials now standing on their own streets. Walking up and down the sidewalks in fire teams and platoon-strength formations. This was no parade that greeted America's citizenry. It was military action.

On a cold Monday morning in late November, the United States of Martial Law was born. The land of the free had become Occupied America.

"Let's play the audio," Lonnie prompted his producer, "while we still have a show." Obediently, an unseen production technician rebroadcast the speech that made history just a few hours ago. Most of the audience listened to the audio on their radios, but paid subscribers were treated to a video that had been recorded as the speaker made his proclamation from a podium in Washington, D.C.

"A very real and grave threat exists in this country," the paternal figure spoke with a firm, direct voice. "We have all seen this threat. We know it is real. We know it is deadly. And we know it cannot be allowed to continue."

The confident speaker turned his head to address the other side of the room. "That is why, as the director of our nation's defenses, I recommended to the President that we take immediate executive action to neutralize the threat of the insurgency that has modeled itself after the so-called Constitutional Killer - a renegade, a criminal, a terrorist who has killed numerous Americans all across this great nation and inspired others to self-radicalize and rise up against our lawful and rightful government institutions."

The speaker half-turned and gestured to another man with lighter gray hair than his own and whose immaculate uniform bristled with a collage of shiny pins and colorful medals. "Over the weekend, I met with Secretary James, the Secretary of the Army. And with General Thorne, the Chief of Staff of the Army. Upon the President's authorization, we have initiated certain emergency provisions of the PATRIOT ACT and the National Defense Authorization Act approved by Congress. I will allow General Thorne to outline some of the details."

With the briefest of exchanged nods, the two men traded places so that the general could utilize the podium's microphone. This was a courtesy to the broadcast audience, as everyone in the White House Pressroom was familiar enough with "Bloody" Thorne to know that the general could easily project his voice to every ear in the room - and the rest of the building, if he chose. Really, his voice could reach the whole block if he wanted them to hear him.

"Thank you, Secretary Warner." General Amos B. Thorne gripped the podium as he briefed the audience, as was his habit. It was a behavior born not from any anxiety or apprehension over public speaking, but to curb his natural inclination to destroy anyone or anything that stood between himself and his objective - including terrorists, buildings, reporters, subordinates, or any angel or demon foolish enough to rub him the wrong way. "The situation is as clear as it is complex. A highly trained fugitive is operating within the Continental United States. He has assassinated several national leaders and a number of federal agents. He operates with an as-yet-determined network of support, which in all probability includes an unknown number of individuals either directly or indirectly contributing to his terrorist agenda."

The general's steely eyes never blinked. "Now, our mission is to find and neutralize this terrorist and to quell any cells that have sprung up - or that will spring up - that might be either linked to him or his agenda of terror. To that end, as of oh-five-hundred hours this morning, the men and women of the United States Army have set up a comprehensive network of checkpoints and security stations from which we can carry out a comprehensive sweep of every major city in order to root out and eliminate this threat." He glared into the nearest camera with unshakable resolve. "If this man, Thomas Jackson Phillips, or his friends are listening, let me be clear: We will find you. And we will stop you. If you turn yourselves in, we will be more lenient. But you have provoked the attention of the most capable fighting force on this Earth, and we will not stop until we have you."

A sea of reporters erupted. Wave after wave of questions crashed upon the front of the press room. Thorn stood as still as a statue, a look of contempt mixed with defiance upon his face. "General Thorne," one voice rose above the others, "what will you do if your men cannot find Phillips?"

The general shook his head. "That just isn't a realistic outcome here. We are on the ground, and we are expanding our control of all lines of communication. Every second that Phillips and his renegades enjoy from this moment on is simply borrowed time."

"But what if he's not found?" another reporter rebutted.

"Then we'll expand our search into the suburbs. Then the smaller towns. Then rural spaces. Make no mistake: the full might of the United States Army has been brought to bear on this operation."

"You said 'the full might,'" a voice from the other side of the press galley chimed in, "does that include intelligence assets? Both military and other agencies?"

"Nothing is off the table," Thorne answered.

"What about air strikes?"

"Like I just said," he scowled. "Everything is on the table. You simply cannot conduct half a military operation. Nor can you advertise to your enemy what your own limitations are. Not if you want to win."

"Are you saying," an accusing voice called from the front row, "that you would authorize military airstrikes against targets here in the States?"

"That is all for now. Good day." As more questions begged for his attention, General Thorne turned away from the podium and marched out of the White House Pressroom.

With a gesture unseen by the audience, Lonnie interrupted the playback. "You all heard this, right? They've just declared Martial Law in the United States."

"This is really unbelievable," Kyp quipped.

"It's unimaginable," Lonnie's eyes flashed. "I mean, there are laws in place to prevent exactly this sort of thing from ever happening. Right? Fred, read us the laws."

Factcheck Fred flipped through his notes. "Well, I mean, the full text of each of these laws - and there are several - would be too time consuming, but we put links to them up on the website for anyone who wants to take a look at them. But I'll just list the laws."

"List them."

"Let me just read the laws themselves."

"List the laws."

"I'm gonna just read this list, because some of these are pretty big deals. I mean, every law is a law, and therefore they're all technically big deals -"

"Yeah," Kyp interjected, "but there's a difference, and I think we all get that, between a little law like the speed limit and a big law like, oh, I don't know, the Fourteenth Amendment."

"Right," Fred clamored. "And these are the latter. These are things like *Posse Commitatus* -"

"Okay," Lonnie broke in, "explain what that is for the audience. Because we can't just assume that everyone is a Constitutional lawyer."

*   *   *

Danny stared into the bottom of his coffee cup as if he were probing the depths of a black hole. His body may have sat in a Metro barista, but his mind was fixated on his nation. "*Posse Commitatus* is just the beginning, Little D."

"So, you don't want sugar?" Derek pinched a white paper packet between the fingertips of his outstretched hand. "Because this could be just about the worst cup of coffee ever."

"You're not even listening, are you?"

"You're the one who's not listening," Derek countered. "I'm telling you straight up: this garbage tastes like they filtered it through a dirty gym sock." Martin ripped open four packets of sugar, poured them into his cup, then added three miniature cups of non-dairy creamer and set to stirring his brew.

"Serves you right for buying coffee made for hipsters. Next time, order something manly." Danny looked around the room. "Preferably from a place that doesn't look like the set of a 90's sitcom." He stabbed his finger into the table top and returned to his point. "*Posse Commitatus* declares it unlawful for US military personnel or assets to be deployed on American soil under any circumstances except during foreign invasion." He gave his friend an accusatory look. "Have the Chinese parachuted into Chicago?"

"No," Derek answered dryly, "but it might be a step up for the place if they did."

"Are these troops looking for *Hizballah* or ISIL cells here Stateside?"

"Now you're just being pedantic." Derek sampled his cup again, frowned again, then ripped open four more sugar packets. "You know they aren't. But what if they find some *Muj* while they're looking for Phillips and his crew? That'd be a good thing, right?"

"The Insurrection Act has been on the books for more than two hundred years," Danny continued. "It says that the president can't just flippantly call out the Army to hunt criminals. Even serious threats like Phillips. That's why we have guys like the Eff-Bee-Eye."

"Fat lot of good the Bureau was against him in Pennsylvania," Derek reminded him. "You saw what happened there. Phillips is a former Special Forces Ranger. We handed them his location and got the drop on him - and he still kicked the dog crap out of those guys." He tried his coffee again, then put the cup down in resignation. "Face it, dude. The Army's the only ones qualified to take him down."

Danny shook his head. "The Army's job is to fight wars overseas. Not police our streets."

"They're not policing them."

"Armed troopers are conducting security patrols throughout neighborhoods and business districts looking for specific individuals," Danny retorted. "Back when we did that in Iraq, folks called it 'policing.' And they busted our balls for it all day long. What's changed?"

"This isn't Iraq. People are scared."

Danny slowly shook his head. "The only people who are scared are the folks who think Phillips is gunning for them."

"Convenient, then," Derek smiled smugly, "that they're also the very people who have the authority to declare war and put the Army in motion. Oh, *and* they sign all of the Army's checks."

"I'll buy your drinks tomorrow night at Black Sam's if you can name me right now the last time Congress actually utilized their Constitutional duty to declare war."

"Does that mean that you and Sandra will actually be coming out tomorrow?" Derek fished. "The last few weeks, the two of you have been a little, uh, nesty."

"Nesty?"

"It's a word."

"I don't think it is."

"It is now."

"Well, whether it is or not, we're not nesty. She's just been settling into the apartment."

"Mmmm-hmm," Derek smiled. "And how's the settling going?"

"Fine."

"She ask you to get rid of the guns yet?"

"What? No." *Why would she…* Danny's mind wondered. *Because she hates them, that's why.*

"Just watch out, dude. They move in, then they take over. Pretty soon, she's picking your clothes and telling you to eat more salad and drink less whiskey."

"Is that what happened with you and Aliyah?" Danny reposted.

"Shut up," Derek groaned. "You know," he said pointedly, "it's cracks like that that make me wish I hadn't fought so hard to stay here."

"Oh, c'mon, Little D. You and I both know that you're not going anywhere." Danny held up a finger, "First off, Aliyah's job at the hospital keeps you both here." He cocked his eyebrow and threw his best friend a sideways glance. "That is, if you still want to be together."

"Of course we do," Little D replied. "And there are hospitals everywhere."

"Secondly," Danny continued with another finger, "didn't you just tell me that you're starting grad school at Hopkins in January?"

"There are colleges everywhere, too."

"Thirdly," Danny ticked another digit, "for better or worse, D.C. is the place to fast-track your career. Hell, even no-talent ass hats like Nick and Jenkins get promoted here in the Beltway."

"With startling regularity." Derek sneered, but it was not because of the bitterness in his coffee.

"See? There you go. A guy with your talents and successes should enjoy a meteoric rise here."

Little D smiled. "It does feel a bit like being a barracuda in a gold fish bowl. You know?" The humor faded from his face as a quartet of Soldiers marched down the sidewalk past the coffee shop's oversized window. "But, you saw how pissed Nick was. He called human resources and had them find me a slot somewhere. Had them on speaker phone while I listened. Five minutes later, he's all 'There you go: Arizona or a pink slip.'"

"So what happened?"

"Dr. Wiley sorted it out."

"See?" Danny offered his best friend a double-shot of enthusiasm. "It's all good, Little D. Don't worry too much about Nick. He's a short term problem. In the long run, he's only a minor inconvenience. He's nothing but a forty-year-old adolescent. Jenkins'll give him the clap, or he'll wrap his Audi around a tree or something. You'll see."

Derek offered the bigger man a meaningful glance. "I was kinda hoping to see you deck him on your way out the door after they fire you. And you know they will."

"I'm not through yet," Danny puffed. "And I found the perfect way to make this suspension nonsense go away."

"Epic ass kissing?" Derek guessed. "And I mean, on a biblical level?" He puckered up his lips in pantomime.

"Better."

Little D looked genuinely panicked. "Please tell me it isn't blackmail. You've got dirt on one of the committee members, don't you? Oh, God, you've been hanging out with Oscar too much."

Darkness fell across Wakefield's countenance. "I'm gonna do what I should've done outside HQ." Danny searched the bottom of his coffee cup, as if he would find something - answers, solace, permission, anything - somewhere in that black abyss. "I'm gonna put an end to this." He drummed his fingers on the cup's paper sleeve. "I'm gonna kill Phillips."

"Lots of people say that -"

"Lots of people run their mouths." Danny looked up from his cup and into his best friend's eyes. "You know how this has to end. He's not coming in. He's just gonna keep going until someone puts him down."

"Dude, the whole friggin' Army's after him. They'll get him within a week. Two, tops."

Danny shook his head. "They're too rigid. Too inflexible. Just like I was while I was running the task force." He slid his coffee away from himself. "No. They'll never find him, unless it's by accident."

"What makes you think you'll do any better? Was it something from the photos that," Little D caught himself before he said Stevenson's name out loud. He looked over his shoulder, then resumed in conspiratorial tones, "that we found?"

"No, not really. Those pics had lots of spaghetti, but nothing really useful. No, it's 'cause I'm free. It's kinda ironic, isn't it? But as long as I'm on this suspension, I'm free to breathe. To move. To do my own investigation - and my own wet work, if needed."

"Dude. Seriously. You'll be lucky to walk away from this review able to get a job anywhere. You press your luck and you're gonna end up in jail." Danny stared into his coffee cup to avoid his best friend's chastising gaze. "I mean it, Big D. Just relax. Make the most of the downtime. Take the bike for a ride."

"I did that."

"Go shooting."

"Did that, too. Zero'd the new rifle. Optics came in this morning."

"Oh, really? You finished the four fifty-eight? How's it shoot?"

"Pretty straightforward. It's pretty much a no-frills gun."

"Except for the part where you can drop anything short of a rhino with one shot." Derek was downright giddy.

"Not quite, but almost. Those five hundred grain rounds make the question of body armor pretty much irrelevant. Even if a plate stops the bullet, the kinetic energy from the impact will take a dude out."

"Man, I wish Aliyah would let me keep a gun in the apartment."

"Yeah, well, you might wanna start with something a little smaller than a four fifty-eight. It's got a lot more recoil than the mil-spec ARs, but it's not unmanageable. All in all, I'd say it suits me just fine."

"Speaking of suits: did you remember to pick up a tux for tonight?"

"A tux - Oh, crap! The fundraiser!" Danny jumped up from the table and nearly spilled his drink as he consulted his watch. "Elbee's gonna kill me."

"That's what these relationships are designed to do," Derek quipped as Danny bolted through the coffee shop's door. "To kill us."

*　　　*　　　*

Randy slipped through the doorway into the gun shop's back room carrying a black, padded case and wearing a grin. "Looks like Christmas came early for my brother from another mother."

T.J. looked up from the workbench he had been sitting at all day. Tucked into the counter's rear corner, Randy's laptop played news reports from a quartet of channels and websites on its screen. A hodgepodge of maps, old training manuals, and sheets of paper with scribbles, drawings, and lists were scattered across the flat workspace where Randy usually built and maintained his customers' rifles. "What?"

"Take a break," Randy indicated the collection of photos T.J. had printed off of the internet: White House pictures; views of the grounds and interior shots taken by people on various tours; pictures of President Fulbright with the First Lady, waving at spectators during his inauguration; President Fulbright leading the White House Easter egg hunt with the First Daughters; President Fulbright and the First Son engaged in a somber discussion in the Oval Office; President Fulbright wheeling his geriatric mother up to a table in the State Dining Room; President Fulbright taking his dog out for a late-night poop break on the White House lawn…

Randy held the nylon bag at arm's reach and presented the gift to his friend. "You know, I should kick your ass for breaking the Beast -"

"Hey," T.J. threw up his hands defensively, "the rifle's just fine. You said so yourself. Now, the scope… that's another matter entirely."

"Busted up all to Hell," Randy said matter-of-factly. "But I've been slipping that cash you bagged into some usable accounts. Slowly, so as to not raise anyone's attention. And that old Colonel Sanders-looking cat was right about ammo sales. They've been through the roof the last few weeks. I can't keep the stuff that you used in D.C. in stock no matter how much I order. Stuff's gold right now. Other brands are flying off the shelf, too. And gun sales are almost triple what they were this time last year."

"Revolution must be good for the gun business."

"Which is why I'm giving you this," Randy jiggled the rifle case.

T.J. took the rectangular bag into his hands. It featured a set of backpack-style straps in addition to the traditional carry handle, a smattering of pockets along the face, and strategically placed areas of MOLLE webbing so that additional accessories could be attached to it as needed. T.J. could tell by the case's weight that it was far from empty. "Dude," he looked at his friend, "you really didn't have to do this."

"I know. But it wasn't that big a deal. And you *did* pay for it. Open it."

The bag's long zipper opened to reveal a black rifle with a familiar pattern. T.J. withdrew the AR-15 and searched for any modifications Randy might have made.

"That's a match-grade trigger," Randy narrated, "just like I put in all of my personal rifles. The nickel-boron bolt carrier group is rated for fully automatic fire - which is good, because we can shoot a semi as fast as a full auto gun." Randy's voice carried more sarcasm than contrition as he issued his false apology. "Matches the finish on the stainless barrel nicely, though. Refinished on the all of the mechanical bits all nice and shiny, too."

T.J.'s eyes bounced from the 1911-style grip panels and sling attachment plate to the selector switch, bolt release, charging handle and scope rings - all of which were a silver hue that contrasted sharply with the rifle's traditional black chassis. "It's very blingy."

"Nothing fancy on the optics. Dot sight with a flip-to the side magnifier. With that seven-and-a-half inch barrel and integrated suppressor, it's set up primarily as a CQB gun anyway."

Most gunfights in the real world were, in T.J.'s experience, Close Quarters Battle events. According to the manual of arms, a gun like this could easily throw 5.56NATO rounds several hundred yards downrange, but a precision bolt-action rifle was the preferred tool for engaging targets past 75 yards anyway. And even though things did not always work out ideally back at JSOC, the ideal was the way the operators preferred to do business when given the opportunity.

T.J. ran a hand down the bench-turned suppressor, then glanced down at the aluminum receiver at the heart of the rifle. To no surprise at all, there was no serial number. *Another gun turned out from a blank here at the shop,* he nodded. *No paperwork. No history. No way of tracing it.* "It's very nice," he nodded.

"Think of it as my contribution to the cause."

T.J. confirmed that the rifle's chamber was empty. It was an old habit, ingrained after years of handling firearms. He angled his body away from Randy so that he could shoulder the rifle while pointing it in a safe direction. He rested his cheek on the stock, aimed at a blank wall, and flipped through the holographic sight's settings until he found the reticle he liked the most. He settled on a bright green circle with a dot in its center. "Thanks again, brother. For everything. And not just for keeping me in the fight. You know, I couldn't do this without you."

"We swore an oath, man."

T.J. powered down the sight and returned the gun to the case's main compartment. "A lot of folks wouldn't take it this far." He opened the pouches on the case's side and made a mental inventory of their contents. An adjustable single-point sling; cleaning instruments, solvent, and lubricant; spare batteries for the sight; and a half-dozen 40-round magazines, already filled, with a few spare boxes to boot.

"Those're seventy-seven grain bullets," Randy narrated. "Sierra Open Tip Match. Like the kind those Eye-Dee-Eff guys used that one time we saw them. They're a few feet per second slower than some rounds, but I figure the extra mass is worth it at close range."

If you say so, T.J. nodded. *Free gun. Free ammo. Don't look a gift horse in the mouth.* The bullets Randy provided with the rifle were almost half again as massive as standard commercial ammunition in this caliber. *If he thinks it'll make a difference…*

"I gave you the five-five-six gun," Randy continued. "Kept its three-hundred twin for myself."

T.J. looked back up at his former teammate. "You change your mind about rolling with me on the next op? Two guns are better than one."

Randy hissed as he shook his head. "I would if I could, brother. But I just don't think I can bring myself to pull the trigger on a gringo."

"What if they were a threat?"

"Oh, *fuggetabouddit*, brother. Some dude jacks me or tries to hurt mine and I'll slot him without missing a beat."

T.J.'s eyes pierced Randy's heart. "You know the folks I'm going after are a threat. They're ruining our country, man. And they're doing it on purpose."

"Yeah," Randy grimaced, "I know that's where you're coming from. And I dig what you're giving off, man. I really do. But from where I'm sitting, there's still a big gaping gulf between shooting a dude in self-defense and rolling against a target on an op." He shook his head. "I'm sorry man. I really am."

"It's okay, man. Just throwing the invite out there."

In truth, T.J. never really understood how some people could support an operation but not want to be a part of it. He knew that a fair number of civilians and even conventional troops paid lip service to supporting a campaign, and some of them even went so far as to contributing from the rear, but most fell far short of standing on the firing line to do the actual work.

Previously, T.J. simply assumed that such people were either weak, cowards, or lairs - maybe a combination of the three. He'd never met a Ranger who hesitated to jump into the fight. Oh, sure, there were always those POGs - Pieces of Garbage - who wore Ranger tabs even while they served in the rear with the gear or from the relative safety of the Tactical Operations Center far, far away from the action. But those guys were not operators - they were never real Rangers in T.J.'s book, and Randy had echoed that same sentiment when they served together at JSOC. All of the guys in the unit did. T.J. could not fully wrap his head around the discrepancy between the old Randy's gung-ho attitude and the new Randy's hesitation, but he could honor his friend and respect his wishes. "Nonetheless," T.J. repeated, "thanks."

"No worries. Now, how 'bout I order us some Chinese delivery and you show me what you've figured out on the President's pattern-of-life so far."

CHAPTER 9

SOFT LIGHTS CAST the posh dining hall in a warm glow that glinted and gleamed off of golden and glassy decorations that gave the massive chamber a ritzy, Christmasy feel. A grand piano, piloted by a dark skinned gentleman who's close-cropped curls were frosted at the temples, played a mixture of soft jazz and slow Christmas tunes softly in the background. A few other musicians, decked out in cheap black suits and clip-on bow ties meant to pass as tuxedos, sat at their stations around the piano upon the stage and silently tended to their instruments and their drinks.

"Excuse me, sir," a waiter who looked like he was barely old enough to hold the bottle in his hand interjected, "but did you have the Krug, or the Dom Perignon?"

Danny looked up from his plate of food - a fine disc of china upon which rested a garlic roasted steak that could fit in his palm, a dollop of chunky potatoes that still retained their red skins, and three steamed sprigs of asparagus, all topped with a thin ribbon of béarnaise sauce - and tried to remember exactly which champagne he had ordered. What was left of the pale, bubbly fluid in the crystal flute ahead of him gave no clues as to the correct answer. And truly, Danny did not care. In his book, one champagne was as good as another. But he had no doubt that the rest of the people around the table not only remembered what they were drinking, but also what he had started with an eternity ago when their food was delivered. Whichever one he chose, he knew that these people would judge him for it. And he knew that they would not forgive him for mixing two allegedly different types of expensive champagne in the same glass.

"The Dom," Sandra offered from his left. "For us both, please."

"Of course, ma'am." The waiter smiled, refilled their glasses, then moved around the large, round table.

"So, Special Agent Elbee," a matron whose black and silver dress looked like the photo negative of her hair and was seated two chairs to Sandra's left smiled, "tell us, dear. Are you working any interesting cases right now?"

Sandra cleared her throat. "Nothing specific," she dodged. "I'm working with the Bureau's narcotics task force right now, while admin's working out the details of my permanent transfer to D.C. But I'm considering a move to a team that specializes in investigating violence against women."

"Goodness knows we need that." The older woman turned to the superhumanly gorgeous brunette at the opposite side of the round table who came along this evening with an unnamed boy toy who, despite wearing a designer tux, looked like he just walked out of an underwear ad. "Why, Angie, didn't you just do a film where you played a woman who was abused?"

Danny held his snicker inside as he wondered to himself, *Exactly how much money does a person have to make each year to call a famous actress like Angela Harrington 'Angie?'* He sliced himself another tiny bite from his miniature steak.

"I did." The previously radiant actress became suddenly somber. "But Nicole, my character in '*The Bridge*,' isn't a victim. She's got a strength - that's what I tried to project, anyway. She's got this strength that helps her to overcome all of this adversity. And celebrating that kind of struggle is why we're here tonight."

Is it? Danny looked around the room again. Politicians and socialites shared tables with businessmen and outright tycoons, with the occasional celebrity or up-and-comer scattered about like so many sprinkles on a cupcake.

"Is something the matter, Special Agent Wakefield?" their table's wealthy matron inquired.

"Oh, no." Out of the corner of his eye, Danny could see that Sandra gave him a look. The Look, in fact. The one that silently growled, *Don't make a scene.* "Nothing at all."

"You look like you've got something on your mind," another woman at the table, whom Danny remembered was a D.C. area psychologist, inquired from his right.

"Just a funny thought, is all."

"I love funny thoughts," the shrink grasped her blonde date by the hand. "Jessica and I both do. Why don't you share yours?"

Danny searched for just the right words while Sandra hid her obvious sudden discomfort with a drink of champagne. "Well, it's just, here we are. Like you said, Angie - I mean, Miss Harrington, at this lovely dinner," he glanced down at the fancy invitation tucked halfway under his plate, "supporting the National Equity Alliance, and I just can't help but think of the irony." He swore he almost heard Sandra *hum* as she returned her crystal flute to the table.

"And what irony would that be?" the therapist pressed with a clinical smile.

Danny kept his tone light. "I mean, c'mon, Doc. Here we are, sitting in the wealthiest city in America - a city which produces nothing, I might add. Now, I'm just some shlum with a job, rowing away all week. Just like everybody else. You know? But this room is packed with multimillionaires." He gestured to Matron Moneybags. "And probably a few billionaires. All talking about how hard life is for the little guy. Like they have a friggin' clue what it's like to actually *be* the guy or gal living from paycheck to paycheck and struggling to make ends meet." He looked at the actress, whose face could have won the Oscar for Most Likely to Stab Wakefield with a Dinner Knife. "You, Miss Harrington. You make, what, ten million bucks per movie?" The Hollywood A-lister looked down, either ashamed for being called out or insulted by the low figure. Danny could not tell which. "And there's nothing wrong with that. Hell, I've seen some of your movies. You do a good job. And people deserve to be paid for their work.

"But here's my point. And it's for each of you. You all come here and spent two grand a plate for dinner served by guys and gals making five or ten bucks an hour, dressed up in cheap tuxes so that they don't look like slaves. You fly to work in private jets or drive European cars back to private villas that cost eleven jibbity zillion dollars. And all the while you come crying to us regular folk about how there's so much inequality in our country, and how the rest of us should all just give more. But how much do you give?

"Did you, Miss Academy Awards, keep the first hundred grand or so - 'cause a gal's gotta live - from your last movie and then donate the rest of your paycheck to battered women's shelters? Or is your service to the women you claim to admire so much limited to pretending to be one on screen?" Suddenly, Danny felt a claw dig into his left thigh. Sandra was the picture of polite thoughtfulness, even though the threat her right hand - invisible under the table - made to Danny's wellbeing was anything but genteel.

The matron stiffened. "I'll have you know," she leaned her head back a bit and literally looked down her nose at Danny, "that my husband and I contribute over a million dollars annually to academic scholarships to disadvantaged minorities."

Danny nodded. "That's quite generous," he sniffed. "Your husband does what again?"

"Walter's company has many holdings," she condescended.

"And what do you do? You personally, I mean. Other than spend Walt's dividend checks?" The matron huffed. "I'm sorry. That's really none of my business. But Joe America gives ten percent of his paycheck off the top to his church, then makes other charitable donations as able. I know folks who take the phrase, '*Give 'til it hurts*' to a ridiculous level. Does that million bucks a year really even put a dent in your checkbook? And does it come from your personal accounts, or is it paid via an allotment from corporate assets?"

"I can't see how that would matter," she sneered.

"It matters, Constance," Walter chimed in with a sour expression on his face as he stared into the bottom of a glass of 20-year-old scotch, "because what Agent Wakefield is trying to insinuate is that our level of giving is not proportionate to our personal wealth."

"All of this," Danny spread his hands to take in the scened with one wide gesture, "is self-aggrandizing bullshit. This snob, dog, and pony show isn't about you helping people. You could do that from home. This is about you being seen and looking like you care. It's about increasing your own celebrity, not improving other people's lives. You get dolled up in clothes that cost more than the average Joe makes in a year. And you make a show of your charity so that people can see you pretending to care. But your so-called charity doesn't actually cost you anything. And it ends the second the cameras disappear. Designers *give* you those clothes so that they can get their name out there and make their paycheck off the backs of Americans who actually have to balance their checkbooks each month. You have so much that even when you do spend, the giving doesn't hurt you. And no matter how much you claim to care about causes like this, you always have a hundred times as much as the people you say you're trying to lift up."

"Well then," Joe Underwear smiled from his perch at Angela's shoulder, "what would you suggest? That we stop?"

"Stop giving? No. Stop with the false piety? Stop preaching about inequality in America while you all live lifestyles of the rich and famous? You bet."

"That is an interesting thought." Danny could not tell if the shrink to his right was genuinely moved or if she was just pretending to consider his opinion so that she could look enlightened in front of her girlfriend. What he did know for certain was that nobody at that table wanted him there anymore. But his opinion could not be unspoken. The damage was done. And it was long time to make his exit.

As Danny desperately searched the room for an excuse to leave, a quiet round of applause - unenthusiastic, but no less polite - passed through the hall. A black man in a sueded burgundy shirt and black slacks took the stage. He cued the guitarist to start a bluesy riff backed by a slow drum beat. A pianist played a series of minor chords.

"Isn't that your ex?" Danny indicated with a thrust eyebrow. Elbee turned toward the musicians just as Lawrence Jackson - *always Lawrence; never Larry,* Danny reminded himself - lifted a trumpet with a brushed bronze finish to his lips and began to blow out a melody that danced across a minor key.

Danny reached into his breast pocket and withdrew a folded one hundred dollar bill. He tucked the c-note under his plate while the other patrons stared at his *déclassé* gesture. "Anybody else gonna hook the waiter up?"

"We don't carry cash," Constance condescended.

"People don't usually leave tips at these sorts of things," Sandra hissed.

"Huh. All these rich folk," Danny mused, "and I'm the only one with any money." He deposited his napkin on his plate. "Well, it's been lovely meeting you fine people, but if you'll excuse me, there's an open floor over there," he held his hand out to Sandra in invitation, "and I believe I owe the most beautiful woman in the room a dance."

Couples slowly swayed and spun around the polished hardwood floor as Danny led Sandra - still seething - along in a subtle oscillating rhythm. Her hands held him almost as harshly as her eyes as they sachet'd in sync with the musical stylings of Lucious D and his backing band. In Wakefield's traditional black tuxedo and Elbee's elegant golden gown, their attire was perfect for the venue. But even though he and his date looked the part, Danny knew to his core that they did not belong there.

"I can't believe you, Daniel," Sandra hissed into his ear. "How could you embarrass me like that?"

Wakefield kept his expression light and his voice soft. "Embarrass you?"

"Acting like that in front of those people."

"Those people don't know you or me. And they don't care. And it wasn't an act," he grinned. "It was the truth. They asked for my opinion. And I gave it to them."

Sandra seethed. "Dammit, Daniel! You knew how important to me tonight was."

"Yeah," he looked to the stage where Lawrence played his own rendition of an older Sting tune on his trumpet. "But what I didn't know what *why* it was so important to you." He looked back into her icy eyes. "Two grand a piece is pretty steep for a fed's salary. And this is a pretty tough soiree to crash. How'd you score the tickets?"

Sandra rolled her eyes. "Fine. I didn't buy them. They were a gift."

"From Lawrence?"

"It's not like that!" she huffed. "Okay, fine. He gave me the tickets. But, it was, like, a month ago. When he and I were still…" Her voice trailed off for a moment. "You know. Anyway, it was just after he landed the gig, and he was really excited. The plan was for me to bring a friend, you know? Like maybe Hudson. But then…"

Danny slowly nodded as her voice trailed off. He needed no reminders about exactly who was involved with whom a few weeks ago, nor did he need to be reminded of how much had changed in such a short timeframe. "I'm sorry, Elbee." He gave her his most sincere and heartfelt look. "I really am."

"Smooth tongued Irishmen," she shook her head. "You should be sorry." They continued to move to the music, but Sandra still held herself back at a distance that told him that she was not quite ready to forgive him. "You know, Daniel, you don't always have to be right."

"I know."

"And just because people don't live up to your demanding expectations doesn't mean they're wrong."

He let that sink in. "You really think I'm demanding?"

Sandra chortled. "Aren't you? Tonight just couldn't be about us. Being here. Among these people. Having a good time. Could it?"

The song transitioned into a bridge between choruses. Danny saw a space in his peripheral vision behind Sandra's right shoulder and cast her at arm's length as the music crescendoed. She followed his lead, moved out to the end of his left hand, then gracefully spun under his arm on the return. Light glimmered and bounced off of her shiny gold dress like an exploding star.

When he caught her hip again, Danny pulled Sandra in closer than before. "C'mon, Elbee. That's not what tonight was ever about. And we both know it."

She pulled her head back, but Danny kept her from retreating. "Oh, really?"

"This was always about being seen," he grinned. "You want these people to see you. You want Darth Luscious there to see you with me - to see what he's missing. To see that you've moved on." He ticked his head back toward their table. "Those people there live in their own little world. To them, you and I are usually even less than a curiosity. But now," his eyes flashed, "now, they'll remember you. All of them. The shrink. Her girlfriend, too. The millionaire, and his wife. That movie star. From the moment we left that table they've been talking about us."

"They've been talking about that hotheaded jackass that I brought." Despite her lingering irritation, Sandra could not help but smile.

"And that lovely lady fed who's so much better off without him," he added. "She's far too smart and talented to let a guy like that drag her down."

"Flattery will get you nowhere," she warned.

Danny gave her his warmest, most sincere smile. "Then stop being so damned incredible."

It is said that ninety percent of communication is nonverbal. So, as their bodies continued to move on autopilot, Danny simply let her see just how deeply he meant what he said. As the music made them sway to and fro, he told her - with his eyes, with his face, with his hands - that in a room full of noteworthy people and famous names, she was the most important person by far. The only person, as far as he was concerned, that truly mattered.

It is also said that the act of communication is the art of taking an idea, wrapping it in a package, and delivering it in such a way that the recipient opens it and sees what the other person thought. In that moment - with the glow of golden lights, the smooth rhythm of music, the movement of their bodies, the scent of each of them filling the other's senses and the softness of his expression - Danny saw that Sandra got it. He felt the muscles under her dress soften just a bit as she relaxed. The space between them shrank into nothing but a memory. Danny closed his eyes, tipped his face forward, and rested his forehead on hers while the band played into the night.

CHAPTER 10

"HERE'S AN INTERESTING little piece that our producers found in the Washington Post," the titular host of the Lonnie Chase Program sang into his antique microphone. "Did you guys see this fluff piece?"

"You mean the one where some D.C. Elites at some fundraiser decided to just up and pay for their waiter to go to college?"

"That's the one, Fred."

"What a crock," Kyp scoffed from his seat at the broadcast table.

"What's the problem?" Lonnie baited his cohost. "Don't you believe in free college for the underprivileged?"

"I believe in scholarships for those who want to make something out of themselves but can't afford to go to college," Kyp countered. "But that's not what this is at all."

"For anyone who didn't catch this story," Factcheck Fred expounded, "which is all over the media right now, by the way… this twenty-year old guy was working as a waiter at a fundraiser last night. You know, one of these dog and pony shows for the rich and famous. By luck of the draw, one of the tables he's assigned happened to be where Walter Standridge and his wife are sitting."

"That'd be the same Walter Standridge whose family has made untold billions trading oil, gold, and various minerals across international markets?"

"That's right, Kyp. Anyway, at the end of the dinner, Standridge and his wife - who are, like, eighty years old -"

"Not that that sort of thing matters," Lonnie interjected.

"Except for the part where at no point in that eighty years did either of them put in an honest day's work," Kyp rebutted.

"True," Fred fought to regain control of his own report. "Anyway. Evidently, at the end of the dinner, Standridge pulled the dude aside and asked him some questions. What his name was, where he was from, and what he wanted to do with his life."

"And, to his credit, the kid's got quite the story."

"Well, Lonnie," Fred whinged, "I'd say it's pretty typical. Raised by a single mom, lots of siblings, no money to spare… Anyway, the dude mentions that he wished he could get a real job, but there's just no way that he could afford college -"

"Because nobody in America can just get limitless student loans guaranteed by the United States federal government," Kyp sarcastically quipped. "Especially if you're a cash-poor minority like this guy reportedly is."

Fred rolled with the interruption. "Or, I don't know, just join any branch of the military and use the GI Bill to go to virtually any school for free in exchange for a four year hitch."

"Everybody wants free college," Lonnie noted, "until you actually offer them free college."

"So," Fred resumed, "Standridge pats the guy on the shoulder and says, 'You wanna go to college? Fine. Go. I'll pick up the tab.'"

"Is that what he really said?" Lonnie sounded incredulous.

"Actually," paid subscribers were treated to Fred's most confident nod via the studio's cameras, "pretty close. Yeah. We've got video of it happening, so we can -"

"Wait," Lonnie derailed the junior member of his broadcast trio, "there just *happened* to be a camera rolling when all of this went down?"

"I smell something."

"No, really," Fred assured his cohorts and the audience. "It really was filmed. And it's not some crappy cell phone video, either. You know, where it looks like the whole thing was recorded by some Parkinson's patient having an episode."

"A real news crew?" Kyp pressed.

"Well," Fred bobbled, "as much as you could call the lifestyle reporter from the Washington Post a real journalist, I suppose."

"How very convenient," Kyp sneered. "A multibillionaire whose company is facing allegations of violating trade sanctions by dealing in blood diamonds, black market uranium, embargoed oil, and other crimes, just up and out of the blue does something nice for one unfortunate soul at a gala, and a camera crew just happens to catch it. And with all of the things going on in our country and around the world right now, this somehow becomes newsworthy."

"So you're saying this is a set up?" Lonnie soberly asked.

"That depends. Is the Post one of Standridge's many holdings?"

"I… I don't know. Fred, could you look into that during the break?"

"Either way," Kyp beamed, "they might as well just show a few seconds of him walking around giving free kittens to orphans. This is just as meaningless. And just as fake. Even if it's totally true, it's all for show." Kyp leaned into his microphone and stabbed the table as he spoke. "It's all a public relations stunt to distract us from what a snake this guy is. Or to make us forget that his wife is the heiress of a family who made their initial fortune strip logging forests that they didn't own after the Civil War, then parlayed that into war profiteering during both World Wars."

"But isn't it a good thing to help those who need it?" Lonnie countered.

"Sure it is," Kyp dug in and held his ground, "but this kid didn't actually work for it. I mean, yeah, he works. But he didn't apply for college, seek grants, earn scholarships, and work his way through the process to better himself. He didn't play the game by the same rules as everybody else. He's getting a break that nobody else is because the right people know him. It's pure patronage. The aristocracy picks the winners, then they make sure they win by rigging the race." Kyp was so close to his microphone that his lips brushed over the metal screen. "Mark my words. This guy will go to a university he should never have been able to afford. He'll slide by on his patron's dime. And in a few years, when he graduates - regardless of his actual performance in class or what his degree is in - Daddy Warbucks will find a cushy chair somewhere in one of his companies where this guy can just disappear and receive a paycheck to do absolutely nothing but be the poster child for socialized college programs. And everyone will call him a success, just because now there's somebody out there making sure that he doesn't fail and make them lose face."

*　　　*　　　*

Danny listened to the radio program stream live on his laptop while he searched the online inventory of every gun dealer in the mid-Atlantic. Most government offices filtered their internet service. It was a policy designed to reduce the amount of time government employees wasted during business hours and using taxpayer-funded workstations to surf social media, watch movies, or download pornography. In practice, however, most offices simply flagged or outright blocked access to any material that management found offensive, such as searches for how to make explosives, online booking sites for escorts, or any media service that was not heavily biased to the Left of center. But Wakefield's suspension meant that he was no longer chained to a Secret Service desk all day. He was, in fact, free to surf the web in the freedom and comfort of his apartment. On his own computer.

Not that that'll give me any real privacy, he grumbled to himself. A voice in the back of his mind - one that was quiet, but could not be fully silenced - made him suspect that his overlords, during the course of investigating him for professional misconduct, might have decided to monitor all of his telephone and internet activity just to see if they might find something that would incriminate him.

Once he had made up his mind to use his plentiful spare time and his own resources to track down T.J. Phillips, Danny set his phone up to spend all day streaming the worst B-movies on the web over his data plan. *That'll give Oscar's buddies at the NSA something to do.* Meanwhile, while any personnel who might potentially be conducting digital surveillance on him complained about his cinematic preferences - which, according to his phone's recent history, leaned toward flicks that relied upon rubber suit monsters and actresses who were clearly not hired for their ability to deliver convincing dialogue - Danny spent the last few weeks on a secondhand, refurbished laptop using a darkweb anonymizer that even the NSA could not trace. He scoured chatrooms, advertisements, reviews, and all manner of websites in a tireless search to find the gun that Phillips used in his assault against Homeland Security Headquarters.

The pictures from Stevenson's jump drive were informative, but ultimately unhelpful in his research. The image of Phillips' rifle was burned into Wakefield's memory. He only saw it briefly, but it stood out in his mind's eye. Danny knew guns, and he knew that Phillips' gun was too special to hide forever. The custom finish, high-end accessories, tooling… all of the details told Danny that his adversary's tool was professionally made.

I spent months working on Vera, he reminded himself. An FBI strike team seized Phillips' trailer in Pennsylvania. It featured a number of firearms. But none of those guns - or any of the ammunition found on site, either - were consistent with the quality of the hardware that Phillips used when he killed Secretary Dagenhart at DHS Headquarters.

No, Danny reasoned, *somebody else built that gun. And they didn't just slap it together for him overnight.*

Gunsmiths were like painters, sculptors, or any other artists or craftsmen. They had preferences. Habits. Their work carried a sort of signature. And as surely as a curator could identify a Monet or a Stradivarius, Danny could tell whether a rifle in a picture was turned out by the same hands that made T.J.'s primary weapon system. Sure, there were trends and fads within the firearms industry, especially with AR-pattern rifles, which were the most prolific sporting rifle in America. But all Danny had to do was find the guy who built their guns just right - the one who claimed to do it first, or best - then check it against anyone who copied the style and see what turned up.

People pay for quality product. So, who wants to sell me a gun just like the Constitutional Killer's? Danny consulted his coffee cup as he clicked on the next in an endless list of websites.

And there it was.

The photo showed an entire rack of AR-15s with skeletonized upper receivers and magazine wells. The patterns in the cuts were exactly like Phillips' gun. Another rack held a half dozen AR-10s - the larger caliber big brother, the exact model used during the Headquarters assault - with the same design. Most of the guns from both racks sported an industry standard anodized blue finish, but some of them featured more festive colors. Matted tans and drab greens preferred by allegedly tactical shooters were mixed among cobalt blue, hot rod red, and metallic orange rifles clearly marketed as Range Barbies and competition guns. The proprietor, a small shop in Fayetteville and just a hop and skip from Ft. Bragg, also showcased a number of Glock handguns and custom 1911s with similarly styled tooling to match.

Wakefield grabbed the nearest phone and made sure it was the one the office knew about. His nose wrinkled at the horrible flick that played on the tiny screen. Morbid curiosity drove him to look up the film's information. More knowledge did not make the cinematic turd any more interesting. *Saber Raine?* he nearly gagged. *Casper Van Dien, whatever soul you may have had has been sold to the lowest bidder.* Danny terminated the streamed movie and dialed a familiar number.

"Homeland," the bright voice quickly answered. "Stevenson. How may I help you?"

"Hey, Dianne. It's Danny."

"You," Agent Stevenson's voice grew quieter. "You're not supposed to be calling."

"I know, but I've got an idea on where you might find Phillips."

"You're supposed to be hands-off." The agent's voice was barely a whisper. Danny had to turn up his phone's volume setting to hear her. "We could both get in a lot of trouble just talking."

"But I've got a lead," he protested. Wakefield wanted to ask her how she could simultaneously feed him and Martin information from a crime scene while at the same time try to stonewall him. But he had to assume that all DHS phones were monitored, and the lines that came into the watch floor were most certainly recorded. Danny did not want to get Dianne into any hot water with the powers-that-were. "Log it as an anonymous tip or a confidential informant."

Static sounded over the speaker as wind blew over the receiver on the other end. "Fine. But not on the phone. In person." Suddenly, Stevenson sounded like her normal self again. "I'll meet you at the same place we did our last exchange. Twenty-two hundred hours."

Someone must've walked up on her while she was talking, Wakefield nodded. *Someone who's gunning for me. Nick, maybe? Or Flowers?* "Fine. I'll see you then."

The phone call ended with an abrupt *click.* Wakefield tore a piece of scratch paper off of a memo pad and scribbled the gun shop's contact information onto it, then paused. *From operator to investigator… and now I'm just a source?* He drummed his pen on the pad and shook his head. *They'll let me keep my job for sure, now. If for no other reason than to avoid paying me the reward money for the tip.* Normally, Danny would have felt more encouraged by the thought of saving his endangered job. But the humility of the situation stuck in his gut like poorly cooked meat.

Danny looked at the guns on the screen, and he could not help but want one. *Well, if I'm gonna be a source, I might as well give them a thorough report.* He consulted his watch. *I can grab lunch en route.* Danny's custom .45 was still packed in his tan soft case with Vera, sitting next to the workbench in the apartment's smaller room. Though they were his favorite guns, they were still dirty from his weekend trip to the range. He pulled open a cabinet drawer and withdrew the 9mm Glock 17 and a pair of spare magazines stored inside amongst various tools. Wakefield tucked the pistol into his leather jacket's interior breast pocket, stuffed the mags into his left outer pocket, and grabbed his keys on his way to the door. *Time for daddy to go shopping.*

*   *   *

"For those of you just tuning in, I'm joined in the studio by Rex Crowley, the District Attorney out of Austin, and I gotta tell you, folks, this guy never ceases to amaze me."

"Well, thanks, Lonnie."

"No, I'm serous here, Rex. Now, for the backstory: my people reached out to your office the second we found out that the feds were investigating us under allegations that we were helping the Constitutional Killer. And that was, what, six? Eight months ago?"

"Right at six months now," the lawyer recalled. "Right at the start of July."

"Right. So, tell us how that meeting led to where we are now."

"Well, Lonnie, I took a look at Homeland Security's allegations and, quite frankly, they struck me as completely unfounded and the product of wild conjecture. So, I met with my boss, the Attorney General for Texas, and we talked about it, and she contacted D.C. and started asking questions…"

"And to whom, just to be clear, was she speaking at this point?"

"That would be the US Attorney General's office," Rex explained.

"Sorry."

"No problem."

"Go ahead."

"Right. So, anyway, Janice - that's Janice Hoskins, the Texas Aye-Gee - agreed with my concerns and asked the guys in Washington to identify for her what legal grounds they had to suspect and pursue you and your company. What evidence? What probable cause?"

"And they had none," Lonnie declared.

"None at all."

"So then what?"

"Well, the D.C. guys hemmed and hawed about how they weren't just going to drop an open investigation -"

"Even though they had no legal grounds to conduct one."

"Right. And while they were dancing the D.C. Two-Step with Janice and my office, a thought occurred to me. And so, we're having this meeting - those had become pretty regular occurrences by this point, which was about two weeks ago - and I said, *'Hey, I notice that you've got a suspect. Everybody knows who your suspect is and he's not one of Chase's guys. Isn't that proof enough that you're barking up the wrong tree?'*"

"Right."

"And, of course, the guys in D.C. are all *'Oh, well, we don't know that Lonnie isn't supporting him -'*"

"Which is not a legal argument."

"Right. It's a fallacious argument. You can't charge a guy with a crime because he hasn't proven that he hasn't committed one. That goes against the foundational ideas of our judicial system. So, anyway, that's when the thought crossed my mind. So I asked, *'Hey, guys, you've locked up this Phillips guy's accounts all locked up. You've garnished his wages - his veteran's pension - and seized the accounts. But I haven't seen where you've filed a formal indictment against him yet.'*"

"Now, tell us why that's important," Lonnie prompted.

"Well," Rex, tried to organize his thoughts. "There's a whole lot of rules that both sides have to follow if a person's charged with a crime. It's a process, and it's complicated, and that's why you're best just leaving it to lawyers - good, competent lawyers - to handle it."

"That's that whole *'only a fool represents himself'* thing."

"Yeah. Well, something like that. Anyway, at each stage of the process there are limits and permissions to what each side can and cannot do. And some of those rules involve the fact that except under the most extreme circumstances the government cannot simply take away the property of a person who has not actually been convicted of a crime ,obviously, unless that property isn't really theirs, or it's evidence in an active case, or some other thing like that."

"Now, I just read something about that the other day," Lonnie shuffled through the collection of papers on his broadcast desk. "Where was it? It's a little obscure thing called the Bill of Rights."

"You're absolutely right, Lonnie. You know - and I'm sure that you of all people are well aware of this, but most people just don't know their rights these days. But fully half of the Bill of Rights is dedicated to outlining your rights when you are charged with a crime. Any crime. Big or small. You have the Fourth, Fifth, Six, Seventh, and really, the Eighth Amendment has to do with the rights of the accused, but this case really doesn't fall within the regular purview of that one."

"That's absolutely right. So, what did they say? The feds."

"Basically," the lawyer drew the word out as his head wagged from one shoulder to the other, "they told me to mind my own business."

"Now, who said that?" Lonnie pressed.

"I really don't think it would be appropriate to name names," Rex resisted.

"You can't name him? Was it a him or a her?"

"I really don't think it'd be appropriate at this time…"

"Okay, fine. So, someone the Justice Department told you to go to Hell.

"Basically."

"Someone high up."

"Correct."

"And that's basically their official stance at the Attorney General's office in D.C."

"Right."

"Then what?"

"Well, that's when I went to the federal courthouse here in Austin and I filed a legal question about the federal government's liberties in this matter."

"A legal question?" Lonnie snickered. "You make it sound so polite. You sued the government."

"Well, it is a legal action, but not really a suit -"

"You charged the Attorney General's office with violating a person's Constitutional rights."

"Correct."

"So, essentially, you charged the Justice Department with a crime."

"Well, it's more like a challenge to their authority, but basically, yes."

Lonnie chuckled. "Do you have a death wish or something?"

"I really don't," Rex smiled at the absurdity of his own defense. "I guess I'm just one of those rare individuals within the judicial system that still believes in the rule of law."

"I mean, come on, man."

"No, Lonnie, really. You know me well enough to know that I'm being honest about this."

"You have always struck me as a straight shooter."

"Thank you. Well, in its treatment of this case - and it's a serious case, make no mistake about it - the

United States federal government has basically thrown out everyone's inalienable human rights and said that, *'To Hell with the law, we're just going to do whatever we want.'* And that's unacceptable to me."

"Really?" Lonnie crowed. "I mean, have you looked outside lately?"

"I have," Rex quietly answered.

"Have you seen the tanks?"

"I have."

"Have you seen the soldiers occupying our streets? And you're telling me that you still believe in the rule of law?"

"It's a travesty, Lonnie. It really is."

"I don't know how much longer I'm gonna be able to broadcast," Lonnie admitted. "They can come in here at any moment and shut me down. Legal or not, Rex, if armored trucks roll up into my parking lot and men with machine guns kick in my door and tell us to turn it off… We're done. Boom. That's it."

"It's unfortunate."

"That's not America," Lonnie declared. "We are living in occupied territory, my friend."

"There's a lot of truth to that. And you and I aren't the only ones who see that."

"What do you mean? I mean, I know that we're not alone in our thinking here, Rex. At least, I hope we're not. But what to *you* mean when you say that?"

"Well, like you said, Lonnie. We all see where this has gone, and a lot of folks just won't have it. We've talked on this show before about what happens with the average American looks to the institutions that are supposed to preserve justice in our communities and come to the conclusion that those institutions are doing more harm than good."

"We have."

"So you and I both know what we can expect next."

"And I pray that doesn't happen."

"But what I mean," the lawyer grew a little unsettled, "is that there are other folks of the same mind on this one as you and me. I haven't had a chance to talk to a lot of my friends in Washington, but my intuition tells me that there are still some people in the Beltway who think that instituting martial law in the States is a step too far. And even our troops are conflicted, Lonnie."

"I imagine they would be."

"Well, I don't have to imagine. I mean, we haven't even had boots on the ground for six hours, Lonnie, and my office has already been contacted by a lieutenant in the Texas National Guard who, when he and his troopers were called up in the darkest hours of the morning, questioned his superiors as to whether that was even a lawful order."

"Amazing."

"When my office opened our doors this morning, Lonnie, our phone was ringing with this guy and his JAG officer on speaker phone asking what his obligations and options were under these circumstances. Now, if our own troopers are confused and conflicted by this situation, can you imagine how murky these waters really are?"

"That's absolutely amazing." Paid subscribers could see the turmoil on Lonnie's already-troubled face stream over the studio's camera. "You're a lawyer - the District Attorney - and you and I both know the reality of the situation."

"You know, Lonnie," Rex leaned into his microphone, "I hope and pray that the good men and women in uniform who are just trying to do their jobs would, if they heard that kind of order, have the courage to challenge its lawfulness. That is their duty: to follow the lawful ones and ignore the awful ones. And they have every right to ask their superiors, if they're not engaged in a time sensitive operation that demands their attention, they have the right and the obligation to make sure that they and their superiors are absolutely, crystal clear on their mission. That includes its objectives, risks, and legality."

"Yeah, right."

"They do, Lonnie."

"They're just troopers, Rex."

"That doesn't matter."

"You're telling me that some Private or Corporal is gonna look at his superiors and ask about their lawful authority and their moral imperative?"

"He or she has that right."

Paid subscribers could see Lonnie as he pulled away from his microphone for a second. Then he leaned back in again. Everyone else in the audience was limited to the sound of a brief silence being transmitted over the airwaves. "You almost made me swear on the air there, Rex."

"You disagree?"

"You know that I love our troops, Rex, but I don't think that the average trooper has the time or the education to think about those sorts of things. It's sad, but I really don't. It's nothing against them personally or professionally. I just don't think their leaders really want them questioning things. That's not what they're about. You know? The military is about order and orders. I've never had the privilege to serve, but I have dear friends who serve and others who are vets, and they all tell me that if you wear the uniform then you fall in line. You don't make waves, you don't make trouble, and the only way you ever single yourself out is when you make sure your bosses know that they can count on you to follow orders better than the next guy." He leaned forward to emphasize his point. "Without question. Without hesitation. And I'm usually grateful for that, Rex. But in this current situation, I'm terrified of the position that might put them in. And what it might mean to the American people."

CHAPTER 11

"THANK YOU VERY much for your business," Randy nodded at the man who walked out of his gun shop with a bag full of ammunition in his hand and his teenaged son in tow. The shop owner waited until the customer's car backed out of its parking spot, then smiled and called blindly to the empty store. "You know, that ammo from the old man is flying off the shelf. Gonna have to order some up before the weekend." He pulled away from the sales counter and ducked is head through the door to the workshop. "How's it going back there?"

T.J. Phillips sat on a padded bar stool in the adjacent back room and stared thoughtfully at a collection of pictures taped to the wall behind the work bench Randy usually used to repair customers' rifles. "You know what they say about a mission like this: If it was easy, everybody'd do it."

Randy nodded. "You'll crack it."

T.J. was less than convinced. "I never really appreciated what those guys in Ess-Two and Ess-

Three contributed until I had to start running missions without them."

"Looked to me like you did just fine up in D.C. without intel or ops holding your hand." Randy grabbed his laptop so that he could add a few cases of the hot selling ammo to his order. There were only a few more boxes left from the batch of light armor piercing rounds that their anonymous benefactor had donated to the Constitutional Killer's cause. "How're you holding up?"

T.J. stretched his torso and probed his flank. "I think I'm all healed up from the drop. Didn't slow me down at all the other night at the community center." He smiled, "Maybe more vets should go to vets for our medical."

"If we got the same care from the Vee-Aye that most people gave their pets, it'd be an improvement." Randy nodded. "I've got a spare scope mounted onto the Beast and got her bore sighted. Nothing fancy. I'll close up a little early tonight so that we can take it and your new kit to the range after work and confirm zeros."

T.J. glanced down at the padded rifle case that held his latest gun and accessories. In addition to being a former Special Forces operator, Randy was a skilled gunsmith who made a halfway decent living after he left the service selling his wares to civilians who, in T.J.'s estimation, did not nearly appreciate the former Ranger's artistry nearly enough. "Sure thing."

The door chime called Randy back to the sales floor. T.J. remained unseen in the rear room, safe to plan his next operation. The fresh customer was a white male of average height, with medium brown hair. He wore the kind of rugged trail shoes favored by operators, jeans that looked like they gave him plenty of freedom to move, and a leather jacket that

Randy instantly assumed concealed a gun. *Watch the right hand.* "Welcome to The Forge," the store's proprietor called to the back of the customer's head, "the mid-Atlantic's source for the finest firearms and training on Earth."

"S'up," the brown haired man nodded, but his eyes remained transfixed upon the rack gun rack nearest to the door - and on the high-end rifles nestled in it.

"Something specific you're looking for?"

The man pointed at one of the pricey guns. "Mind if I test the grips?"

Randy slid around the guy and plucked one of the AR-patterned guns off the wall. "We build those all in house," he bragged. "Free float barrel. Slim fore end with spare rail sections. Titanium parts. Nickel boron bolt carrier group. I've got a few different trigger packages you can choose from."

"Is it okay if I dry fire it?"

"Go right ahead," Randy handed him a Snap Cap, a spring-loaded dummy round that could be chambered to protect the gun from any potential wear and tear and from the possibility of a negligent discharge while shooting without ammunition.

The stranger confidently cycled the rifle's charging handle, fed the Snap Cap into the chamber, set the stock against his shoulder, pointed the gun at the back wall, and smoothly pressed the trigger. He smiled with the rifle's *click*. "That's nice. Real crisp. Clean break."

"You're not gonna find a nicer Aye-Are-fifteen south of three grand," Randy smiled. "I turn those receivers out myself. Mill out all of the extra material so that it's as light as possible. If that gun was a car, you'd be sitting in a Ferrari."

The man in the leather jacket hefted the gun to feel its weight. "It's really well balanced," he nodded, "a lot lighter than you'd think." Then he handed the gun back to the shop owner. "That's one Hell of a rifle, bub."

The proud gunsmith set the rifle back into the wall rack with its cousins. "Name's Randy," he held out his hand."

The customer shook it. "Danny." Then he looked back at the rack. "You do all of the custom finishes, too?"

Randy nodded. "Back in the day, guns were all just blued. I remember back in the war it was a big deal to grab a can of Krylon and make your M-4 tan. Black stands out against the sand, you know. Now, you can get 'em in any color under the rainbow."

"What about calibers?"

"Standard build is chambered in five-five-six," Randy pointed. "Obviously, that's the most popular. A couple of bucks more and I can set you up with a three hundred Blackout or common pistol calibers. I do a fair number of nine-mils. On the high end, we're looking at four-fifty-eight, six-point-five, or even a fifty Beowulf upper that I can hook you up with. That's the upper limit for that series rifle."

"I see a couple of Aye-Are-tens over there," Danny slid over a step. "Right by the bolt guns."

"Oh, if you want a big bore," Randy plucked one of the beefier rifles out of the rack and handed it to the eager customer, "that's the way to go." He gave Danny a wary eye. "That is, if you know how to shoot it."

"I really dig the 1911-style grip," Danny said approvingly as he shouldered the adjustable stock.

"You shoot a 1911? Well, I'm glad you like it. That weapon system is my own design. As a matter of fact, I just put in a bid for a contract to supply those to the pipe hitters on base as an upgrade to the Ess-Are-twenty-five. And you know, some guys blink at the lighter gray or some of the other colors, but at night, just about any color turns dark. And the gray really works at winter time or in an urban environment. You know, for SWAT guys and the like."

Danny ran his hands along the rifle's chassis as he inspected the gun's mill work and admired its artistry. The AR-10's flat gray finish was a little bit smoother than the bronze he put on Vera. *Better temperature control in my workshop would probably reduce the orange peel.* "I shoot a lot of different stuff," he sniffed, "but my 1911's my favorite." His thoughts leapt back to the attack at headquarters; to the skeletonized AR-10 that Phillips had carried during the firefight. The showroom model lacked a scope, but aside from the optics, the killer's rifle was exactly the same design as the gun in his hands. Phillips used one that was brushed nickel instead of a darker stone gray, but it was the same platform; the same details; the same workmanship. The details were all too similar to rule out the obvious conclusion. "It's a little underdressed," Danny said wistfully as he handed back the hefty rifle. "What kind of glass would you suggest?"

"Well," Randy's smile became more genuine. This customer was obviously hooked. The store owner tried to hide the dollar signs in his eyes as he led Danny to a shelf with various scopes, lasers, and mounts. "That depends on what kind of shooting you plan to do. If you're gonna shoot at night," he plucked a boxed scope off the shelf, "then you'll need a big enough objective lens to let in plenty of light. Something like -"

Randy turned back to see Danny's humorless eyes staring at him over the sights of a plain Glock pistol pointed right at the gunsmith's face and held in a professional grip. "Just don't," Danny shook his head. His voice was calm, quiet, and deadly serious. "Be smart here, brother. Keep your hands where I can see them and tell me where he is."

"Where who is?" Randy forced calm into his voice. "Gotta tell you, man, most folk'd see holding up a gun store as suicide."

"This isn't a hold up. Just keep your hands away from your guns and stay right where you are." Danny expanded his peripheral vision to take in a little more of the shop around him, but kept his eyes fixed on the man in front of him. "I'm Special Agent Wakefield with Homeland Security. And you're Sergeant Randall Edwards, formerly a buddy of Sergeant Thomas Phillips with a certain codenamed team at Jay-Sock." JSOC, the Joint Special Operations Command headquartered at nearby Ft. Bragg, and its personnel had been at the center of the Constitutional Killer case almost from the beginning. Wakefield was not about to ignore the overlapping threads that potentially tied Edwards to the man who so desperately needed to be brought to justice. "You know Phillips. You know what he's been up to the last few months. And we both know he's been getting his kit from you lately. Give him to me and I'll walk away."

"Look, brother -"

"Don't play, Edwards. I recognize your handiwork from the gun Phillips used to shoot at me and my 'mates. Saw it up close a few weeks ago. Found the same guns on your website. And here. Exactly the same. You're the artist. Like you said: it's your design. It's your signature. It's how I found you.

So let's not play. I don't know when you gave him the rifle and right now I don't care. But do I hope for your sake, from one vet to another, that it was a long, long time ago. 'Cause if you bullshit me right now and we find out that you supplied a known fugitive with the gun he used to kill federal agents…" Danny shook his head in sympathy, "Well, I hate to see the special kind of hole they put you in. Or the amount of prison rape a good lookin' guy like yourself suffers."

"It ain't rape if you're pitching." Randy held his hands perfectly still, but the smallest glint flashed in the former Ranger's eyes.

Danny shot sideways to his left as a dark figure popped through the doorway near the customer service counter and fired two quick rounds at him. The shots passed behind Wakefield by the narrowest of margins. His pistol lurched uncontrollably to the side, causing him to reflexively pull his finger off the trigger to avoid an inadvertent discharge. Something crashed into his right temple. It felt like a sledgehammer, but even while his sight dazed and returned, Danny was pretty sure that it was Randy's fist.

Momentum carried Danny into a display case, which shattered on impact. His 9mm pistol retraced the direction from which he fell, but all he saw was Edwards' heel disappearing through a doorway as he bolted to the back of the shop. Glass crunched as Danny pushed himself back to his feet and gave chase.

The Forge's back door burst open. T.J. covered the alleyway behind the shop with quick, athletic strides. Two steps behind him, Randy slipped his second arm into a backpack strap, then called forward. T.J. tossed a short barreled rifle back to him without looking. Randy snatched the gun midair and slapped the bolt closed on a loaded magazine without missing a beat.

Randy led them around a corner to the left, then angled for the next right turn down the alley. Randy skip-pivoted through the turn to complete a visual circuit and check for their inevitable pursuit. "T.J.!" he called as he dashed after his faster friend.

"Gotta get clear," T.J. ordered from the point position. "You know that."

The pair of former commandos sprinted around yet another corner, zig-zagging their way through the block. "You could'a slipped out the back quietly," Randy called out between breaths. "I was trying to buy you time to get away."

Phillips' feet ground to a halt fifteen yards short of the alleyway's end. "Fed had a gun on you, bro."

"I had it under control."

T.J. shook his head and sucked a deep breath. "I couldn't leave you behind, brother."

"Look, T.J.," Randy skittered up to his former teammate and took a moment to ventilate and catch his bearings. "I appreciate it, I do. But I told you, bro. I ain't in this fight. I can't do this. Not to our own."

T.J. stood gobsmacked for a handful of heartbeats as he tried to reconcile his memories with his reality. Then Wakefield burst through the alleyway's mouth with his gun drawn and shouted orders for both men to stop.

The former Rangers doubled back toward the gun shop and tried to purchase distance between themselves and their pursuer. "Pretty fast for a white guy. Circled the whole block and cut us off."

"T.J.," Randy's voice was filled with concern, "I've got nowhere to go, bro. This is all I've got." Randy's legs slowed, then sputtered, then stopped altogether as he faced his own shop's busted back door. "This life I've built," he huffed, "it's all I have."

Phillips had no reservations with dropping anyone who tried to stop his mission, but preferred not to engage and adversary on their terms. The g-man had the initiative. For all T.J. knew, the guy from the shop was just the bunny - the guy used as bait while the rest of the team prepared to take the target down hard. There could be dozens of feds closing from a preset perimeter. *That's standard operating procedure. That's how we used to do it all the time.*

Training and experience let T.J. and Randy spend microseconds like hours. The veteran commandos knew that the two best responses when engaged were to either utilize overwhelming force or the exact opposite of whatever fight the attacker seemed prepared to carry. "They want us here," T.J. announced. "Time to get off the X."

"We're going back into the X!" Randy chastised.

"Blow through!" T.J. ordered.

Wakefield cleared the last corner between them and angled for his quarry. He saw his suspects' guns held instinctively at the ready, so he fired a single hasty shot in their direction from about twenty yards out. His 9mm bullet shattered a brick between T.J. and Randy. Acting purely on instinct, the Rangers ducked back into the gun shop and laid down a volley of covering fire.

T.J. scooted backward to the shop's front entrance with his sights trained on the doorway through which they had just leapt. "You still think that guy's one of ours?" he challenged.

Randy hissed an unending stream of curses. "Fine," he spat. "Fine. That's how it is, then." He shook his head like a rattle, then blew out the last of his reservations. "Okay, bro." Somewhere, deep inside Randy's psyche, a switch flipped. "It is what it is." He thumbed his .300Blackout rifle's selector. "Let's rock 'n roll." Randy dropped his hips, shouldered his rifle, and walked out his own front door with his face painted in grim determination. He knew it was the last time he would see this shop and all that he had built. "I hope you speak Spanish."

Danny did not feel like getting shot. *Not if I can avoid it, anyway.* So he bypassed the Forge's back door, which he assumed was covered by at least one of the men he was chasing, and rounded the building to approach the front entrance. It was his least worst option if he was going to bag his target. *Going through the front door is suicide,* he seethed, *especially if they've already seen you go through it once today.* It was a horrible idea, but his only other choice was to let the most wanted man in America - the man who murdered government officials and killed Wakefield's career - walk away. Again.

A pair of tan armored Humvees rolled up into the Forge's parking lot at the exact moment Danny stepped around the building's front corner with his gun drawn. It was also the exact moment that two gunmen, well-armed and obviously trained, walked out through the barred door at a brisk pace and with their guns ready.

Shouts bellowed forth from both of the Humvees as Soldiers ordered the gunmen to stand down. They were immediately answered by a stream of *thwack-thwack-thwack* as rapid shots fired from Phillips and Edwards rained metal on them. The incoming fire washed across the Humvees' bulletproof windshields and up-armored doors. Spiderwebs pocked and marked the panels and rendered them opaque, but the ballistic material held up to the barrage.

Shards and sparks splashed off the vehicles as the two commandos moved laterally in tandem, away from the freshly arrived troopers - most of whom had the good sense to keep their heads down and stay inside their trucks to avoid being riddled with bullets. As the two pipe hitters moved to their left - further away from Danny - the rear, driver's side door to the truck on Danny's right swung open. A young man in tan camouflage and body armor stepped out and stayed low to the ground as he moved along the leeward side of his vehicle.

Stay down, stay down, Danny begged in his mind. *Incoming fire has the right of way. Don't be a friggin' hero.* Danny took careful aim at the withdrawing commandos as they punished the grunts in front of them for their insolence. In three or four more seconds, they would punch right past the troopers and be in the wind.

Thirty, maybe thirty-five yards, Wakefield estimated. It was the extreme range to effectively engage a target with a handgun, but there was no time to jockey into a better position. He fought to control his heavy breathing… *Can't let 'em hurt anyone else…* forced his hands to relax his grip… *Can't lose 'em again…* took careful aim at the nearest target… His polymer pistol punched once, twice at the closest shooter.

One of the commandos - Edwards - stumbled and fell to his knee. He tried to raise his weapon again, but had difficulties. *Tango down*, Danny noted, *but not out.* The Glock sounded again, almost of its own accord, as soon as the front sight fell upon a target.

Something hit Danny in the torso like a building, only it left his chest on fire. Danny closed his eyes against the pain's white hot intensity. Then it hit his chest again. He was not sure, but he thought he screamed as his legs collapsed. Danny focused all of his energy on not passing out. His field of view shrank, then went completely black. Wakefield's world was filled with the sound of explosive typewriters, then a scraping sound of something dragging along gravel. Finally, the whole universe wrapped around him like a muffled blanket that ushered him into quiet darkness.

CHAPTER 12

A FAMILIAR WHITE mask stared into the camera. Comic features painted onto the false visage in stark colors graced the viewer with a humorless, macabre grimace - a twisted and sinister imitation of an expression that was usually much more comforting. "The time is coming, my brothers and sisters," a digitally scrambled voice warned, "when America's tyrants will fall." Light played off of a black, leather-gloved hand, which made it more visible against the speaker's blank, shadowy background. "We will tear them from their high places and burn them down to the ground. And freedom will rise up from the ashes to restore our nation." Guy Fawkes' image faded. In its place, a graphic depicted a stylized eagle as it sprouted forth like the legendary firebird, its plumage replaced with red and white streaks that trailed a starry blue field.

A single mouse click froze the video. "I don't know," the woman at the controls stared at the computer screen. "Don't you think the phoenix metaphor is a little over the top?"

Her partner sat behind her in a cheap canvas chair. "Nobody ever paid for 'under the top,' Heather," he noted. "Or would you call what he's been doing up to this point 'subtle?'" He drained what was left from his water bottle. "Look, if you think about it, it's layered. Right? I mean, this whole thing basically took off in Phoenix… am I right?"

The former Airman made a sour face. "Oh, no you didn't just use that pun." She threw a pen at the guy who was a virtual stranger a month ago, but with whom she had become quite close. Heather turned back to the computer and gave their handiwork another evaluative look. Her fingers drummed on the desktop. "I dunno, Lance. It just doesn't seem like the way he'd do it."

The Army veteran, clad head to toe in black, looked down at the Guy Fawkes mask perched on his lap. "If Phillips wanted us to do it his way then he'd've been here already."

"Maybe we should wait."

Lance shook his head. "We did wait. Look, I'm all about giving a guy fifteen minutes of dude time. I mean, that's just common courtesy. But we waited. And then we waited some more while we scripted, shot, and edited this whole thing. They're not coming, Heather. And if he's done being the Constitutional Killer, then somebody else'll have to step up."

Heather consulted her phone for the hundredth time in three hours. "I wonder where they -"

Heather's apartment door flew inward. Both veterans jumped at the sound. A white flash and concussive *BOOM!* knocked them both to the ground in a stupor. Muffled voices might have yelled at them from a thousand miles away, but the flash-bang grenade left them in an incoherent stupor. The constant ringing in their ears drowned out any hope of understanding anything anyone said. Shapes moved around them, barely discernible through clouded eyes and double vision. Each suspect was jerked, rolled, bound, and rolled some more.

By the time the world around them became coherent again, Lance and Heather sat back to back in the middle of the room. Their hands and feet were secured with industrial strength plastic binders. And they were completely surrounded by large men in combat fatigues and tactical gear, each with their gun pointed right at them.

"Corporal Lance Matthews," a man who wore a Second Lieutenant's subdued gold bar on his tac vest barked, "Staff Sergeant Heather Combs. You are under arrest under the charges of treason, sedition, and lending material aid to terrorists. Do you have anything to say for yourselves before you are remanded into custody?"

"Hey," Heather's head swung from shoulder to shoulder. She still seemed a little dazed. "Don't we have the right to remain silent or something?"

Lance, more accustomed to rougher treatment than his former Air Force counterpart, perked up. "We need to see a warrant. And a lawyer, Lieutenant Jerkface."

The officer squatted so that his mouth hovered only a few inches from the former Soldier's right ear. "Oh," he barked, "look here, fellas! The guy who's been taking a dump on his country wants some Constitutional rights! Well, I'm sorry, Corporal Matthews, but we ain't cops! And you ain't civilians! You're enemy combatants!" Lieutenant Jerkface's voice suddenly became softer, though far from soothing. "And after we've done introduced you to some nice people," he sneered slowly, "and they've asked you some nice questions," he drew a deep breath and let the menace of this threat sink into their minds, then resumed barking. "You're gonna face a military tribunal! And then, you'll be executed like the scumbag traitors that you are!"

Heather's shoulders heaved under the weight of heavy sobs. For his part, Lance was not surprised. From the moment he first agreed to help Phillips and Edwards, he knew that a day like this would probably come. But he never doubted for a second that he did the right thing. So he held his head as high as he could while his former brothers stood ready to hand him off like some *Muj* Tango on his way to Camp Godknowswhere. *Probably GITMO,* he he sighed.

Halfway to the door, Lieutenant Jerkface turned back to the captives. "Unless," his voice was suddenly calm. Reasonable. Like a normal human being. "Unless, that is, you give me something."

"What do you want?" Heather managed to ask between tears.

"Oh, c'mon, Heather," Jerkface coo'd as he came in closer and lower so that he could meet her own gaze with his cool, baby blue eyes. "We all used to be on the same team, girl. You know how this works. I gotta take a bad guy back with me, but there's only so much room in the back of the truck. *Capisce*? Now, all you gotta do to ride in the front of the truck with the good guys," he cast a sideways glance behind her, "is tell me who the real bad guy is."

"Don't listen to -" Lance's warning was cut short by a mook's dirty leather boot to his solar plexus.

"You know the drill, honey," Lieutenant Jerkface continued. "You're either with us, or against us. So, what's it gonna be?" The officer smiled as he held out one empty hand, palm up. "Are you a source," then he held up the other hand to balance the imaginary scale of life's dichotomy, "or a Tango?"

* * *

Randy focused on his breathing as he laid in the hospital bed with his eyes closed. Padded nylon straps bound his wrists and ankles securely to the bed rails. Machines *beeped* and *hummed* in the background. The sound of his door as it swept open, then closed again with a dull *clack* broke Randy's respite.

"Sergeant Edwards," an official sounding voice spoke over the *clap… clap… clap* of worn footfalls on hard tile, "the doctors tell me that you should be awake."

"My first name ain't Sergeant," he corrected with a dry throat. "It's Randy. I was honorably discharged over two years ago."

"Well," the other man humorlessly replied, "I guess old habits die hard." The voice was closer, right at the foot of Randy's bed. "Felony assault, aiding a terrorist, about a dozen different felony weapons charges…"

"It ain't what it looks like."

"Really?" The man's voice was incredulous. "Do tell. 'Cause it looks to me like you never really left the war, Sergeant."

Randy slowly opened his eyes. Everything about the visitor screamed *Federal Agent.* His close cut red-brown hair and regulation shave. His cheap suit and the thin shirt that obviously came in the same box as that God awful tie. His self-righteous voice and face. This guy looked, smelled, and sounded like a cop.

All of Randy's senses felt just a bit off - like he was still half asleep. *Could be pain meds,* he reasoned. *Could be something else they have me on.* Though his body sluggishly resisted his efforts, Randy still tried to offer up a hostile stare. "Never got a chance," his throat and mouth felt like they were lined with chalk. *Did they tube me? How long was I out?* "Came home, but folks treat you different. Like you're broken. Or toxic. Vets just can't catch a break."

"Spare me the sad story," the fed answered. "You were caught providing material aid to a known fugitive - including unregistered firearms. I have to wonder exactly how many guns have illegally crossed your door since you opened shop."

"Army taught me two skills," Randy slowly retorted. "Leading people and shooting them. Couldn't find work doing the first one when I got out. Too much experience, not enough degrees."

The fed shook his reddish crowned head. "The Army didn't teach you to assassinate our own leaders."

Randy closed his droopy eyelids again. "Actually, they did. Funny, ain't it? We take out an anti-American politician over there and folks call it regime change. Give us medals. Do it here and it's assassination."

"Don't play the patriotic crusader with me, Edwards. You shot at American troops. Guys just doing their job. Guys wearing the same uniform you used to."

"Used to train guys out in Mujistan," the stoned vet grinned with a memory. "Local boys who were supposed to guard their country against warlords and terrorists. Gave 'em guns. Gave 'em uniforms. And as soon as we'd teach 'em how to shoot, you know what they'd do?" Randy mustered as much fire as he could and drove it toward the fed with his stare. "They'd shoot at us. Right there at the range." His eyes closed again. "And you know what the brass said? Every time one of us got taken out by some *Muj* bastard who was too much of a coward to face us on the battlefield? They'd say, 'Do your duty, no matter the cost.' And we'd go do it again, even though we knew that it meant that within a few weeks, another one of us would get shot in the back." Randy's head swam as he shook it, as if he could feel his brain sloshing around inside his skull. "American troops do their duty. No matter the personal cost. And they don't raise arms against American citizens on American soil."

"Then how do you explain what you and your boy Phillips have been doing?"

"T.J.'s defending the Constitution," Randy sighed. *Why am I so sleepy?* "I'm supporting."

"Well, while you were under, we rounded up the rest of your little cell. Combs rolled on the rest of you in exchange for leniency. Told us everything you've been up to for the last few weeks."

Randy knew that he should be upset, but he was not. Perhaps the sedatives kept him cool. Perhaps it was the echo of a voice from his past. *Everybody breaks,* some sergeant taught him somewhere along the way. *Women break first. Then they'll use the skirts to start breaking the guys. Finally, they'll use you each against each other. Hold out as long as you can. Keep the faith. Support each other, no matter what. Then come home with your honor intact.*

"It's all coming apart," the fed smiled. "Phillips left you behind."

"I told him to leave me."

"Now Combs is singing like a bird."

"She's gotta do what she's gotta do."

The fed offered up a cocky chuckle. "Hell, I don't even need you. You know that, don't you? I don't need to offer anyone any more deals, Edwards. But if you made things go easier for the good guys, I'd make sure this all goes easier for you."

"I'd take it as a professional courtesy if you didn't."

Randy's mind worked backwards through his life, and about how all of that had been undone. He had a good thing going at the gun shop, but it was gone. He used to hunt bad guys, but now he was called a terrorist. He served with pride and honor in the Army, but now he would be labeled a traitor and criminal. He had a family once, a million brothers and sisters in uniform, but now he was alone.

The steady *beep… beep… beep* of his heart rate monitor reminded Randy of something. A rhythm, steady and familiar. It was cadence. Each *beep* fell on the left foot as his life seemed to march inexorably forward to its inevitable conclusion. *Maybe,* he wondered, *it's time to stop fighting.* He searched himself for the meaning of ideas such as honor and duty. He asked himself what they meant to him. *Or maybe, there's only one fight left to fight.*

Beep. If I die in a combat zone.

Beep. Tell my mamma I'm coming home.

Beep. Pin my medals upon my chest.

Beep. Tell my momma that I did my best.

"My only regret," Randy eased into his restraints and let his head sink into his hospital pillow, "is that I have only one life to give for my country."

CHAPTER 13

A COLLECTION OF machines *hummed* and *beeped* in the background of the Intensive Care Unit. The room in which Wakefield laid was painted in sterile white and adorned with faux wood furnishings and accents in pale colors that made it easier for the staff to wipe up blood and other body fluids. Sunlight filtered through the flimsy curtain that half covered the large room's window. And stretched across that pane of glass was a panoramic view of the next wing's exterior brick wall, maybe six or eight feet away from this one.

"I'm fine, Elbee. Really."

Sandra remained in her seat, unconvinced. "You were shot, Danny."

"Well, yeah… but only a little."

"Twice," she squeezed his hand harder in scorn.

Danny blew out a puff of air and shook his head lightly, as if the whole ordeal was less interesting than a mild breeze. "It's no big deal. I took it in the vest."

Sandra frowned, then drove a finger into a spot about an inch below his right nipple and pressed none-too-gingerly on a tightly bandaged rib. Danny winced in pain as electricity arched through his chest, along his spine, and somehow managed to oscillate simultaneously between his ears and his buttocks. "And who the Hell wears a bulletproof vest when they're off duty, anyway?"

"Obviously, people who don't want to get shot at the store."

"You've never worn one off duty before."

"Well, you know how rough things can get in the Carolinas."

"They dragged you into the ambulance unconscious," she pointed.

"Naaaaaah. I was totally conscious." He blinked slowly. "Okay, mostly conscious. I was aware. I remember answering the medic's questions."

"You're high as a kite right now," another voice sounded from the private room's door. The new speaker was fresh to the conversation, but he was certainly no stranger to either Sandra or Danny.

"Father," Danny looked away from his girlfriend - who had not left his side since she arrived - to see his boss from the Secret Service's Analysis Division. He smiled at the familiar face. "Are you here to give me my badge back?"

"Why would I do that?"

"Because I found Phillips. I got him. He was there. They brought him in, right?"

"Well, you're half right. But that ain't it."

"Then why are you here?"

"I'd ask you the same question, Danny boy." Dr. Wiley was not related to Danny by blood, but the two shared a bond that was tighter than most mentor-protege relationships. It was more caring, more honest, and sometimes much more blunt. "Do you know where you are?"

"In a hospital in Fayetteville?"

"You're suspended. You know that."

"I know that," Danny slowly echoed.

"So, what're you doing investigating the case that you got kicked off of?"

"I'm not."

Jonas held a white paper bag with stylized red script along its side far out in front of his body like some sort of pagan offering. "I brought you chicken," he bribed the younger man. "Just be straight with me and you can have it."

"Nuggets or strips?"

"Nuggets."

Danny brightened. "I love nuggets."

Jonas walked the snack over to Danny's outstretched hands, but passed on the empty chair on his side of the hospital bed. "They don't have you on propofol, do they?"

"Nah," Danny dug into the bag and produced a tasty morsel. "Just a banana bag to keep me hydrated."

"And oxygen for pain," Sandra pointed to the medical tubing that fed gas into his nostrils. "And antibiotics, anti-inflammatories, and -"

"That's just procedure," Danny gleefully popped a chicken nugget into his mouth.

"It's also a sedative," she persisted. "You're in pain."

Danny frowned. "I wouldn't be if you'd stop poking me."

"Danny," Wiley cut back in, "the truth, son. What're you doing chasing Phillips?"

Wakefield woofed another nugget. "I wasn't," he answered as he chewed. "I was just gun shopping."

"You build guns," Jonas shook her head. "You don't buy them."

"Gotta buy the parts somewhere," he countered.

"There's an internet for that."

"Sometimes you gotta try it before you buy it."

"There are closer places than friggin' North Carolina," Wiley chided.

"Well, Father, it's not like I had anywhere else to be, now, was it?"

"I ain't buying this, Danny. And I'm telling you as a friend, the Assistant Director sure as Hell ain't gonna believe you."

"I found this guy on the internet," Danny innocently shrugged, then swallowed. "Saw that he had some interesting uppers. Thought I'd check it out."

"Your instructions," Jonas growled, "were to keep quiet and stay in town. And what happens? You get in a shootout with the most wanted man in America and wind up in the hospital two states away."

"Nobody said I couldn't leave town. Besides, it's only two states if you live on the Baltimore side of D.C. From my place in Virginia, it's just one."

"This isn't a joke, Wakefield! It ain't funny and I ain't laughing."

Danny's face grew serious. He nodded, then pulled his hand out of Sandra's so that he could gesture during his explanation. "You're right, boss. Fine. Look, I could see from the videos online and what I remembered from the attack that Phillips' gun was high end craftsmanship. I figured it was custom and started searching the web for a gunsmith who did similar work."

"Which led you to Sergeant Edwards," Jonas nodded. He seemed to calm a bit.

"Right. I saw some of his rifles online. They were the same basic pattern as Phillips' gun. The way they were tooled, the pattern they were milled, the way some of them were configured… Then I looked Edwards up on social media and found out he was a Special Forces Ranger back in the day. That ties him back to Jay-Sock. Directly back to Phillips. I just knew he had to be helping Phillips, you know?"

Jonas rubbed his face in an attempt to wipe away some of his frustration. "So why didn't you pass this on to the task force? Let the FBI do the heavy lifting?"

"I tried. Gag order, remember?" Danny knew that any mention of Stevenson's name would land everyone involved in hot water. "Called the hotline," he offered up, "and they just ignored me anyway." Wakefield tried not to sound sheepish, but he felt a little tired - whether from his injuries or the meds, he could not tell. "Besides, there's a big difference between seeing something on the 'net and having actual eyes on the scene. I figured it wouldn't hurt to check it out. Figured Flowers and the board couldn't ignore a firsthand report if it helped us bag the actual bad guy."

Wiley heaved a heavy sigh. "Oh, they're certainly not ignoring you now." He heaved a heavy sigh. "I don't even recognize this country anymore, Danny boy. Political assassinations. Martial law. This is the United States! Not some Latin American crap hole or third world African cesspit. We used to -" something caught in the older man's throat. When his voice came back, it was much softer. "We used to be better than this." Jonas leaned over and took Danny firmly by the hand. "Son, they're gonna take you in on charges of obstruction and interfering with a federal investigation. As soon as the doc says you're good enough to travel, you're on a transport to the Butner Federal Medical Facility. I made it here as quick as I could so that I could warn you in person."

Sandra leapt to her feet and produced her cell phone. "How long until they get here?"

Danny slumped again in his bed and closed his eyes against the world as it crashed around him. "They're already here, aren't they?"

Jonas stepped back from the bed. "Saw a pair of black Suburbans pulling into the rear as I hit the door. They're probably checking in at the nurse's station now. They'll come get you as soon as they've set up a secure path for your exit. You've got three minutes, tops. Five if you're lucky."

"Let me get this straight, sir. I shot the guy in Miami who shot at me, so I got in trouble. I *didn't* shoot the suspect in D.C. 'cause he wasn't shooting at me, but I got in trouble anyway. Then I shot a suspect here who was shooting at me and everybody else. And I got shot. And I'm in trouble."

"Right."

Wakefield hissed and shook his head. "Is there some combination of shooting bad guys or not, and me getting shot at or not, that ends with me not getting in trouble?"

"I don't think so, son."

And they expect me to play by the rules? Danny seethed. "You need to leave, Father."

"Don't do anything stupid, Danny boy."

"Just gimme a minute with my girlfriend, would you?" Jonas nodded humorlessly, then sachet'ed out the ICU room. Silently, Danny prayed that the senior executive might be able to stall the agents at the door. "Elbee, quick. Listen. I need you to do something, and you're not gonna like it." As he outlined his request, Sandra grew more and more uncomfortable in her seat.

*   *   *

T.J. shuffled along the tree line that ran around the perimeter of a park on Fayetteville's outskirts. A sharkskin jacket from BOB - the Bug Out Bag he grabbed during the evacuation - helped him stave off the cold and conceal his short carbine as he evaded pursuit.

They got Randy, he cursed in his mind. The scene played itself over and again in his mind. He forced himself to hold a nondescript pace, just slow enough to avoid the appearance of fleeing something. His jaw instinctively clenched at the mental image of his former teammate and current confidant falling to the ground. Somebody - *was it the infantry guys or the fed?* - landed a shot that hit Randy in the liver just a few steps before they were clear of The Forge's parking lot. T.J. had dragged Randy a handful of paces before his brother from another mother just went slack and laid on the ground.

The sight of Randy ejecting his own rifle's magazine hung invisibly in front of T.J.'s eyes. *Just go,* he had coughed as he handed T.J. all of his ammo.

I ain't leaving you behind.

You have to, Randy's disembodied voice echoed for the hundredth time since he actually spoke the words. *I got minutes. Maybe.* The last look T.J. saw on his buddy's face was a grimace. *If they roll me, they'll do first aid. I stay, we both make it. Maybe I live. You keep fighting.* Pain racked through the ghost of Randy's body. *Otherwise, bro, we're both out.*

The hours spent evading detection since the firefight had begrudgingly led T.J. to the conclusion that Randy was probably right. When they were downrange, they both saw what proper medical care could do for guys with gunshot wounds worse than Randy's. And every step T.J. had taken since then told him that hauling Randy would have slowed him down just enough to get caught - and delayed treatment long enough to probably kill his friend.

We almost made it, T.J. spat thick fluid from his pallet. Just then, something in the park caught his eye. Not something, he realized, someone.

Next to a nondescript bench along an empty jogging path, a lone man sat in a familiar looking - *government-issued*, T.J. realized - wheelchair. He was a big guy with a knit cap and an unkept beard on his face. A hooded sweatshirt and cheap jacket insulated him from winter's cold, wet air. A drab, green poncho liner, universally nicknamed a Woobie by American Soldiers - was tucked tightly around his lap to keep his legs warm.

Leg. Singular. T.J. saw that only one foot rested in the chair's footplates. The big man was easily ten years younger than T.J.. Something inside him compelled the fugitive to stop. Not fatigue. Curiosity, maybe. Or something else. Entirely on instinct, T.J. angled for the guy. *They ain't lookin' for two dudes chillin' in the park,* he reasoned. The closer he got to the wheelchair, the more its occupant reminded him of Randy. *Maybe it's 'cuz he's white. Maybe 'cuz he's hurt.*

"S'up?" T.J. greeted the guy from a few paces away.

"What's going on?"

"Same ol' same," T.J. shrugged as much as he could without flashing the rifle tucked inside his jacket. "You?"

"Pushing through."

T.J.'s mental radar incessantly sounded. "You look familiar. Do I know you?"

The white guy sniffed and shook his head. "Nah, brother. Nobody knows me."

"Mind if I sit?"

"Help yourself," the big man gestured to the bench at his side. He casually scanned the area while T.J. sat for a much needed break. "Busy day?"

The odd nature of the question tickled the hairs on the back of T.J.'s neck. "Fits and spurts," he forced a chuckle. "You?"

"Meh." Though he reached out his hand in friendship, the big guy's eyes searched the horizon again. "I'm Mike, by the way. Lucky Mike. That's what they call me."

"Who calls you that?"

"People who come here," Lucky Mike finally met his eye. "People looking for me. And what I got."

A suspicious thought dawned upon T.J.. *He's a damn drug dealer.* The last thing T.J. needed in the middle of an escape and evasion drill was to be around the type of gringo the cops were always looking for. "Look," he started, "if you've got people -"

"Relax, brother." Lucky Mike smiled. "Just cluing you in. In case anyone stumbles by." He sniffed again. "I ain't had *people* since I got back."

Another piece of the puzzle working itself out in T.J.'s brain clicked into place. "Back… from the war?"

"Yep." Lucky Mike patted his Woobie where his right knee must have been at one time. Before. "Lost this guy in Sadr City."

T.J. realized why his mind subconsciously drew him to the stranger. The gringo was a brother he had never known. He looked at the big guy in a new light. "Army?"

Lucky Mike's smile faded with a nod. "Sixty-two Foxtrot," he clarified. "Crane operator."

"In Sadr?" From somewhere within a sea of troubled memories, a particular story washed upon T.J.'s shore. "You get that building Bremer's Wall?"

Bremer's Wall - a colloquialism among American ground forces in Iraq named for its author - was the classic product of ill-informed intellectualism born from people in leadership positions who were long on ideas and short on experience. After Muqtada al Sadr became famous among Shi'a insurrectionists for leading *Mujahideen* that called themselves *Jaysh al Mahdi* - loosely translated as the "army of the coming Messiah" - in a campaign of endless IEDs and rocket attacks that killed a host of Coalition troopers, the Good Idea Fairy decided to erect a giant concrete wall around the neighborhood in which the bad guys liked to hang out - nicknamed by Coalition Forces as Sadr City.

Shoot *Muj* in the face? No. Rain bombs on bad guys? Might offend people. Build a big wall? Oh, that was the thing to do.

So, on orders from a career diplomat with no military experience at all, the US Army ignored the cost of building enough 20-foot tall, steel-reinforced concrete barriers to erect a perimeter more than 15 miles long. And because some political appointee felt that killing terrorists was too aggressive an action for a war, thousands of America's sons and daughters spent many hard days and too much of their own blood slowly building a box around more than 10,000 very angry *jihadists* armed with surplus Russian assault rifles and military grade ordinance courtesy of their masters in Tehran.

In the aftermath of the Battle of Sadr City, Muqtada al Sadr became famous and moved to Tehran for religious studies in the hope that some day he might become *Ayatallah.* Washington elites patted themselves on the back and sold the media tales about passive measures and non-escalation. Generals and colonels in Tampastan pinned medals on each other's chests and dictated their own memoirs. And the men doing the heavy lifting on the streets of Baghdad filled the Euphrates with their own blood from when the Shiite hit the fan.

Another nod. "Yep. We were laying T-walls when my crew got hit. Some Muj appeared outta nowhere with an Are-Pee-Gee. Hit my crane while we had an Alaska wall up in the air."

"I'm sorry, brother."

Lucky Mike blinked back images that T.J. knew played out in front of his eyes. "Yeah, well, I didn't get the worst of it." He sniffed again. "Anyway, you know how it is." After a companionable moment, he drew a deep breath. "Look, I know who you are. Hell, man, if I still had my other leg I'd've joined the cause. You know? What you're doing is right, man. Cleaning house. You ain't got nothing to worry about from me."

"I appreciate that, man."

Lucky Mike looked hard over one shoulder, then the other. "But I also know that the local cops like to swing by here before they stop for dinner, tryin' to catch folks in the act. Oh, they ain't caught me yet. I'm careful. But they ain't been here yet tonight." He jerked his head. "Why don't you make yourself look like a good Samaritan and push me around, rather than some street thug trying to score Oxy."

"So, you *are* dealing?"

"You got another way for an unemployed vet with endless 'scrips to pay the rent? 'Cause if you do, I'm all ears. You think I wanna be out here doing this? Ain't got much choice, though."

"Sorry, man, but it's been a bad enough day already. I don't wanna add to your problems."

"Think nothing about it, man. Vets help vets. You can tell me all about it on the way back to my place." T.J. considered his options, then stood. "Oh, and hang your pack on the handrails. Anyone sees it, they'll think it's mine."

"I've, uh…" T.J. jostled his carbine inside his jacket.

"Tuck it under Woobie." Mike whipped the poncho liner off of his lap and kept watch while T.J. hid his short carbine among the wounded warrior's natural lines and creases. He quickly tucked the utilitarian cloth back around his thighs before what was left of his legs got cold, then shared memories with the fugitive while T.J. wheeled him out of the park. The duo were barely two steps from the sidewalk when a police cruiser rolled into the lot behind them. Mike cast the cop car a curt not. T.J. threw a wave in the officers' direction without looking back at them. The two veterans walked casually down the road, rounded a corner, and slipped anonymously away.

"That was close," T.J. breathed.

"They don't call me Lucky Mike for nothing."

CHAPTER 14

A PAIR OF FBI AGENTS in stereotypical dark suits and tan trench coats hovered next to Danny's bed. One was a white male with red-brown hair, the other was a clean cut black male. But their identical builds, ages, and the matched expressions on their humorless faces practically made them twins.

"Do everyone a favor, Wakefield," Coppertop warned. "Don't make a scene." The ginger gumshoe gestured with his head at two DHS SWAT operators, fully kitted out in tactical gear and armed with M-4 carbines, who stood ready for action by the door. "This is a hospital."

"I wouldn't dream of it," Danny calmly replied. He remained motionless in his bed while the nurse nervously disconnected his heart rate monitor. "I do have just one question, though." Shaky hands extracted his intravenous drip and left a slight burning sensation in the back of his right hand. "But tell me this: Who shot me? Phillips or Edwards?"

The candy striper shuffled back to the hallway as quickly as her feet could carry her.

The smug agent snickered. "Actually," a smile crept across his mug as Agent Coppertop fitted Danny with a pair of handcuffs, "it was one of ours. One of the Soldiers who responded to the call."

Danny frowned as a familiar expression echoed in the back of his brain: *Friendly fire isn't.* "Trooper got a name?"

"The only thing you're getting today," Coppertop sneered, "is a ride to a more secure facility. Now, get on your feet and let's go."

Disappointment washed over Wakefield's face. "C'mon, man. You're not even gonna let me get dressed first?"

"Saves us the hassle of another search."

"That's cold, man." Danny shook his head. "We're on the same friggin' team." He looked over at Coppertop's silent partner. "I guess fratricide's the order of the day, eh?"

"Play stupid games," the dark skinned officer replied, "win stupid prizes."

Danny eased himself out of the bed. The cold, antiseptic floor tiles turned his toes into popsicles. His legs were still a bit wobbly from hours in bed. *Wouldn't put it past them to've slipped me a little something in my IV bag when I wasn't looking.* Danny's head was still clearing. *Something to keep me compliant.* "This is ridiculous, man. My ass is hanging out the back of this gown." He held his cuffed hands out in front of himself like Oliver Twist clutching a soup bowl. "Please, at least let me put on some pants."

"Let's move."

The staff at the Cape Fear Valley Medical Center gave the agents a wide berth as they transited the hall with their prisoner. Danny knew that their pedestrian route had been cleared of all nonessential personnel, but he could not help but feel as if those busy people still managed to find the time to stare at his exposed backside as he was paraded before them in nothing but a flimsy, open-backed gown. He grinned as he put a little wiggle into his walk - just a little strut so that the ladies would have a nice show. The security detail slipped down a service stairwell and exited the hospital via a loading dock where a pair of black Suburbans sat idling with drivers ready. Danny was loaded into the lead vehicle, then the cadre maneuvered around the building and into the night.

A sea of reporters, whom Elbee had anonymously tipped off about Wakefield's location, stood between the fed's Suburbans and the hospital's exit. The path to open road was congested with bodies. Both vehicles were trapped by an army of American reporters with questions, microphones to pick up the answers, and cameras to carry the word around the world. The drivers were given pause by a host of jackals hungry for any morsel and desperate to be the first person to post a story for the news-starved public.

For the first time in his life, Wakefield was actually happy to see the press. "Gotta love a media circus, eh boys?" Danny tapped on his tinted window with his steel bracelets and held his hands aloft in full view of the bodies that crowded around this door. "Hey, any of you guys got a Sharpie? Or lipstick - I don't judge. I just wanna write my address on the window so that these clowns can watch you all rape my apartment tonight. It'll be all over YouTube. We'll be viral by breakfast."

Agent Coppertop, who rode with him in the back of the Surburban, tried to pull Danny back into his seat. "Sit still, Wakefield." Impatiently, the driver revved the truck's big engine in an attempt to intimidate the pedestrians. Few in the crowd responded.

Danny wiggled against his restraints and pressed his face against the window. "I'm being set up!" He yelled. "I did my job! And now they wanna kill me!"

"Shut up!" Coppertop yanked him away from the window as the sport utility vehicle finally crept forward. "Don't be an ass. We're not going to kill you."

"I know that," Danny fell back into the seat. Out of sight from witnesses, he smiled at the agent - who was clearly in charge. "And you know that. But they don't know that. And they're not interested in the truth. They're only interested in a story that they can sell. In thirty seconds or less, that little soundbite is gonna be bouncing all around the globe. Like it or not, Phillips made me recognizable after the D.C. attack. And here I am - thanks to you, getting more and more famous by the second." He frowned in thought. "More famous? Famouser? Is that right? Is that a word?" He shook off his curiosity at the rules of grammar and gave Coppertop a meaningful look. "Your bosses are gonna get a lot of questions about me now. Best not do anything to arouse suspicion." During his banter, Danny noticed the Suburban had finally made its way out of the jam and approached the highway.

"You're being taken into custody for questioning," Coppertop reiterated. "Pending the Attorney General's decision on exactly which charges to press, you'll be held over for arraignment." The agent cast him a disapproving look. "As spritely as you are, it looks to me like you're on the mend. I can't see us needing to take you to the fed med." The ginger g-man called up to their driver, "Let's just head to the prison." The driver echoed the order to the other truck over the radio and both vehicles changed directions.

"What colored jumpsuit do they issue in this county?" Danny joked.

"Oh, no. Not some cushy county jail," the red haired agent shook his head as the Suburban turned onto the highway and picked up speed. "You're going to federal prison."

"I hope you like to eat runny eggs," the tactical officer in the front passenger seat snickered.

"And penis," the driver chimed in.

Danny slumped into his seat. "I never caught your name, by the way."

"Special Agent Rick Gardner."

"You're with the Bureau, right?"

"Yep."

"Figures. The smugness gives it away." Danny took a calming breath and forced himself to relax. "I'm sorry, Rick. Truly, I am. One professional to another."

"Just sit back and enjoy the ride. Don't make this any more difficult than it has to be."

Danny closed his eyes. "You're taking a fellow agent in for doing his job. You know that, right?"

"Starting a firefight with a suspect isn't your job."

"That's funny, Gardner. 'Cause *not* shooting at that same guy is exactly what got me in trouble in the first place." Danny cycled another slow breath. "Tough spot, huh? Can't shoot 'em… Can't not shoot 'em…"

"You know you have the right to remain silent, right?"

"I'm sorry." Danny listened to the sound of the road as the Suburban accelerated along the highway.

"At some point, Gardner, you're gonna have to make a choice."

"What choice?"

"A choice," Danny looked his fellow agent in the eye, "as to which is more important to you: catching bad guys, or following orders."

"Our orders are to catch bad guys," redheaded Rick reminded him.

"Not today they aren't." Danny gave him a quizzical look. "Tell me something, Gardner. Am I being punished for doing my job, or for failing?"

"That's not for me to decide."

"Well, what do you think?"

"I think," Gardner smiled, "that bringing you in tonight pretty much seals my next couple of promotions."

"That's too bad. I mean, it's too bad that you're so wrapped up in yourself that so long as things are going well for you, you don't care that the rest of the place is falling to shit." Danny shook his head. "But hey, as long as you've got yours, I guess it's okay if Rome burns. Eh?"

Gardner retreated as far as his seat would allow him. "Please shut up."

"Sorry," Danny laid back. "Sorry about everything."

"Yeah?"

"I'm sorry I took this case," Danny sighed. "Sorry I didn't drop a Hellfire on Phillips in Pennsylvania. Sorry I didn't shoot him when I had the chance. Sorry I found him again today. Really sorry some infantry idiot shot me." He chuckled. "But mostly, I'm sorry about the fact that I never really lost consciousness at the hospital."

Gardner looked at him in confusion. "Why's that?"

"'Cause that means they never had to give me a Foley."

"A what?"

Danny lifted his pale, paisley hospital gown and loosed a stream of bright yellow urine over the front seat cushions. Acrid fluid splashed all over the driver's shoulder, spraying his shirt, face, and neck. Without a Foley device - a catheter - to automatically drain his bladder, the former Marine had simply withheld the urge to urinate until after he knew his fate - and Wiley's visit only encouraged him to hold it until the most opportune moment.

Gardner lurched to clamp down on Danny's little fire hose, but the driver freaked out and instinctively jerked away from the urine stream. The Suburban swerved from one side to the other, then slid sideways as the driver overcorrected the skid. Tires bought purchase on pavement as the truck slid across the concrete road along the wrong axis. The truck flipped up onto the driver's side and dropped Agent Gardner hard against his door. Danny hung in midair by his seatbelt while the Suburban ground along, then slammed into a concrete highway divider.

Danny tucked his knees, hit his buckle's release, and fell squarely onto Gardner's chest. The winded agent *huffed,* then went slack. Danny quickly found the redheaded fed's Taser on his belt and shot the guy seated in the Suburban's front passenger seat in the neck. A signature *tick-tick-tick-tick-tick* sounded as 50,000 volts arched into the DHS SWAT officer's body. The weapon wrought havoc on the man's already stressed nervous system and quickly robbed him of consciousness.

While the electronic weapon recharged its capacitors, Danny knelt down and relieved Agent Gardner of his sidearm. In exchange, Danny traded his own handcuffs - which he had unlocked a mile ago with a key that Father palmed him back in ICU during their handshake before the feds came into his room.

A quick check showed the driver to be unconscious, but alive. Gardner stirred under Danny's weight, so the former Marine sent the agent deeper into dreamland with a powerful right cross to the face. He hurriedly retrieved Gardner's spare magazine and was rewarded to find a can of pepper spray - the nice kind, not the cheap stuff from the surplus store - on the agent's belt, too.

Gotta work fast. Danny knew that the feds in the other vehicle would work quickly to secure the scene and help to their teammates. He also knew that the accident had already been called in, and that dispatch would reroute any and all available units in the area to his position in order to render aid.

Danny reached up to the unconscious operator in the front passenger seat and pulled a cylindrical grenade off of the guy's vest. A quick pull of the pin, then he tossed the steel canister through the Suburban's shattered windshield. The grenade skittered, bounced off the concrete wall in front of him, then rolled along the pavement. A heartbeat later, sparks shot from the grenade and a plume of smoke billowed out onto the road.

Give 'em something to think about. Danny fetched another grenade - this one from the driver - and chucked it out the compromised rear window. The smoke was harmless, but Danny hoped that it would give the feds pause to worry about what was going on in the Suburban as they inevitably advanced to secure the vehicle. The rules of engagement, they all knew, prohibited any of them from taking a shot unless they had a clear sightline on the target. It was

Danny's most sincere wish that everyone would do their job today.

"We're cutting live to our Channel Three Eye in the Sky, where Three for Me's own Janelle Davidson is watching events unfold. Janelle, can you tell us what's going on?"

"Thank you, Daviona," the intrepid reporter hollered into her headset's built-in mic. "I'm here onboard the helicopter as we fly over the scene, and you can see where the Suburban that we believe is carrying Agent Wakefield has overturned. Now, you can see through our sky cam as we circle overhead that agents from the second vehicle have spread out and are making their way to the wrecked truck with guns drawn. It looks like they're yelling commands to whoever might still be in the other truck. There's smoke everywhere. They're yelling - it's really hard to see in the dark, Daviona. It's dark and there are shadows and smoke and debris all over the place. It looks like they're pulling people out of the wrecked truck. I see what looks like an agent who might me injured, but I don't yet see Wakefield…"

Danny raced through the bushes as quickly as his bare feet could carry him. He slipped onto an auxiliary road not far from the freeway just in time for a car's tires to *screech* in front of him. The car, a mint green Volkswagon Beetle, stopped inches shy of Danny's knees. He quickly padded to the driver's door and was met by a waifish coed with a knit skullcap pulled over her jet black locks.

"Federal agent," Danny announced as he threw open the door and extricated the driver. "I'm commandeering your vehicle."

"Hey!" the young girl squealed, "you can't do that!"

"Bunch'a good guys behind me," he blindly pointed back the way from which he came. "They'll sign for it."

"Screw you, pig!"

On another day, another person under other circumstances might have utilized this encounter as an opportunity to counsel the naive collegiate about how misguided her prejudices against law enforcement officials were. That thoughtful and caring person would probably have told her about how her liberal arts professors were more interested in programming her as a professional protestor than teaching her anything about truth or some combination of knowledge and skills that she might find useful in the job market. And if that adult was extra kind, they would have mentored her and coached her along a path that would allow her to see the world more clearly and make informed life choices.

Wakefield flipped the safety on the pepper spray in his hand and maced the mouthy coed until the can ran dry.

The previously brave social justice warrior screamed and melted like the Wicked Witch of the West. Danny dropped the can, pushed the nag aside, and hopped into the compact car. "My name's Gardner. Just tell them I said it's okay." The fastest of the uniformed officers had just barely made his way into the bushes when the mint green Beetle leapt to speed and raced down the road.

It's better than running, Danny told himself as he whipped the little green car around a corner, *but there's no out-driving the cops, Not on their own turf.* He shook his head, drifted around another turn, then desperately stomped on the accelerator pedal hard enough that it threatened to punch through the floorboard. *Not in this thing. That's for sure.*

Danny thought he noticed a helicopter overhead earlier. He knew that the chopper would relay his every move to the local police on the ground and whatever federal agents were still engaged in the chase. He knew that the freeway would be crawling with pursuit cars, so he pushed the little Beetle through a whiplash-inducing turn down Elizabethtown Road, which was heavily wooded on either side. He coaxed all of the speed he could out of the Beetle's tiny engine and checked the dashboard clock. *Nineteen thirty hours.* The night was young, but there were precious little distance between Danny and his pursuit. *Need to lose this thing, fast.* Itchy fabric rubbed against his bare hindquarters. *And I need to find someone who will trade me Gardner's gun for some pants.*

CHAPTER 15

"YOU'RE A DAMN TRAITOR!" the red-faced civilian bellowed.

"Look, Mr. Green -"

"That's *Mayor* Green, Captain Hartman."

"Mayor Green," the humorless Soldier corrected himself, "you need to understand that I'm just following orders here. And my orders are to secure these streets."

"This ain't Baghdad, Captain Hartman," the older man fumed. "It's Paducah. My town. An' I told you to get yer men an' get yer trucks off a' my streets."

News of the three-way firefight between the Constitutional Killer, Special Agent Wakefield, and a team of troopers out in North Carolina spread quickly through all manner of news channels. All across the nation, in big cities and small towns alike, people began to find their voice, and that collective voice was decidedly unhappy. The loss of their liberties had reminded the American people of what freedom actually was. It required the presence of armed troops on the city streets for folks to realize the value of that lost liberty - and to realize that freedom was not so free after all. And so by ones and twos at first, and then in greater and greater numbers, people all around America took to the internet, the airwaves, and the streets in scenes that mirrored this confrontation at the heart of downtown Paducah, Kentucky.

"My orders -"

"Yer orders're illegal!" Mayor Green cut him off.

"They come from the top, sir."

"Well, that don't make 'em right!" The portly man waved an angry finger at the contingent of men and women in front of him. He easily cast a shadow twice as large as any of the troopers at the intersection, but did so without the benefit of tactical equipment or body armor. "Now, as Mayor of this city, I'm ordering you to return to base."

"I can't do that, Mr. Mayor," Captain Hartman shook his head. "My orders come from Lieutenant Colonel Richardson. And his come from General Boone. And his come from Secretary James. And his from Secretary Warner. Until I receive a direct communique indicating that martial law has been lifted -"

"Now, lis'en here son. An' you lis'en real good." Mayor Green's face turned redder and redder with each breath. Veins in his neck and forehead pulsated with each heartbeat. "I've always supported the troops. Ain't nobody gonna tell you different." The middle aged man's hands shook as he fought to contain the righteous indignation that built up inside him. "An' there ain't a man or woman in this town that wants to see this go any further than it has. But yer on the wrong side of your oath on this one, son."

"I will remind you, Mr. Mayor, that curfew is in effect." The junior officer, barely thirty years old, let his eyes sweep from one side of the gathered crowd to the other without the slightest movement of his head. "All civilians are ordered off the streets by twenty-hundred hours local time." The furrowed eyebrows behind his clear safety glasses carried the full seriousness of his warning. "Eight o'clock," he clarified for those unaccustomed to military time. "Which is in three minutes."

"This is America!" Mayor Green boiled. Several of the citizens who had gathered around the exchange shouted their agreement with his sentiment. "We're Americans!" More voices concurred. "This is our town! These are our streets!" The portly man crossed his arms and planted his feet on the pavement in the middle of the intersection. "*You* leave! NOW!"

"Mayor Green," the Army captain threatened, "your attitude and demeanor make me suspect you might be a rebel sympathizer. I'm afraid that if you don't clear out now, I'll have to report you to my superiors." While the town leader remained silent, several members of the crowd vocalized invitations for Captain Hartman and his men to copulate with themselves utilizing some rather imaginative methods, groupings, and equipment. "Sergeant Reynolds!" he blindly barked back toward his platoon. "Have your men clear this street." Several Soldiers filtered up from the background with their M-4 carbines held at the ready.

"That ain't gonna happen," Mayor Green pursed his lips as he shook his head. "Don't do this, son.

You're about to cross a line that you can't return from."

Captain Hartman made a show of checking his watch with an overly dramatic motion. "Two minutes," he announced.

"Ladies and gentlemen," a dark skinned man in his mid-twenties called out from behind a velcro tab with three chevrons, "please return to your homes immediately."

"This is our home!" a matronly woman shouted back. "Why don't you go back to yours?"

"One minute, twenty seconds!" Captain Hartman stood with his left hand in front of his face and his right hand on the grip of the M-32 grenade launcher slung across his chest.

Enlisted men started pushing against the folks in the front of the crowd, trying to shoo them away. But the civilians would not have it. "Please clear the street," Sergeant Reynolds pled, "or we will have no choice but to remove you by force."

"One minute!" Captain Hartman called. "Sergeant! MOPP Two. Now!" The NCO echoed the order to his troops, who all produced gas masks from their belts and assumed the proper Mission Oriented Protective Posture while their commander quickly moved to mount the Stryker armored vehicle parked behind him. In a well-practiced maneuver, the troopers on the street swept their helmets off and pulled the straps to their gas masks over their heads - which, for a split second, left their hands upon their heads and their vision completely obscured by black, vulcanized rubber.

A split second was more time than it took for the civilians nearest to them to grab each Soldier's rifle - hung uselessly by a sling and unretained in front of their armor carriers. A few of the troopers were driven to their knees in the struggle. Sergeant Reynolds' assailant held the NCO like a human shield. The muzzle of a previously concealed pistol pressed against the black sergeant's temple.

"Captain Hartman," Mayor Green called, "by the authority vested in me by the city of Paducah and the great state of Kentucky, you and your men are under arrest for violation of the War Powers Act. Chief Patterson, take these criminals into custody."

Dean Patterson, the Chief of Police for Paducah, Kentucky, nodded from Mayor Green's shoulder. "Sir," he called up to the Army officer, "step out of the vehicle, place your weapons on the ground slowly, and raise your hands." Captain Hartman paused. Then he exchanged a knowing look with Sergeant Reynolds.

Sergeant Shadaran Reynolds slumped in his attacker's grip, drew his M-9, and fired blindly behind his own hip pocket as quickly as he could. He did not need to see if any of his shots landed. He only needed to make his insurgent captor jump. He only needed for people to look his way for a second - the exact second when Captain Hartman loosed a volley of capsaicin grenades into the crowd around them.

Noxious gas poured out of the grenades. Chemical agents wafted through the crowd. Civilians gagged until they fell to the street crying, coughing, screaming.

And then another shot rang out. But instead of a painful - yet non-lethal - 40mm gas grenade, this shot propelled a bullet from a gun.

Perhaps that shot came from within the foggy irritant that lingered over the street. Perhaps that shot came from a window overlooking the scene. Perhaps that shot came from one of the light cavalry troopers. Or perhaps from within the rabble that crowded the streets around the intersection. Nobody knew. Nobody cared. Because once that shot was fired, it was joined with more gunfire from both sides of the skirmish.

Shop windows up and down Main Street shattered as rounds from US Army rifles and machine guns ripped through them. Captain Hartman's Stryker *ping*'ed as small arms fire fell on his vehicle like rain drops.

For a moment that stretched into eternity, American citizens exchanged gunfire with Soldiers wearing their citizens' own flag on their shoulders. When the shooting finally died down, bullet holes pocked storefronts and tore into the nation's soul. Men and women cried out on the sidewalk as they joined the hallowed dead of Selma, Athens, Gettysburg, Lexington, and Concord.

A new chapter of American history was written in blood on the streets of a small Kentucky town.

*   *   *

Sandra carried Danny's effects home from the hospital in a cheap, flimsy, plastic bag. Even with her badge, the nurses would not release Wakefield's clothes to her until after some unnamed official at DHS approved Elbee's request. The pistol Danny took down to North Carolina was still in official custody - *He did shoot a guy with it,* Sandra reminded herself - but at least his clothes were not going to stay bundled up in a trash bag, tucked into an evidence locker in a warehouse in Quanico.

Four official vehicles parked next to the door. She shook her head as she trudged into the apartment building from the parking lot. Sandra listened to the news on the radio in real time as they reported on her former partner's escape. *Former partner turned fugitive.*

A lone agent was posted at the building's door. He watched Elbee as she approached. He let her pass after a quick flash of her badge. *He looked surprised that I was alone.*

D.C.'s cold November air snuck into her jacket as she cleared the doorway. *Honestly,* she shrugged, *so am I.* Elbee had more than half expected to see Wakefield, half naked and standing on the side of the road, flag her down during the long drive back from North Carolina to the D.C. Metro. But she did not, and she tried to quell the quiet question within her head as to which disappointed her more - the fact that Danny ran from the authorities or the fact that he had not run to her. *I wonder if they know that I called the press. Or Derek.* Sandra shivered, then ascended the stairs with squeaking shoes.

Elbee saw more agents at the apartment door as soon as she cleared the stairs. Two men, kitted out in full tactical gear and with M-4 carbines held muzzle down across their chests, stared at her as she approached. From the sound of things, there were plenty more past the open door. Derek stood in the hallway, clearly unable to gain entry.

"Sandra," Little D gestured at the gorillas. "I, uh…" Words failed Derek - not that Sandra needed any explanation. She knew why he was there. *Daniel planned this from the beginning,* she shook her head. *But whatever pre-planned idea they had, he didn't plan on Derek getting stopped before they could pull it off.*

"Gentlemen," Elbee flashed her badge to the agents.

"Ma'am."

"Step aside, please."

"Sorry, ma'am, but we can't do that."

"I live here," Sandra clarified.

"Yes, ma'am," the brute answered, "but we're effecting a search warrant. The scene is secure."

"My badge says Federal Agent," she pressed.

"Orders, ma'am," he growled. "Nobody in or out but Task Force personnel."

"Special Agent Elbee," a catty voice sounded from inside the door. "What a surprise."

"Jenkins," Sandra stared lasers at Special Agent Carrie Jenkins, the smug female that worked with Wakefield in the Secret Service's analysis center before the Constitutional Killer struck. Neither Danny nor Derek had a high estimate of their female colleague, and Elbee learned quickly after meeting her that Jenkins earned their ire. "What're you doing here?"

"After the fiasco a few weeks ago," Jenkins sneered, "the task force needed some new help." Elbee knew that somewhere within the DHS some opportunist would use Wakefield's misfortune as a stepping stone for their career. The fact that a hack like Carrie had pulled the maneuver off made it all the more distasteful. "So I'm helping with the search and seizure of anything that might be pertinent to our case."

"Is the task force investigating Phillips, or Wakefield?"

Jenkins pursed her full lips. "Well, between his arrest for obstruction, assault, and now escaping federal custody and his already shaky suspension, your boyfriend's been added as a person of interest to that investigation." A petty smile showed just how delicious Danny's contemptible coworker found the whole affair. "And since Nick got me a spot on the Task Force…" she let her voice trail off for a moment, then she perked back up again. "Oh, I'm sorry. Where are my manners? Were you here for something in particular? Some of the military gear, weapons and ammo we've boxed up and sent to Quantico, perhaps?"

"Of course not," Sandra knew Derek well enough to know that he was bluffing, but she kept that opinion to herself.

"You sure you don't wanna put together a little care package for America's most wanted fugitive?" Jenkins mocked. "I bet that's why his little butt-buddy was here." The bitter agent glared at her coworker. "I'm telling Nick that you were here when we got here, Martin; that we caught you skulking around. You: a guy with a romantic relationship with a woman from a nation that produces Muslim extremists, who also happens to be a known associate to a federal fugitive, engaged in suspicious activity at the site of a federal investigation related to domestic terrorist activity." She hummed in glee. "Nick's gonna have your ass for sure this time. Screw reassignment. You're gonna be flipping burgers by the end of the month."

Sandra's fist balled and shook. "Get the Hell out of my apartment, bitch."

"When we're done." Jenkins kept her eyes locked onto Derek. """You know, for more than a year now, I've heard you and Wakefield run your mouths about how awesome you are. I guess you're not such slick shit after all, are you? Some chump's running rings around you. Either that," she grinned wickedly, "or maybe you two are helping Phillips. If he even is the real killer." She shared her toxic smile with Elbee. "I mean, with everything that's been going on lately, it kinda calls to question all of the progress you two allegedly made on the case while you were sniffing each other's tails." Jenkins' poorly-dyed red mop turned back into the apartment. She surveyed the progress made by her teammates. "We'll probably be a few more hours, deary. Your boyfriend had quite the arsenal here. More than we got from Phillips' trailer. Cataloging it all slowed us down a little bit, but we'll get through it all." Carrie gave her a menacing grin. "I sure hope all of those guns come back clean when we run them against the databases. Might complicate your career prospects if they don't. Don't you think?" Jenkins turned back into the apartment to resume her supervisory role. "If you're going to hang around," she called over her shoulder without looking, "why don't you be a peach and get us some coffee?"

"Why don't you go fu-"

"Forget about it," Derek grabbed Sandra's arm. "C'mon. Let's just get out of here. We'll pick up Aliyah and get some drinks."

Sandra breathed fire through her nostrils and watched as Jenkins stood in a room full of busy people. Wakefield had used Carrie Jenkins as an example of the exact stereotypes and stigma about women in the workforce that Elbee had fought against her whole career. And here, right before her eyes, Sandra saw all of those negative opinions being revisited, reinforced, and rewarded. She hated the negative impact it had on Daniel. But even more, she hated the negative image it painted of women in their profession - or any profession, for that matter. *You think you're hurting the man,* she fumed, *but you're really just hurting the cause.* Dejectedly, Sandra sighed and followed Derek to the staircase.

"We'll lock up behind us," Jenkins sang as Sandra walked away.

For a moment, Sandra simply stood outside of the apartment while the world swirled around her.

"Just let her do her thing," Derek pulled on her elbow. "Let her play her games. Don't sweat it. She sucks at her job almost as much as she sucks -"

A single tear in the corner of Sandra's eye cut Derek's quip short. "It's not fair," she whispered.

The younger man gave her arm a reassuring squeeze. "Life rarely plays fair. C'mon. Let's go get a drink."

"They're gone now," Sam still managed a smile as he delivered the latest round of drinks to the three unhappiest people in his bar.

"Who?" Aliyah asked.

"The feds who followed you in here," he indicated the empty table nearest to the Black Sam's door.

Aliyah looked startled. "What feds?"

"Plainclothes guys, *mhboob*," Derek answered for Sam.

"Why didn't you tell me we were being followed?"

"We're not being followed," he clarified. "Sandra is. Anyway, I didn't know for sure. I just suspected."

Sam nodded to confirm Derek's theory. "A pair of them. They left a few minutes ago."

"If they were undercover," Sandra inquired, "how'd you know they were feds?"

"One beer each," Sam shook his head. "Barely touched their drinks before they left. Paid in cash. No change. Terrible tip. Might as well have worn hats with 'Eff Bee Eye' stenciled on them." The wise barkeep looked at the trio that sat before him. "Do try to cheer up, guys."

"I thought sad people bought more booze," Sandra countered from her seat in the booth.

"Frowns are bad for business." Sam snatched empty glasses and bottles from the table. "Drags everyone else around you down. Those two feds who followed you all in here were already sucking all of the fun outta this place." Sandra sampled her glass, then looked up in surprise. "*Apfelwein*," Sam answered her question before she could ask it. "Apple wine. From Germany."

"Do you ever just order something, Elbee?" Derek demanded. "Or do you just drink whatever he brings you?"

"I like it," she smiled as she took a second sip.

"Me, too," Aliyah offered. "Well played, Sam. An excellent choice, as always."

Sam beamed with a roguish grin. "Like I always say: I know what the ladies like." Satisfied for the moment, Sam returned to the bar with the trio's empty bottles.

"Now that things are cooled down," Derek whispered over a heavy handled mug with a liter of lager with a healthy head in hushed, conspiratorial tones, "I can finally let you off the hook."

"What do you mean?" Sandra suspiciously raised her eyebrow.

"Okay, so, you said that Big D asked you to text me from the hospital."

"Right. He said you had a spare key and that you'd know what to do. So I did, just as soon as I got back to my car."

"Well," Little D confessed, "I was already there."

"While they were loading him up?"

"Actually, I got there just after you left town." Sandra still looked confused. "By the time you got to North Carolina, I'd already done what Danny needed me to do."

"Which was what, exactly?" Aliyah asked.

"It's best if I don't say. Plausible deniability."

"Well then why bring it up at all?" Sandra stabbed.

Derek made a calming gesture with his hand. "I just wanted you to know that everything's taken care of."

"I don't know what that means," Sandra shook her head.

"You don't need to know," Derek tried his best to soothe her, but it clearly was futile. "Look, the less you know, the better for everyone involved. I just didn't want you feeling like you failed or something."

"*Mhboob,*" Aliyah whined, "what are you talking about? Failed what? I know that *Daniyal* is in trouble," she begged. "Please tell me you aren't involved with something stupid."

"Big D's just doing what he thinks is right."

"And just what is Daniel planning to do?" Sandra pressed. "He's a wanted fugitive. His Jeep's been impounded, the apartment's under surveillance, and Jenkins and her boys took away all of his guns."

Derek shook his head. "When the time comes," he took another pull from his drink, "I think we'll know what he's got up his sleeve."

CHAPTER 16

A PRACTICED AND scornful frown hung upon Father Crane's face as he shook his head at the tired man in dirty rags. "You come walking into my church," he scalded, "wrapped in rags and stinking of shame, and you have the nerve to ask me for sanctuary?"

Danny pulled at the tattered clothes he obtained from a homeless bum he found in southern Virginia. "I'm sorry. They kept my clothes down in -"

"I don't give a damn about your clothes," the priest countered. "I care about your behavior, son. I care about what they're saying on the news. About what you did."

"I was wrongfully arrested."

"Then you sort it out during the hearing," Father Crane chastised, "you don't assault cops."

"I have a job to do."

"You're on suspension!"

"But I found him!"

"Then you should'a called it in and let your teammates handle it. With numbers. By the book, Danny. You know that."

Wakefield knew. He knew what it felt like to blindly follow bad leads into dead ends. He saw firsthand what Phillips was capable of in Phoenix, and what it meant to be forced to let him get away. He knew the fear and frustration of watching a teammate get shot - like happened to Agent Collins during the West Virginia raid - only to learn that the target was another Dry Hole. He knew what happened to the FBI team in Pennsylvania when they tried to apprehend Phillips. He lived through the attack at DHS headquarters - watched powerlessly as Phillips killed Secretary Dagenhart right in front of him. He knew all of this and much, much more. And he knew that he would do anything he could if it spared another good guy from knowing it, too.

"Somebody's got to stop Phillips."

"That's what they're trying to do."

"Yeah, well, they suck at it."

Father Crane's eyes went narrow. "Oh, really? And are you helping or hurting, Danny? What do you call what you're doing?"

"I had him," Danny persisted. "I *had* him."

The Catholic priest's eyes went wide. "Outnumbered and outgunned in a running firefight through the city streets. Is that what 'having' him means? Is that what you call it?"

"I just need a place to lay low for -"

"No." Father Crane crossed his arms. "You show up here with the cops on your ass and blood on your hands -"

"I went out of my way to *not* hurt those guys!"

"- and in a stolen car."

"*Commandeered*," Danny corrected. "Commandeered. It's a law enforcement term."

"And when you start acting like a cop again instead of a felon, you can start talking like one to me."

Danny's face skewed. "Actually, there's some fuzzy language pertaining to lawful orders that makes all of this somewhat ambiguous -"

Father Crane seemed to rise up into the air atop an imaginary lectern. "I studied a lot of languages at Saint Mary's," he looked down his nose. "Latin. Greek. Hebrew. None of them were as befuddling as the two step your tongue is dancing right now, boy."

"I'm just saying that I'm not totally wrong here, is all."

"Unrepentant," Father Crane spat. He shook his head. "The privilege of sanctuary is a grace reserved for innocents in genuine need, Danny. Abuse victims. Refugees. Not willful criminals trying to dodge jail."

"But I *am* in genuine need -"

"What you need," the priest cut him off with a raised hand, "is to get righteous again - with the law *and* the Lord. Then we'll talk about your place in this church."

Wakefield processed that last bit with a long breath. The priest's mind was clearly made. "Yes, Father." He sighed, then made for the door. Halfway to the chapel's exit, he turned back to his priest. "One more thing, Father Crane."

"I won't bless you," the holy man admonished.

Danny dug the keys to the green Volkswagon that he commandeered - that he *stole* in North Carolina - out of his pocket and tossed them at the priest. Father Crane caught them effortlessly. "I'd consider it a personal favor if you took care of that for me."

"The authorities -"

"Government officials aren't the only ones who can make things right," Danny pointed. As he departed, Wakefield resigned himself to the course his actions had set him upon and steeled himself against the plummeting night temperatures. *I may not have started this, but I'm the one who's got to end it. There's no changing that now.*

The air would be cold. He knew that. The night would be hard and the road long. He knew that, too. But Danny shuffled his feet, sang a cadence in his head, and set out on the only path he knew that could make things right again.

* * *

Agent Stevenson poured over the file sprawled across her desk and shook her head. "Any sign of him at any hospitals between here and Bragg?"

"Nothing," a tired voice answered from a few chairs down the line. The task force was supposed to operate around the clock, but the night shift was hard to keep manned. A lot of analysts snuck off to the J. Edgar Hoover Building's more distant and quieter corners during the early morning hours to steal a few precious minutes of sleep away from prying eyes. And though the practice was prohibited by policy, in reality it was rarely punished - so long as nobody was caught napping on the watch.

Dianne Stevenson was bright enough to know that she lacked the certain *je ne sais quoi* that made gifted folks stand out from their peer group. She was smart, but no genius like Martin. She was pretty, but not gorgeous like Elbee. She was fit, but not tough like Wakefield. All of her life, Dianne had been good enough, but never great; respectable, but not legendary.

She was also a dedicated law enforcement professional who was determined to push her career forward. So she worked hard. And she volunteered to take the jobs nobody else wanted - including the graveyard shift at the Hoover watch floor - because those jobs came with the opportunity to prove herself. What Dianne lacked in random talent she more than made up for in tenacity and persistence, which was why she was happy to lead the night shift, even if it required her to triple her caffeine intake and pour through her former-colleague's personnel file, comb through his personal life, and contribute to a manhunt for a guy that she used to think she could trust.

Dianne scanned the watch floor and found an under-tasked face. "Hey, Rich!" Agent Rich's head jerked to attention at her summons. "Double check the Vee-Aye clinics. And any Veteran Service Organizations who might have open doors this late. Especially the small ones. Wakefield's a vet. He might think they wouldn't report him if he dropped by."

"On it."

A thought struck her. "And can somebody check his church? He's Catholic, right? He might try to claim sanctuary."

"I'll check all of them between here and North Carolina," another voice acknowledged.

"Thanks, Pierce." *Learn their names,* Dianne reminded herself. *Learn all of their names. Can't just be good. Gotta be good, but gotta act like the boss. Then they'll treat you like the boss. Then, someday, you'll move on from the crappy work details to the good jobs.*

Oh, Wakefield, Dianne shook her head as she read the confidential file - including his sealed psychiatric notes - for the fiftieth time, *how could I have misjudged you?*

CHAPTER 17

OSCAR TIED THE THIRD trash bag as tightly as he could - because some rubbish was too disgusting to risk simply double-bagging it, even with extra thick, commercial grade plastic. Then, for good measure, he plucked a roll of duct tape out of his utility drawer and applied it liberally around the bag's opening to prevent any accidental leakage from the closed maw. Satisfied with is handiwork, he dropped the black bundle next to the ladder to the surface and locked his front door.

Years ago, Oscar dropped a significant portion of his savings from working at the National Security Agency as an investment in a small Maryland winery whose product he enjoyed. The squat cryptologist insisted that the arrangement remain completely anonymous. He also insisted that the majority of that investment was used to repair and update the grounds near the distillery - a landscaping renovation that included the installation of a series of bunkers and chambers buried deep enough underground to allay any apprehension that the analyst might actually be spied upon himself while he lived there.

The grotto was built with more than sheer privacy in mind. Comprised of a series of concrete and steel tubes laid upon their sides and finished with painted stucco laid over a copper mesh that blocked out all signals, its scale worked well for a man of Oscar's short stature, as he was barely one inch taller than the American Medical Association's official measure for dwarfism. And the den was decorated in warm woods and furnishings that gave the home an atmosphere that was as comfortable as its locale was uninviting.

It was, in short, the perfect place to hide. Perfect for a misanthropic introvert such as Oscar. Perfect for a federal fugitive like Danny.

Wakefield toweled the gaps and crevices in his ears as he padded barefoot out of the bathroom. "It's true what they say: a good shower really is worth four hours' sleep." His brown pants, made out of the same warm, durable fabric as fire hoses, hung from his hips unbuttoned. "I think I used up all the hot water."

"Well, Chumly, at least you don't look or smell homeless anymore." Clad in a plaid robe that almost reached his ankles and fluffy house slippers that looked like bunnies, Oscar glared at the main portal into his subterranean home. "Where on Earth did you get those foul rags?"

"Traded some wino a pistol for them."

Oscar's nose wrinkled. "You and I'd've both been better off if he shot you once he got the gun. Saved us both from the smell."

"Didn't give him the bullets," Danny smiled as he pulled a black, long-sleeved shirt from a familiar backpack and slipped it over his refreshed frame.

Little D did good, he mused. *Grabbed my rifle case and BOB before anyone else got to the apartment. Left the rest of the guns so that DHS would have something to do. Wild geese for them to chase.*

The shorter man shivered. "What kind of dumbass street rat trades his clothes for an unloaded gun on a night like tonight?"

Danny secured his belt and stretched. His head almost touched the ceiling in his diminutive colleague's shrunken-scaled home. "Didn't give him a choice, either."

Oscar looked at the clock on his shortened wall. "Look, Chumly, I know what's going on. You're on some sort of Grail quest that you feel honor bound to complete. I get it. Hell, I even think it's a good idea. That's why agreed to pluck your bags up out of Derek's car while he smoke-screened the clowns searching your apartment."

Danny looked at the luggage that rested on the leather couch: his BOB - Bug Out Bag, a hefty black backpack filled with all of the gear he needed during the worst of all imaginable emergencies - clothes, first aid, hygiene kit, radio, meds, and so forth. Next to BOB sat his range case, still loaded with his new bronze AR-458, his matched custom 1911, and all of the associated ammo and accessories. Satisfied, he nodded. *Nobody who knows the first thing about me would ever think for a second that I didn't have any guns in the apartment. But with these,* he mused, *with these I'm still in the fight.* "But?" he raised a suspicious eyebrow at Oscar.

"But, it's one in the morning," Oscar huffed.

"I understand. We could probably both use some sleep." He cleared his backpack and gun case from Oscar's couch.

"There's that," Oscar's head bobbled from side to side, "and the part where I don't need you bringing any unwanted attention around here."

As if on cue, the buzzer to Oscar's intercom sounded. The paranoid NSA analyst flicked a switch, consulted the image from a security camera pointed at the surface hatch, then keyed the system's microphone. "C'mon down." He punched a series of commands into the panel which unlocked the doors, watched the subject for a moment, then turned back to Danny. "Relax, Chumly. I ordered myself some delivery while you were delousing."

"I thought you were going to bed."

"I am," Oscar insisted as he unbolted the inner hatch. The door opened to reveal a fair skinned young woman. Danny guessed that she was around twenty-two, though the plunging cleavage beneath the black blazer buttoned below her breastbone drew his eye away from her face. His gaze was carried further down her alluring lines and along a set of lovely legs that started at the jacket's hem line and stretched for an eternity in both directions.

Danny looked back up into the brunette's eyes, framed within a pair of oversized black glasses. Her chestnut hair was twisted in some sort of complicated braid held in place by a pair of black sticks. "I've seen pictures of your sister, Oscar," he smiled, "and this ain't her."

"I'm Devon," the porcelain figure smiled as she stepped through the doorway. "Are you -"

"No, he isn't," the dwarfish man interrupted. "But I am."

The bookish brunette's smile never changed as she shifted her gaze. "Of course you are. Nice to know I'm at the right place." She looked back up at Danny. "This isn't a problem for me, but the booking only said there'd be one of you. So, if you're both gonna -"

"He's leaving," Oscar tossed Danny a set of keys. "Take the Cherokee, Chumly. Plenty of baggage space. Top it off when you get back."

"You bet." Danny found his all weather hiking boots and gathered his bags. "Thanks again. It was nice to meet you, Devon."

The young woman produced a business card from within her jacket and handed it to Danny as he exited. "A pleasure," she smiled. "Give me a call sometime."

"And grab the trash on your way out," Oscar chided.

* * *

Sandra slept in fits alone in the Daniel's bed. When she woke, tears burned the pillow and forced her to shift the bedding that she had grown accustomed to sharing. Jenkins and her lackeys left Daniel's apartment in disarray after their search. Sandra wanted to put things back together again after they left, but when she started the bitter task, she was not sure where some of Daniel's things went. That's when the crying started. It had not stopped since.

She flipped the pillow and flopped her head back down. Daniel's leather jacket was still clutched in her hands like a security blanket. *You couldn't just leave it alone, could you? Couldn't stay out of it and let others do their job?* Pools welled up once more in her blue eyes.

Oh, Daniel, Sandra shook her head. *Do you have any idea what you have done? What this will do to your career? To us?*

CHAPTER 18

"THANKS FOR JOINING the Lonnie Chase Program. It's Kyp and Fred, covering for Lonnie on this, the day before Thanksgiving," the senior co-host's baritone voice rolled into his microphone. "And we're so thankful, so very thankful around here this year."

"And not just because Lonnie's not here today," Factcheck Fred quipped from his chair.

"Though that has lightened the mood around the studio."

"Well, something needs to be light around here," Fred chuckled. "At my house, we've been pre-eating for the holiday -"

"Pre-eating?"

"Yeah. It's our new thing. Think of it as the culinary equivalent to a pre-game workout. You know how you always overeat on Thanksgiving because that's the one day that you get all of those great foods, right?"

"So you just can't say 'no.'"

"Exactly. So, to avoid overdoing it tomorrow, we've been enjoying all of our favorite traditional Thanksgiving dishes early."

"That seems very thoughtful. When did you start this?"

"Halloween." Paid subscribers saw Fred's matter-of-fact expression via the studio camera, contrasted with Kyp's snicker.

"Looking at you, I'd say it's really not about avoiding weight gain."

"Oh, heavens no," Fred waved. "It's just so that we don't get sick tomorrow after we gorge ourselves."

"So, it's like training for a marathon?"

"Right," Fred's face remained deadpan. "Every bite of sweet potatoes is like a step on a long path -"

"To diabetes," Kyp finished for him. "Speaking of celebrating the holidays, our producer just brought us word over the break that several of the Army units assigned to street security and searching for Thomas Phillips have apparently stood down."

"Well, not several," Fred corrected his colleague. "One."

"One that we know of," Kyp countered. "And if we know about one, we have to ask ourselves how many more we haven't heard about yet."

"We also have to ask why they've done it. I mean, nobody wants to see this occupation end more than we do, but it does raise some questions."

"It's probably because they're tired of getting into firefights with Americans," Kyp offered. "In the last few days, there've been - what, fifteen incidents?"

"We're tracking eighteen," Fred clarified. "Eighteen shootings and more than three dozen protests across the nation," he checked his notes, "which have resulted in more than fifty people killed - three of them US Soldiers, the rest civilians - and upwards of two hundred people injured."

"That's quite the casualty count," Kyp shook his head. "And it's all Americans shooting Americans."

"Well, a few of those numbers came when protesters in Cincinnati hit a Hummvee with a Molotov cocktail, but still… You see, this is part of what makes a civil war such a difficult thing to stomach. It's all your own people. On both sides."

"We're up against a break here, but I when we come back, we're going to hear from a Soldier who knows firsthand how hard a situation this is. Corporal Jesse Spears was one of the troopers who responded to a call of shots fired in Fayetteville which led to a shootout where one of the Constitutional Killer's accomplices was captured and the Special Agent who used to be in charge of this investigation getting shot…"

* * *

"It's a goddam mutiny."

"Secretary James," a dark skinned officer with a silver eagle on one collar and a gold pen, sword, and wreath on the other cautioned his superior, "that's not a word we use lightly around the JAG Corps."

"Oh, really?" The Secretary of the Army glared across his desk at the lawyer who stood before him. "And tell me, Colonel Richards, exactly what legal term the Judge Advocate General would use to describe a Captain who violates a standing order from his superiors and sends his troops home for the holidays?"

The military lawyer subtly shifted his weight from one leg to the other in order to avoid a cramp while he stood. "For now, sir, I'd call it a delicate situation."

"Is this what passes for soldiery today?" Secretary James stabbed. "Have the ranks of the United States Army been filled with a bunch of pussies who can't stay engaged in a combat deployment because it interferes with the holidays?"

"Sir," Richards cycled a careful breath, "there have been a number of legal challenges to the current operation here stateside."

"Colonel, I don't give a rat's -"

"The outcome of those cases, sir, may well determine whether this entire campaign is even deemed legal." The lawyer carefully considered his words. "I don't want to sound like I'm overstating the situation, sir, but we may well be writing history here."

"Now you listen here, Colonel, and you listen good. Just because some ACLU chickensh -"

"I'm talking about objections from within the Army itself, sir. As well as some other voices who have raised concern."

"I. Beg. Your. Pardon?"

You may indeed be begging for a pardon, Richards kept to himself, *before this is all over.* "Sir, a number of troops have sent petitions up the Chain-of-Command, and several unit-level JAG officers from various branches and regions are already reporting challenges to their orders."

"You can't be serious."

"As you know, sir, our troops are conditioned to follow all lawful orders. Well, sir, that includes being taught how to recognize them. And we're getting a lot of feedback from the line. Questions as to whether the entire task order to deploy personnel onto our own territory constitutes an unlawful order."

"It's lawful because I said so!"

"I'm afraid, Mr. Secretary, that it's a little more complicated than that." Colonel Richards reminded himself that Mason James was a political appointee, not a veteran, and as such might not respect or understand the responsibilities and obligations that came with his office. *Be patient,* he breathed, *walk him through it.* "And I am duty-bound to inform you, sir, that at this point it is too early to predict the Pentagon's final determination."

The Secretary of the Army looked incredulous. "Are you telling me that we can't even enforce an order to our own troops issued from this office?"

"Sir," Richards fingered his folded beret behind his back, "I'm saying that at this moment, a compelling argument can be made. Counsel has been called into play, sir. And it's not just Captain Tucker's case, sir. Questions have been filed from NCOs, company-grade, and even command-level officers from all over."

"Who?" the Secretary glared daggers. "You tell me which sonso'bitches signed their own warrants -"

"Sir, I'm not sure it would be appropriate -"

"You've gotta be goddam kidding me." Secretary James looked like he wanted to throw something heavy at the Army lawyer.

"Sir," Richards wished for more steel in his bones than he felt like he actually had, "I am duty-bound to remind you that Army regulations specifically protect our troops from reprisals in these sorts of circumstances." He swallowed. "And to advise you that if the JAG ultimately determines this operation to be a violation of policy or law, not only will troopers like Tucker be vindicated, but there may actually be significant legal ramifications."

"Meaning?"

Just pull the bandage off quickly. "Sir. You, the Chief of Staff, and every commander in charge of this entire operation may face charges under the Uniform Code of Military Justice, federal, and civil law. Sir."

Mason James' face alternated between an enraged red and a flush, ghostly white. His silver hair seemed to lighten as he sat and considered several possible futures and his life, and the ramifications he faced should each of them play out to their full fruition. His eyes seemed anchored to the executive writing pad atop his desk. "Get out."

Colonel Richards straightened and curtly nodded. Without another word, he spun to his right with military precision and walked out the door to the Secretary's office. Once he was in the hallway, he pulled his cell phone from his pocket and dialed the woman he hoped could improve his mood.

"Hey, Babe. It's me…"

*   *   *

Yvette Richards roamed slowly but purposefully through the Phillips Memorial Gallery in DuPont Circle. The building was empty save herself and a couple of employees who busied themselves somewhere out of sight. Weekday afternoons typically had light foot traffic, which made them the perfect time for her to inspect her subordinates' work getting the place ready for the next gala.

Her cellular phone was held up to her ear, but her attention was focused upon the trio of canvases before her. "Well, honey, you just do what you have to do," she absently commented as she thought about the guests she anticipated over the holiday weekend. *Do I want their eyes to drift from one painting to the next, or to linger?* Three oil paintings by the hottest cubist visionary in the hemisphere hung against a blank wall. Concealed lights bathed the bright images in pools that had to be carefully tuned to provide illumination that was sufficient and complementary, but not overpowering.

Friday night's gotta be perfect, she reminded herself. Yvette's instincts told her that a big show during Thanksgiving weekend would be just the thing to draw snobs and bigwigs from all around the D.C. Metro area - and their donation dollars - into the gallery. *A good show,* she smiled, *and I might even be able to slip myself a little Christmas bonus.*

Yvette's husband, the military lawyer, asked a question that she barely paid attention to - something about picking something up somewhere - when her eyes fell upon the absolute last sight she wanted to see just before a big event in her gallery. Leaning against the wall, doubtlessly discoloring the paint on the corner, her ex-husband stood with his arms crossed and a frown upon his tired face. "I'm sorry, Jaycen," she grumbled, "but I've gotta go tell Christine to re-tune the lights in the Bruce exhibit." A pause. "Yes. I'll pick it up on the way home." She ended the call without listening for a response, then hissed at the man in front of her in a whispering yell. "What the Hell are you doing here, Danny?"

"S'up, Yvette?"

"Jesus, Wakefield." Yvette's normally nutmeg visage darkened with a scowl. It was a look with which Wakefield was well acquainted. She shoelessly stomped across the polished hardwood floor. Black nylon struck against manilla stain with each pounding step, as sharp a contrast as any image in any painting on any wall. "Did Christine tell you I was back here?"

Danny took in the exhibit and nodded. "This is nice, Yvette. When we got married, you were just another starving art student struggling to break out. Now look at you." His gaze returned to the black mid-length skirt and dazzling, multicolored blouse that looked like it was wrapped and draped over her thin frame. Danny could never guess the label, but he knew expensive designer clothes when he saw them. "Curating a place like this. Living the dream."

"You don't know the first thing about art, Danny. You never have and you never will." Yvette stabbed a manicured finger into his chest. "And you made it pretty clear on the phone the other day that you're not interested in me or my life." She folded her arms across her svelte torso. "I've seen the news, Danny. You're a fugitive. What do you want?"

Wakefield stuffed his hands into his lightweight tan jacket's pockets and shrugged. "I want it to be over, Yvette. The running. You know I didn't do anything wrong."

"That's not what they're saying on TV."

"Well, they're wrong." He sighed. "Look, I'm tired. I've been constantly moving since Fayetteville. I need a break."

"You need to turn yourself in."

"I don't know," he cringed.

"It's either that," she pointed, "or get dragged in. You know, I bet it's nice being white and wanted. If you were a brother, they'd just shoot you and be done."

"Look, Yvette - you really don't want to start down that road with me right now."

She held up the phone, still in her hand. "Don't I? What do you think the reward would be for turning you in? Hell, I should do it just for the publicity."

"You don't mean that."

She glared at him. "It'd be great exposure for the galley. Get the name in the headlines."

"Yvette," he wrapped his hand around the phone in her fingers and locked eyes with her. "Don't."

"Give me a reason." The space between them slowly disappeared. Her empty hand found his shoulder; his, her waist.

Their history was all out there again, another painful display in a gallery devoid of attendees. All of the tension, all of the fury, all of the conflict that had marked their relationship and ultimately doomed their marriage hung in the air between them. Arguments punctuated by wild nights; all passion and energy; it was a dance that could be equally positive and destructive. Yvette closed her eyes and leaned in to close the last inches between them.

"No," Danny pulled back and slipped out of her grasp. "Yvette, I can't." He shook his head. "If I let myself, it'd be no different than when you…" He let his voice trail off. "Look, I thought there might be a place here. You know? A storage room or office or something. Somewhere that I can catch my breath and grab a some shuteye."

"What?"

"After you phoned the other day, I thought that maybe I could call on you for a favor. That's all I came here for, really."

Yvette shook her head. "It's an art gallery, Danny. Not a bed and breakfast."

"I understand." Danny left a thousand words unsaid as he stood motionless for a heartbeat, then shrugged again. "Look, I better get going."

"Maybe Jaycen could -"

"I'm on the government's hit list and half the Army is on the streets," Danny chuckled. "Colonel Richards is the last person that I need to see right now."

"He's a lawyer, Danny."

"Yeah, for the Army. The same Army that shot me." He hissed a breath through his teeth. "At this point, Yvette, I'm not sure how many of them are on the right side."

"You can trust Jaycen," she adamantly announced.

"I couldn't trust him with my wife," Danny turned to head down the hallway toward the stairs. "I won't trust him with my freedom."

Danny drove Oscar's Cherokee a few blocks down 21st Street from the gallery before he pulled into a hotel parking lot. Smiling, he pulled a piece of black plastic from his pocket. His ex-wife's current husband's name was imprinted near its bottom edge. *Never let the wife borrow your credit card,* he chuckled. Danny dialed a familiar hotel hotline from memory on the burner phone from his Bug Out Bag, then pressed the number for the nearest location.

A chipper voice answered before the second ring. "Thank you for calling the Dupont Circle Residence Inn. How may I help you?"

"This is Lieutenant Colonel Jaycen Richards," he calmly replied. "My wife and I have family coming in for the holidays, and the house is already full. Please tell me you have a decent room available tonight."

"Wait just one moment while I check, sir…"

CHAPTER 19

T.J. PUSHED LUCKY Mike through the door into a cheap ground floor apartment that was even smaller on the inside than it looked from the hallway. While the fugitive set the locks, Mike rolled across the littered floor. "It ain't much," he apologized, "but you can crash here or bounce out. Whatever you need, brother."

"Thanks, man." Being forced to leave Randy behind left T.J. feeling rattled more than the incoming fire had. Randy was yet another person left injured, dead, or ruined in T.J.'s wake. He shook his head at the thought. "I probably outta move on down the road, though. You know?"

Mike sniffed and nodded, then dug T.J.'s carbine out from under the Woobie wrapped around his useless leg-and-a-half. Then, to T.J.'s amusement, the handi-capable veteran reached into the folds of material where his right knee used to be and withdrew a subcompact Springfield XD pistol, which he placed upon a battered end table. "Suit yourself, man. Can't blame you for runnin'. But I know some folks who'd be sad to see you leave."

T.J. unloaded the carbine, then broke it down for storage into the Bug Out Bag with which Randy had gifted him."Really?" *We left the rifle bags at the shop. Got to take stock of my new inventory.*

"Yeah, I mean, you're famous, dude. You've really started something, man."

"That ain't always a good thing." T.J. dug through the oversized backpack. *Must'a left the tac vest back at the shop,* he shook his head. *Still got the gun and one spare mag. No other ammo. Clothes on my back, plus a set of digital urban pants and a black assault shirt. A change of socks, and a knit cap. An MRE, two protein bars, some instant coffee and a bag of butterscotch drops. First aid and survival essentials.* His eyes widened just a bit when he spied a trio of pre-packaged cubes, each roughly two inches on a side. *Looks like I'm not the only one who was squirreling away C4.*

"Well, people are rising up. You saw the news. Folks're standing up and taking to the streets."

"You mind if I use your latrine real quick?"

"First door on your left," Mike pointed. His voice followed T.J. easily enough through the tiny apartment and it's thin walls. "Yeah, man. I was at a demonstration last week. It was kinda weird, you know? Surreal. I mean, not so long ago, we were the ones standing on the street corners and running security patrols. Now look at us. We're insurgents! In our own country, man."

T.J. made use of the facilities while Mike rambled. On his way back from the bathroom, he noticed another wheelchair neatly folded and stowed next to the bedroom door. The hairs on the back of his neck bristled. "You got a roommate, dude?"

"What?" Mike looked at T.J. in confusion. "Oh, that. No, man. Don't sweat it. That's just my Sunday chair. You know? The nice one that I use for special occasions." He patted the mobile seat in which he rode. "This one's my daily beater. I don't take the nice ride out to the park. If some punk gets stupid, I don't want any holes in it." He withdrew a plastic bag from a pocket behind his own seat back. The bundle rattled as he dropped it on the table next to his 9mm.

The wheels of T.J.'s mind whirled as his eyes danced between Lucky Mike, the spare chair, and the Bug Out Bag. Images flashed across his vision, pictures and video clips from hours of studied media footage. "Dude," he swallowed. "You said you believe in the cause?"

Mike raised his chin and fist in solidarity. "All the way."

"I hate to do this," T.J. slowly said, "after all you've done. You helped me, man. And you've already given so much for your country."

"We took an oath, dude."

"And I have no right to ask this of you…"

A quartet of thunderclaps sounded from the apartment door. *Cop knock*. That was what people called it. The angry voice that chased the beats through the hatch made it clear as to why they did that. "Police department! Open the door!"

Lucky Mike snatched the XD from the table. "Somebody must've noticed you with me," he shook his head. "I'm sorry, man."

Acting on reflex, T.J. donned his backpack and slapped his carbine back together. "Grab a cushion," he nodded toward the ratty couch next to Mike. "Use it to smother the flash-bang."

T.J. knew that his time in Special Operations had given him vastly superior experience with raids than anything his wheeled wingman could have possibly gained from his time in more conventional units. The standard procedure for a Knock and Call was to establish presence, elicit surrender, then make dynamic entry - usually by way of busting the door off its frame and tossing a flash-bang grenade into the room to incapacitate the occupants - and overwhelm the targets. Even a Special Operator could only do so much against a team of trained adversaries who held the initiative and had a plan. T.J. clearly hoped that by removing the stun device from the equation, the two of them could make a good showing of themselves against the inevitable team of pipe hitters prepared to burst into the apartment.

"Just a second!" Mike grabbed a well-worn cushion with his left hand. "I'm coming! Don't shoot! I'm disabled!" Mike held his subcompact pistol at the ready and whispered to T.J.. "There's no way out, dude." He jerked his head to the back bedroom. "Make your own exit."

T.J. shook his head. *No,* he resolved. *Not twice in one day.*

"Open the door! Now! Or we will break it down!"

"Alright, alright! Chair only rolls so fast!" Mike's face became downright hostile as he glared at T.J.. "Go," he whisper-yelled. "Go now!"

T.J. died a little more inside as he realized that Mike was right. *There's only one way.* "Thank you."

"This is your last warning!"

"It's been a good run." Mike jockeyed his chair a little and steeled himself for the inevitable. T.J. slid down the hallway, ducked into the bedroom, and scooped up Mike's second wheelchair. He reached the rear wall at a dead run and kicked through it with all of his might.

At that exact moment, something like a train slammed into the apartment's door. A metal canister sailed through the air and landed in the middle of the small living room. Lucky Mike dove to the ground in a Heisman-worthy tackle with eyes closed, teeth gritted against the pain he knew was coming, and the cushion between himself and the grenade. The sound of T.J.'s second kick - which freed a stud in the wall and ripped an improvised doorway through the drywall on both sides - was overshadowed by the muffled *boom!* of the flash-bang under Mike.

On the other side of the wall, T.J. burst into the adjacent apartment's bedroom. A teenaged meth-head laid unconscious on a pile of blankets in the corner. T.J. bolted through the addict's apartment - which was laid out in a mirror image of Mike's - with the wheelchair in tow. The *pap!-pap!-pap!* of small caliber gunfire sounded through his ragged portal, quickly chased by the familiar *pow!-pow!-pow!* of a group of AR-15s as they answered.

T.J. cleared the hovel's kitchenette, then punched through another wall and found himself in the living room two doors down from Mike's. Children's toys crunched under his booted feet as he maneuvered to the back room. *One more apartment between me and the street.*

A large, tattooed, bald man met him in the hallway with a stainless steel magnum revolver in hand. The white mope cocked the pistol as he raised it to eye level. "Freeze, nig-"

T.J. let his carbine swing on its sling as he reached up with his right hand, grabbed the revolver around the cylinder, and plucked the pistol from the portly man's meaty hand. Without breaking his stride, T.J. reversed his hand's direction and *cracked* the overweight man across his fat face with the butt of his own gun. A leathery-looking woman in a tattered t-shirt screamed as T.J. stormed through the bedroom and dove out the window.

T.J. came out the other side of the building from the handicapped vet's apartment at street level. Two squad cars and four uniformed police officers, reinforced by a pair of tan Mine-Resistant Ambush Protected trucks and eight armed and armored troopers, looked up at a black man carrying reverse-gripped revolver in one hand and a wheelchair in the other in utter disbelief.

It was often said that people under extreme stress perceived time in a manner that was not entirely rational. The entire universe could whirl by in an instant. Conversely, a single heartbeat could last an eternity as the mind relived a lifetime of joys and horrors.

At one point during the war, Sergeant First Class Thomas Phillips stood in front of a street vendor's donkey-driven fruit cart in a nondescript market in some random Iraqi village. His uniform was miles away, as was his gun. He was undercover, just coming off a rotation conducting surveillance on a possible meeting point for some targets. No sooner had Phillips chosen some dates from the cart than a dozen al Qaeda fighters appeared, seemingly out of nowhere. The vendor - a boy who could not have been a day over fifteen years old - dropped the change from his hand and fell to the ground as the terrorists whipped out their AK-47s and sprayed fire throughout the market. Maybe they were insurgents engaged in some sort of reprisal; probably, somebody had told them the *Amerikan kafirs* sometimes went there. Coins hung in midair as time stopped completely for the Soldier.

The gunmen did not target Phillips directly. Nothing about them told him that they even knew who he was. But as he stood there in the open with nothing more than a desert snack in his hand, Sergeant Phillips saw muzzles flash and casings fly in impossibly slow motion. And in that moment of dilated time, his trained mind told him that none of the rickety cover available would stop the 7.62mm bullets that would inevitably come his way. *God,* he prayed, outside of conventional time, *if today is my day, let me die worthy.*

Alone, exposed, and impossibly outnumbered, the Special Forces Ranger snapped his wrist and threw the dried date held uselessly in his right hand. It sailed through the air more slowly than the laws of physics should ever have allowed. And then the fruit impacted one shooter in the face and exploded in a wet mess. Phillips swore that he saw it hit the *Muj* in the eye.

Startled more than injured, the insurgent flinched just long enough to stop shooting - just long enough for Phillips to throw another date, which hit another al Qaeda fighter - this one square in the chest. Like David hurling stones at a team of Goliaths, the hopeless man stood alone and chucked missiles at his foes. He felt no fear, just a sense of peace at a life lived to completion and for a purpose… mixed with a small appreciation of the absurdity with which that life was about to end.

At the very second one of the *Muj* zeroed in on the insolent, fruit-flinging infidel, crimson geysers erupted from all of their chests. A barrage of bullets poured through the terrorists as Phillips' teammates, nested in a mud-sided apartment that overlooked the street, raked them with return fire. A half dozen bodies fell, cut down by a hail of 5.56mm light armor piercing rounds that rained down from above him. And so far as T.J. Phillips was concerned, no man in history ever received a more divine deliverance from his enemies.

No longer desperate, Phillips stood beside the cart in wonder. The sight of his fallen assailants was soon overtaken by the wailing lament of citizens who held their dead in their arms, and shouts that blamed him and his brothers for what had happened burned him more than the unforgiving desert sun ever could. The moment was gone. Time and the hearts of men returned to their cruel, normal state.

As a dozen of his countrymen raised their rifles toward his direction in impossibly slow motion, the memory of that day in Iraq flashed through T.J.'s mind. His heart had barely contracted for what he knew would be its last beat when Phillips prayed a prayer that transcended time and space: *God, if today is my day, let me die worthy.*

Alone, exposed, and impossibly outnumbered, the veteran tossed the inverted revolver held uselessly in his right hand. It sailed through the air and tumbled end-over-end more slowly than the laws of physics should ever have allowed. The shiny pistol drew twenty-four eyes up toward it, well above T.J.'s head, as it gleamed in the artificial light. He felt no fear, just a sense of peace at a life lived to completion and for a purpose… mixed with a small appreciation of the absurdity with which that life was about to end.

"Grenade!" Phillips shouted in his most soldierly voice. He matched desperate action to desperate words and dove to his right with absolutely no hope of survival.

And a dozen men before him, each trained to react in a very specific manner to very specific stimuli, all dove to the ground, too.

T.J.'s body barely hit the frost-encrusted grass before he recognized his miraculous deliverance. He let the wheelchair fall, rolled into a firing position, and fired round after round parallel to the ground. His practiced trigger finger pressed the switch four times each second. A stream of bullets flew out of the semiautomatic rifle as he swept and raked a thin band of airspace between the unyielding pavement and the unwelcome vehicles before him. It was not a large space, and it was full of targets.

Phillips filled the air with jacketed lead. He forsook his sights and raked his rifle in a sweeping arc. Rounds *pop*'ed against flesh and armor alike. Some created small founts of splatter and gore when they struck home, others sparked off the ground with friction and ricochets. Still others produced no visible result. But by the time T.J.'s gun finished its track, there was very little movement along the ground before him.

Fueled by desperation, Phillips pushed himself up from the ground, scooped up the wheelchair, and bolted into the night. The wails of his fallen assailants and the shouts of his would-be pursuers faded as he disappeared into the darkness, just another shadow on a cold winter evening.

CHAPTER 20

NIGHTTIME IN D.C. was no less hectic than the daytime. Holiday shoppers added to a full night life. Diners and visitors wove through sidewalks with shoppers. At least, they did until the servicemen at checkpoints throughout the city shut down the streets and imposed the Metro's curfew.

Dressed down for an evening in the town, Jaycen Richards wore a comfortable yet stylish green, knit, long sleeved polo over a warm wool undershirt, plain black pants, and thickly woven peacoat as he consulted the uniformed officer next to him. Jaycen's civilian attire was markedly more casual than that of his wife, who hung up her phone and shook her head above her designer dress.

"My mother," Yvette summarized as she stuffed the phone in her designer trench coat's pocket, "says that Madison can stay the night with her in Baltimore."

"Great." Jaycen stepped closer and rubbed her upper arms in his warm hands. "You're sure you're okay?"

"I'm fine."

"'Cause you'd have every right to be rattled."

"I said I'm fine, Jaycen."

"Is there anything you need to tell me?"

"No," she furrowed her eyebrows at him. "I told you everything already. Danny came by the gallery acting weird. I sent him off. Two hours later, I was getting something out of my purse when I realized the credit card was gone. That's when I called you."

"And you're okay?"

"Of course I am. Why wouldn't I be?"

Jaycen's dark eyes looked deeply into her lighter irises. "You were face to face with one of the most wanted fugitives in the nation," he pointed. "That would leave anyone feeling a little unsettled."

"He's my ex, Jaycen. I can handle him."

"He's a trained killer who put a team of feds in the hospital."

"Oh, Jaycen. You said yourself the other night that after the scene a few weeks ago, you didn't think he had it in him to pull a trigger anymore."

"He's still a criminal," the military lawyer persisted. "Unless… he isn't?"

"And just what is that supposed to mean?"

"Major Clark here just told me that the only charges on the card he lifted from you - I still don't know what you were doing with *my* credit card, by the way - were to this hotel, just a few blocks from your office, and to a gas station to buy a pair of inexpensive phones. The kind often used as burner phones. Disposable communications for would-be criminals and people engaged in other illicit activity.

He registered the user names Mr. and Mrs. Smith to the numbers."

Yvette took a step back. Her frown transformed to incredulity. "Just what are you saying, Jaycen?"

"I just wanna make sure you're not tied up in any of this, Yvette."

"Jaycen. I told you -"

A lean man with light brown hair and a clean pair of digital fatigues interrupted the conversation before it could delve too deeply into uncomfortable territory. The subdued gold oak leaf on his rank tab and the name tape velcro'ed above his breast pocket identified him as Major Clark, Commanding Officer of the tactical team that would conduct tonight's raid. "Excuse me, sir. Ma'am." The Major's face was a case study in professional soldiery. His voice was crisp, with clear enunciation. "Intel is still reviewing footage from the gas station's security cameras. We're looking for hours either side of the time stamp of the transaction where the target's card was used."

"*My* credit card," Jaycen reminded him.

"Yes, sir. Anyway, we have visual confirmation of a figure that we've identified as Special Agent Wakefield in the gas station. We observe him approach on foot, conduct the transaction, then leave. Again, on foot. No other activity. No contact other than the cashier."

Richards was visibly disappointed. "No vehicle?"

"No, sir. Not within line-of-sight of the cameras, anyway. Pedestrian the whole way."

"No car. No plate to trace," Jaycen reiterated. "No closer to tracking his movements."

Major Clark shook his head. "Not at this time. But, we've got the hotel room he booked. I've got an intel guy in plainclothes in there right now. He's pumping the front desk for real-time updates." He gave the JAG officer a meaningful look. "Says they just got a call from the suite booked to your card."

"Suite? Nobody told me that he booked a suite."

An anonymous sergeant in the corner snickered. "Colonel pay. Must be nice."

"Dude ordered room service," Major Clark continued. "For two."

"You're ex either *has* company," Jaycen shook his head at Yvette, "or he's expecting it."

"Don't look at me," she fumed. "I'm the victim here. I don't know what's going on. I told you everything."

"Major Clark."

"Colonel."

"I realize I'm not a line officer."

"Colonel?"

"But are your men ready?"

"Always."

"I would like my credit card back, Major." Jaycen growled. "Before he orders Pay-per-View."

"Or rents a car," Yvette sniped.

Clark nodded, then keyed the mic on his radio. "All teams: silent countdown to breach. Ten seconds, then go. Mark."

A flurry of voices answered over the radio. One answer came from the platoon on Wakefield's floor, whose leader divided into a pair of squads that waited at opposite ends of the hallway. A similar acknowledgement followed from the platoon leader whose men moved from a service door into the lobby and waited to respond to escalation. It was echoed by the mobility commander outside, who sent a pair of Hummvees to the hotel's front door while the rest of his vehicles bracketed the corners where O and P Streets intersected with 21st and 22nd Streets, locking down the entire block.

Colonel Richards counted down in his head. *3… 2… 1…*

"Execute," Clark announced.

Corporal Plank - point man, Able Squad, First Platoon - was a competent and well-trained infantryman. He first joined the Army for the chance to make something out of himself and maybe get the chance to kill some terrorists. The free college money did not hurt, either. God knew there were few opportunities waiting for him back in southern Maryland. And everybody knew the Navy sucked.

Tonight, though, Plank was tickled by the thought that he and his buddies would be stomping some Leatherneck-gone-bad a new mud hole. Interservice rivalry ran deep between ground forces, and the scuttlebutt among the guys was that this Tango had turned Jodie - military slang for a guy who stole a trooper's girl from behind his back, and was thus viewed by most troopers as a special form of cowardly traitor. Word was that Objective Jodie was in the hotel trying to score with some officer's wife. So Plank quickened his pace just a bit as he guided his squad down the hallway and made sure that his was the first foot to hit the target door.

Plank stomped the hatch hard enough to splinter the structure and throw the portal wide open. He and his teammates stormed into the hotel suite with their guns at the ready. A chorus of *Down! Down! Down!* echoed off the walls.

Penetrate and exploit, their instructors had taught them. CPL Plank flew down the suite's entryway and swept through the sitting room while he quickly scanned for threats. He was confident that his buddies had his back and would neutralize any dangers that he might have missed. He knew full well that the second quartet would split off and secure the latrine to the left, just as surely as he knew that the door to the second chamber - identified by intel as the Tango's sleeping area - would yield to his boot.

Plank charged through the last door and into the hotel suite's deepest hole ready to shoot. *Down! Down! Down!* the chorus of Soldiers hollered. If Objective Jodie planned to resist, Sergeant Rich had told the team that this was where he would most likely make his stand.

The room, partitioned from the rest of the suite by a wall that almost reached the ceiling, was not very large. It held a short dresser along one wall, a single chair, and a queen-sized bed. And on that bed laid the team's reward.

"Say again?" the incredulous Major demanded.

"Dry Hole," the voice on the other side of the radio repeated.

"Intel said he was right there," Jayson seethed.

Major Clark keyed the microphone again. "Ess-Ess-Eee?" Clearly, the major hoped that a quickly conducted Sensitive Site Exploitation could provide some clue as to where - and when, how, and exactly *why* - their target had fled.

"Uh, sir," the platoon leader answered. "There's really nothing to report. The room's empty. Other than the bed, it doesn't look like it's been touched."

"What about the bed?" Major Clark desperately dug for clues.

"We're taking pictures now, sir. But, uh, I think this was all BOGINT."

Bogus Intelligence. One bad tip could sour an otherwise spectacular operation. One false lead, one exaggerated report, one source, or operator who was more interested in pleasing their handler than in reporting the truth could ruin everyone's day. Most guys who stayed in the service long enough fell prey to it from time to time.

An icon on his laptop told Major Clark that his team had just emailed him a photo. He clicked on the symbol to download the image. A picture from inside the Marriott suite painted itself onto his screen. The veteran Soldier shook his head at the sight of a set of hotel towels and washcloths folded and arranged on the bed in the shape of a giant, three dimensional phallus - all in full, digital technicolor detail. The strike force commander rolled his eyes at the display of juvenile humor. *Oh, that's not going away anytime soon.*

"Major Dick," Yvette recalled aloud.

"Excuse me?" Clark asked.

Jaycen was not amused. "It's an old nickname." The frown on his face made it clear to everyone that it was a nickname that Jaycen Richards would rather not have heard again. "I think we're done here, Major." He turned to his wife. "I don't know who's screwing with who here, Yvette, but we're leaving. Now."

*　　　*　　　*

Danny reclined the driver's chair in Oscar's Cherokee. He found a place to park in some random neighborhood in Waldorf, Maryland. He dug blindly as he reached into his Bug Out Bag in the back seat, guided by touch and his own memorized checklist of the backpack's inventory, until he found his prize: a plaid, lightweight, flannel blanket. He withdrew the tightly folded bundle and spread the blanket over his body for added protection. *Cold air outside will rob all of the heat from in here in no time,* he warned himself. Automotive glass was a terrible insulator, but Danny's options were limited if he wanted to avoid wrongful imprisonment.

Wakefield knew firsthand how his hunters worked. He knew their procedures. He knew how they thought. And he knew that if they thought they had a line on him for even one second then they would follow it to whatever end. Danny took Yvette's credit card specifically to lay a false trail for his pursuers to follow. And while they spent valuable man hours on a wild goose chase and running down every rabbit hole attached to it, Danny knew that he could risk a little rest.

Oscar called it the Law of Conservation of Intellectual Energy. The misanthropic midget explained his theory to Danny once over a bottle of hootch in his underground hovel. People could only think about so many things at a time. They only had so much emotional and mental capital to invest in any endeavor. There were only so man hours in a day to spend doing anything. As Oscar's theory went, the more of these precious and perishable resources a person spent on *this,* the less they could spend on *that.* Oscar used this tool to maximize his workflow and make his efforts as efficient as possible, but Danny also saw how it only proved how valuable distractions were when used against his adversaries. *Give them something to do. Let them waste their time, energy, and money chasing false breadcrumb trails and ghost leads. Hide your real activities within a flood of false reporting so that they can't tell the good gouge from the BOGINT. And that's how you maintain freedom of movement.*

The former Marine snuggled under the blanket, a souvenir from a trip to Ireland, and allowed himself a smile. *Credit cards are too easy to trace.* A part of him was almost insulted that anyone could think of him as so amateurish as to actually use his ex-wife's stolen plastic. *Going to Yvette for help is predictable,* he frowned. *What kind of a dolt do they think I am?*

He giggled and wished that he could see the looks on their faces when whatever action element conducted the inevitable Knock and Call on his fake hotel room. *At least I left a little something for your Dry Hole.* In his mind, the only way the prank could have been better was if the Residence Inn used green linens instead of white. *The Green Weenie,* he recalled the nickname grunts held for the Corps when things in the service got painfully stupid, *sticking it to you yet again.*

His government salary did not afford him a luxurious lifestyle, but Danny had, over they years, managed to tuck a some emergency cash into his BOB. He had hoped that with any luck, a few of those bills - folded and discreetly slipped to one of the hotel maids on her smoke break - would help bring some modern art into the world. *My little gift to the direct action team,* he smiled at the prank. *Stick* that *in your gallery, Yvette. A new piece for your two-bit Thanksgiving show…*

Inspiration made Wakefield shoot upright in his seat. *The big show,* he mind processed. *On Thanksgiving.* Quickly, he rolled up the blanket and half-stuffed it back into his BOB. *That's it.* He returned the seat to its upright position, started the engine and pulled the Cherokee out of the parking lot. *That's where he'll be.*

CHAPTER 21

"MR. COFFIELD FROM the National Reconnaissance Office to see you, Mr. Secretary."

"Thank you, Dorris. Send him in. And then head home. It's late." A skinny head topped with dirty blonde hair and dominated by big, round glasses poked his head through Secretary James' office door. "Come in, son."

Powered by lanky legs, Michael Coffield crossed the room in a few long strides and an expression of awe upon his face. He hid most of the awe he understandably felt as he stopped between the big executive desk of the civilian in charge of the largest fighting force on planet Earth and a chair opposite it. Michael stretched his right hand out from the end of an arm that seemed to be able to extend well beyond his frame's proportions. "Mr. Secretary."

Mason James briefly took the man's hand, then gestured to the chair. "Please, sit."

"Yessir."

The wiry man reminded Secretary James of the bookish bird from the old Loony Tunes cartoons.

"You know why you're here?" he asked with a raised eyebrow.

"Yessir." Coffield held a zippered padfolio on his lap with both nervous hands. "We got your request this afternoon."

"I sent that request to the Army."

"Yessir. And they immediately reached out to DARPA. General Stubbs was aware of my previous work there under Admiral Poindexter."

"Did you work closely with John Poindexter?"

"With all due respect, sir, 'close' might be overselling it, but we did interact routinely."

"And what'd you think of the Admiral?" James tested.

Coffield stiffened a bit in his seat. "Admiral Poindexter was a patriot, sir. Professional, loyal, and focused on the mission. He oversaw my retirement ceremony from the Navy. I was proud to serve under his leadership."

"Relax, son. Just testing the waters. John was a friend of mine. And what, precisely, did you do under his command?"

Michael seemed to relax a bit. "I was on DARPA's You-Aye-Vee project team. Originally enlisted in the Navy as an Aviation Technician working on F-18s, but I got into Unmanned Aerial Vehicles after a few years and stayed with it. We did a lot of systems review, test and evaluation, and mission suitability stuff with them at DARPA. I stayed there for a few years as a civilian contractor after my retirement. Then En-Are-Oh picked me up to run their You-Aye-Vee Are-Tee-and-Eee - that's Research, Test, and Evaluation - cell."

"I see," Secretary James steepled his fingers. *A UAV RTE guy. This should be good.* "So, when I asked

Army Intelligence for a way to maintain surveillance while withdrawing troops…"

"The brass came and asked us to field a solution," Coffield finished for him. "I was told this tasker was the highest priority. Time sensitive."

"Son, we wouldn't be in my office this late at night - let alone the night before Thanksgiving - if it wasn't urgent."

"Yessir."

"So you have one?" Mason wasted no effort trying to hide his incredulity.

"A solution? Yessir. It's pretty straightforward, really." Michael unzipped his leather notepad. Inside, a tablet computer came to life. "In addition to my work with drones and avionics, I also do a fair bit of computer coding. Started off writing commercial apps in my off time. You know, games and such."

"Time sensitive," the Secretary repeated. "Less preamble. More point."

"Sir," the skinny man went even more pale, then cleared his throat and continued. "I spent the last year and a half writing up a new series of command and control protocols that became a prototype guidance tool for our drones."

"Which ones?"

"All of them, sir." Coffield flipped through a series of graphics on his screen until he reached a particular slide. "We've worked out a way to control every drone on any mission from a single workstation with a dedicated uplink. From Dragonfly platforms up to Global Hawks and beyond."

Secretary James cycled a thoughtful breath. "What do you mean, 'beyond?' I thought Global Hawk was our big momma."

Coffield beamed. "Not even close, sir. Not anymore. Global Hawk is still the Air Force's go-to long-endurance drone. That's why they're used for dedicated surveillance missions." His finger played across the tablet's touch surface until a wireframe diagram appeared. "But this is Icarus."

Secretary James looked unimpressed by the multi-segmented flying wing in the picture. "Looks like something from a high school science fair."

"It's based off the design from NASA's Helios platform, which was decommissioned a few years back. It's virtually all lifting surface. The variable geometry flying wing allows us to optimize lift. Onboard sensors analyze the air currents in flight and adjust the wing's configuration in real time, making our flight profile as efficient as possible. Maximizes her endurance. Propellers are driven by brushless motors fed by a series of batteries that are recharged by these solar cells, which cover the entire topside of the airframe."

"What kind of loiter time are we looking at?"

Michael smiled. "Indefinite."

"No, I mean per plane."

"So do I, sir."

Mason James frowned. "Bullshit."

"Sir," Michael continued, "even with a wingspan of nearly 450 feet, by using carbon fiber and other ultra-lightweight materials, we've kept the total mass of the entire bird to around 2500 kilos - well less than 6000 pounds. It weighs about the same as your wife's sport utility vehicle."

"How do you know what my wife drives?"

The UAV king grinned. "Doesn't everybody's wife drive one? Anyway, that weight includes the payload: several organic sensors of its own, plus signal duplicators and re-transmitters that snoop and slave every drone within Icarus' broadcast range to my bird - and, therefore, my desktop. With modern power management systems, Icarus can orbit over an area for days, weeks, or months. I've had one running circles about 60,000 feet above Nevada for a hundred and thirteen days straight now. Just gonna leave it up there until breakage forces us to land her."

Secretary James looked hungry - and not for the turkey dinner that awaited him over the holiday weekend. "You're telling me that you can use this thing to fly any drone in our inventory?"

"Not just any of them," Michael shook his head. "All of them. Any in particular or all at once. Well, everything within its broadcast range. It's basically a low flying satellite. One that I can re-task to any location on Earth. And from there, I would have at my disposal the full arsenal of unmanned systems." Coffield smiled. "We're also having the various operators install the code as part of the command and control software into all of our unmanned ground, sea, and undersea platforms. All in the name of standardization and, efficiency, and compatibility with other systems. That effectively gives me access to every drone in service today - and, of course, all of their capabilities. Command and control. Intelligence, surveillance, and reconnaissance with whatever sensors you can imagine. The full spectrum of imagery - full motion video, day or night, IR, RADAR… Plus SIGINT. MASINT. Anything."

"How many of these things do we have?"

"Do you mean operational, or available?" Coffield defensively waved a hand. "I'm sorry, Mr. Secretary. I don't mean to sound like a smart ass, but it's just, well…" He shrugged, then seemed to resign himself. "Since you're a Cabinet member, I guess you have clearance." The bookish man sighed. "En-Are-

Oh was planning to start fielding them on surveillance ops over Russia and China this fiscal year. As soon as the budget comes through." He smiled sheepishly. "If you've got some friends in Congress who could smooth the checks out -"

"And just where are all of these - what did you call them? *Icarus*? - drones?"

"They're in a secured storage facility, sir."

"Where?"

"I'm sorry, sir, but it's Top Secret."

"Where?" Mason humorlessly pressed.

"I'm not sure I'm at liberty -"

"Let me make this clear, son. You're about to walk out of here. And when you do, you're going to have a new job. Either it's working for me, or it's handing out mints at Chick Fil-A. I'll give you exactly three seconds to choose which one you like better."

Coffield stiffened, but he did not hesitate. "Edwards Air Force Base."

Secretary James smiled as a plan clicked into place in his mind. "Call your friends at Groom Lake."

CHAPTER 22

"WELL, IT'S OFFICIAL. *Daniyal* has ruined Thanksgiving."

Derek adopted his most soothing voice. "Don't say that, *mhboob*. It'll all be fine."

"No, Derek, it will most certainly not all be fine," Aliyah fumed. "That *khaliilon khara* was responsible for bringing the turkey. How in *al Jahiim* am I supposed to cook a turkey in this tiny oven?"

"It's just a breast. Not a big bird, *mhboob*. Follow the recipe and everything will be fine."

Aliyah shifted back and forth from one side of their apartment's cramped kitchen to the other. "Is there any word on him?"

Derek shook his head and took another pull from the dark glass bottle in his hand. "They're clueless. You know, right now the Task Force is spending almost as many resources trying to find Big D as Phillips."

Aliyah hissed and tossed the thawed turkey breast into a baking bag. "He should've just shot that *kalib* when he had the chance."

"Phillips was using Dagenhart as a human shield, *mhboob*. Big D couldn't risk hitting her."

"Not that it matters anymore." Aliyah growled as she looked up into the pantry. "Can you reach the garlic for me?" Derek obediently plucked the spice from a shelf that was too high for his beloved. She added the requisite amount to the bag. "Alright. One half bottle of dandelion wine, one half cup of butter, three tablespoons of garlic, and… does that look like the right amount of pepper to you?"

"Looks great. We'll let it sit overnight, then toss it into the oven in the morning."

"Fine. And the candied yams can wait until then. I'm done for tonight. Ugh, did I tell you? When I went to the market, some *sharmuta* kept looking at sweet potatoes and then just dropping the rejects in with the yams!"

"The nerve of some people." Derek consulted his phone. "Oh, hey, work just texted. Excuse me for a second." Aliyah made a *shoo*'ing gesture as Derek stepped away from the breakfast bar and headed down the short hall to their bedroom. There, he dialed a number from his contact list.

"Homeland Security. Agent Stevenson speaking. How may I help you?"

"Hey, Dianne. It's Derek. Did you just page me?"

"Yeah. Hey, Derek. Look, I don't know exactly what's going on, but Nick Brown just called and said that he needs you to come in first thing in the morning."

"You've gotta be kidding me." Derek ran a hand through his hair. "Aliyah's gonna be pissed."

"I'm sorry. Doesn't sound like you've got a choice."

Derek rolled his eyes and deactivated his phone. *Looks like Big D's making his move.*

*　　　*　　　*

A commuter bus' headlights lit I-95 as it rumbled up dark highway. The driver kept the cabin lights turned off so that passengers could steal some sleep on the way to their destinations. Few people used shuttle buses anymore, and anyone who was forced to move around during the wee hours of the morning deserved the rest.

In a cheaply cushioned bench at the back of the bus, T.J. pulled the stitching out of the wheelchair's padded seat. He worked carefully, but quickly. There were less than a dozen people on this bus, including Phillips and the driver. The passengers were spread out, which gave him a decent amount of space to himself. And nobody was awake anyway, save Phillips and the driver.

Dim red light from a filtered flashlight guided the Patriot's hands. *Cut. Pull. Cut. Pull.* He pocketed the freed threads so as to leave no trace of his deeds on the bus. Whether they were the misdeeds of a terrorist or the brave actions of a liberator, only history would tell. But T.J. had seen firsthand the effectiveness of a device like the one he had in mind. It was at a mud hut turned into a school in some random village in Afghanistan. When the smoke cleared and the dust settled, the surviving village elders had certainly learned the lesson that the Taliban warlords intended.

The wheels on the bus went round and round. T.J.'s knife worked back and forth. Time marched inexorably forward. All of the people on all of the worlds in all of the universes in all of existence, set into motion by events both cosmic and personal, raced toward their inevitable conclusion. The moon had already set in the west. The sun was still invisible, hung lower than the eastern horizon. But darkness would not last forever. Eventually, there would be light.

T.J. dared to hope that maybe after the flash and crash, the smoke and fire, anyone left standing would finally be able to hear the cries of his people. His face drifted forward a few inches until his forehead rested on the seat in front of him as the toll from the last few days's events finally started to catch up with him. Phillips willed himself to ignore the fatigue and the frustration. He forced his hands to keep moving. *Maybe,* he dared to hope, *I'll still be standing when it's over.*

CHAPTER 23

SECRETARY GARRET Ambercrombie Lehman, the newly confirmed head of the Department of Homeland Security, confidently stood with his hands on the wooden podium. On a bad day, standing upon the dais in the White House Press Room made him feel like a condemned prisoner facing a firing squad. Reporters' microphones could be just as deadly as rifles. But this evening, the Secretary of Homeland Security felt like Santa Claus as he gave the greedy children before him a present he knew they would gobble up with glee.

"And so," the Secretary smiled into the cameras that rebroadcast his words across the nation and around the world, "we have decided to scale back our operations for the foreseeable future. The National Guard and select reserve units will remain on base at strategic locations, alert and ready to respond to any threat or indication as to where any terrorists might be." The head of Homeland Security made no mention of the fact that instead of armed troopers on the streets, Americans would be watched henceforth and until further notice by swarms and flocks of UAVs in the skies above the United States.

He never alluded to the idea that from this point forward, every movement, every action, every word… everything done by every American would be quietly observed, collected, recorded, analyzed, and evaluated by his office. Neither Secretary James' nebulous fleet of drones nor the new era of domestic surveillance they were about to usher in were topics for tonight's press conference. Nor would he bother to mention that he had just ordered the installation of a network of sensors for a new Ground Warfare Acoustical Combat System on top of every major building in Washington so that his office could detect, locate, and push assets to any gunshot in the Metro. No, tonight was about making Americans feel free again. So he gave them their bread and circuses. He made a big show of standing down the troops. And all the while, his new initiative would come online and help usher in a brave new world.

It might not be real, he reasoned, but they had to believe it. Nobody in office - elected or appointed - wanted the stigma of being the person to change America into a police state, but there were very real dangers out there. No one in their right mind wanted terrorists, murderers, and rapists on the streets with good, law-abiding citizens. Too much freedom allowed thieves, fugitives, and ne'er-do-wells to move among the citizenry like so many wolves among sheep. No, for the people to be truly free, they had to be free from the myriad dangers that inevitably followed in freedom's wake - whether the people wanted them or not. And that was Lehman's gift to the American people: the Tree of Liberty, version 2.0, remade shiny and new for the modern era, complete with digital updates and all wrapped up with a red-white-and-blue bow, just in time for Christmas. It was a gift they could not refuse - and a gift that Lehman or his successors could take back again as they deemed fit.

"I have chosen this course of action after careful advisement from Secretary James and General Thorne, and it is our unanimous agreement that the situation at this time no longer requires a large scale presence on American streets. Effective immediately, our forces have been ordered to stand down and return to their regular duties."

"Mr. Secretary! Mr. Secretary!" A choir of voices raised in unison.

Secretary Lehman chose one reporter at what seemed like random. "Go ahead, Claire."

"Mr. Secretary," the CNN correspondent spoke above the fading voices of her peers. "Is this a policy change in response to criticism that by deploying US Forces on American soil that the administration has somehow overstepped your bounds?"

Beside Lehman, Secretary James stepped closer to his own microphone. The other two speakers gave him their attention and assent. "This has always been a part of our overall strategy. It was never our intent to conduct a longterm engagement here Stateside."

"But what about reports that troops ordered into this operation were issued orders for months - or even a year - of action?"

From Secretary Lehman's other flank, General Thorne retorted. "Deployment orders vary in length by branch of service. Those brave men and women who helped secure America's streets for the past few weeks were simply given standard deployment packages. As we have seen in the past, in some situations those orders can be extended," the Army's Top Soldier consciously avoided any reference to the years-long engagements in Iraq or Afghanistan, "or shortened, like Grenada or Panama, depending on operational developments and mission needs."

The reporter's turn spent, the rest of the press pit erupted in another chorus of "Mr. Secretary! Mr. Secretary!" Secretary Lehman selected another token Oliver Twist.

"Mr. Secretary, has there been any news as to the whereabouts of the Constitutional Killer or the missing Secret Service agent who was responsible for his escape?"

Lehman grew more somber, but still projected an air of confidence. "We are currently chasing a number of leads…"

*   *   *

T.J. locked his left knee as he walked from the bus station. It was a simple trick that changed his natural gait to a limping swagger. Added to his disheveled clothes, backpack, and the lingering smell of a few days literally spent on the run, and the veteran looked just like any other street urchin. He did nothing to hide the fatigue from his face. *The more tired I look, the more I blend in around here.*

The denizens and passersby in America's wealthiest city could not be bothered to care about a dirty person as he ambled down the swept streets. They would not sully themselves by making eye contact with a seemingly homeless man. Anyone out and about on this Thanksgiving holiday had better things to do than to invite such a depressing sight into their lives as a lone, crippled veteran walking through the alleys and back streets with a half-assembled wheelchair. The few people T.J. saw in the morning midtown shuffle made an active attempt to avoid seeing him. There were more pressing matters that demanded their valuable resources - their time, attention, and money.

The most wanted man in America walked through the nation's capital completely unseen. T.J. moved through hazy daylight cloaked by his own people's indifference. But the Patriot was undeterred. He turned a corner and aimed for a shelter where a familiar, charitable sign offered him a much needed respite. Burdened by his load and his purpose, Phillips limped into the humble alcove and disappeared once more.

CHAPTER 24

"BUCK GREENLAW HERE, bringing all of you early risers up to speed on the latest developments in the most talked about case in America today.

"You know, here we are, Thanksgiving morning. And really, it's not just a day. It shouldn't be a day, anyway. It's called the 'holiday season,' and the whole season really ought'a be about friends and family, and all of the stuff that comes with this time of the year. The turkey, and the mistletoe, and time together. It should be a time of peace, and joy, and all of that good stuff. And I hope that all of our listeners on the Lonnie Chase Network find that for themselves this Christmas season.

"And yes, I said 'Christmas season.' I know that some people are offended by that word and everything that it represents - Christ, Jesus, and all of that - but I don't care. Honestly, I don't. If somebody calls this program - and I've told my producers this for years now - if somebody calls in and tries to tell me that I can't say the word 'Christ' or use the name 'Jesus,' then my producers won't even put them through. And if you're one of those people - I hope you're not, and you're probably not if you're listening to this program. Unless you're lost. Or curious. Or some sleeper or spy from another network or the US government who's trying to figure out what we're saying.

"Or maybe you're a person from the other side of the spectrum who's realized that Progressivism really is, at the end of the day, nothing more or less than a mental disease. Because it is, by definition, a mental disorder. When you consciously choose to reject objective facts and instead insist on living in denial and a world constructed solely on unsubstantiated ideas and an ideology that has been repeatedly and demonstrably shown to be false... you're delusional. You are. You're a mental patient. And back in the day, if you were delusional like that then the nice men in white coats would come for you, put you in a straightjacket, and toss you into a padded room until you came to your senses. Now? Now, they just make you the head of the Dee-En-See. Now, the inmates are running the asylum. But hey, to each their own.

"Anyway, if you're one of those people who gets all offended whenever anyone says, 'Christmas,' or claims that we have to keep religion out of the holidays, then I hope to see you working on December twenty-fifth. Really, I do. If you're offended by the celebration of Christmas then I expect you to be at your desk all day on the twenty-fourth, and bright and early on the twenty-fifth, holding down the fort for those of us who appreciate the holiday for what it is - a Holy Day. That's where the word comes from. But I digress.

"What Christmas present did the feds give the guy who was leading the hunt for the Constitutional Killer? Special Agent Wakefield, the guy who was leading the investigation. What did they stuff in his stocking yesterday afternoon? Two days before Thanksgiving? They shot him. A decorated combat veteran. A former Marine who, according to everything that we've been able to find out, has served this country since he was old enough to raise his right hand and take the Oath of Office. They shot him. Reports are a little sketchy at this time, but it appears that one of their jack-booted thugs shot him on the street. And it looks like he was actually about to arrest the suspect, Tom Phillips - who, by the way, got away.

"You know, some folks'll call me a conspiracy theorist for thinking it, and maybe I shouldn't say it out loud, but it kinda makes you wonder - it does me, anyway - how much of this is about catching a killer and how much of it is about control. You know? Controlling our own population. There. I said it. And you know what else I'll say - and my producer is over there shaking her head over her cup of coffee, 'cause I've talked to her about this and she thinks I'm nuts. Even *she* thinks I'm going to far with this one, folks, but I have to wonder if maybe this Constitutional Killer, this Master Sergeant Thomas Phillips, isn't somehow getting played. Maybe he's a stooge who's having his strings pulled by powers-that-be. Maybe he's a total patsy.

"Wouldn't that be hilarious - if the whole thing is a shadowy operation by the government to clean house? And after everything our government has done - the things that we know about, the things they wish we didn't know about, and the things that we haven't even heard of before because they're so secret, can you really look me in the eye and say that some of the individuals within our government are not above killing their own? Because we know that they are. They've done it before. They'll do it again. And if they'll do that to each other - if they'll do that to their own kind - then what hope do you and I have? Eh? Whay makes you think they'd hesitate to snub some of us out if they thought that we might get in their way? Now if they kill me tonight, you'll know why. 'Cause I said it.

"Hopefully I'll get to eat a nice turkey dinner before I go. There are worse ways to die, really. It may not be as fancy as the White House Thanksgiving Dinner, where the Fulbrights and all of their zillionaire cronies will be yucking it up in ultra luxury on the taxpayers' dime, but it doesn't have to be. My beautiful wife of thirty-five years makes the best turkey. It really is to die for. I don't care what they pay the White House chef, there's no way he or she could do better. And I have to wonder, you know, how many homeless people and starving people in D.C. could be fed and housed tonight for what the First Family is gonna spend on just one meal. Kinda seems to me like maybe some people's priorities aren't the same as yours and mine. Doesn't it? Like their values aren't our values anymore? I wonder if they ever were.

"This is what you get with these people. This is what you get, ladies and gentlemen. And no, I won't acknowledge any of your other made up genders, so don't ask me to. This is what you get when morons in Washington make stupid decisions like declare martial law, and they take stupid actions like they always do. And I, for one, am sick of it.

"You know what I want for Christmas this year? I'm gonna pretend that I'm sitting on Santa's lap right now, and I only get to ask him for one thing. You know what I want for Christmas? I want the Attorney General of the United States to file charges against every single one of these sons o' bitches responsible for this travesty. Only I pray that it doesn't take until the end of the year to do it. You know? I hope I don't have to live in Occupied America, like some Polish Jew hiding from the brown shirts, until somebody in Washington pulls their head out of their ass and actually does the job they swore to do. The job we pay them to do. But no, that's not gonna happen. There's nobody actually working in D.C. until after New Year's. They're all on vacation. Christmas vacation. They're all in recess. They're all on break. They're all traveling with family or headed back to wherever their mansions are back among the little people, their constituents. The Senate confirmed Lehman as the new Secretary of Homeland Security after about five minutes, then adjourned for the season. They can't be bothered to even pretend to do their jobs. It's sickening.

"Meanwhile, though, us regular folks? We do our jobs. And later in the show I'm gonna bring in a very special guest. We're gonna talk to the Dee-Aych-Ess operator who actually took the killer's call - the real criminal, not the guy who got shot by the feds. She works at the Department of Homeland Security as a switchboard operator. And I'm amazed that kind of job even exists, honestly. I'm surprised that hasn't been automated by now, and another group of hard working Americans replaced by the digital age. But that's not what we're gonna talk about. I mean, we might. If she wants to. But she's the one who actually took the call from the Constitutional Killer on that day earlier this month when he attacked the Dee-Aych-Ess building and killed the Secretary of

Homeland Security. And what an amazing story she has, so stay tuned to your Morning Buck. But first, we've gotta pay the bills.

"Our sponsor for this half hour on the Lonnie Chase Network is Goldstein Financial Group. You know, silver and gold isn't just a Christmas carol; it's a solid investment - literally and figuratively. And lemme tell you what the folks at Goldstein Financial are doing . From now until New Year's Day…"

*   *   *

"I'm sorry, *mhboob.* Really I am."

"What could possibly be going on that they would have to call you in on Thanksgiving morning? And then keep you?"

"Aliyah," Derek tried in vain to sooth his girlfriend, "it's all part of the job."

"It's that Nick the Dick, isn't it? Oh, you and *Daniyal* were right about him. He's such a *sharmuta.*"

"*Afwan, mhboob.* I'll be home as soon as possible."

"*Ramili* isn't answering her phone either."

Derek stopped to think for a second. *Who is Ramili? Ramili… like sand. Sandy. Oh.* "Well, maybe she went up to Jersey to be with her family."

"Without even calling," Aliyah pouted over the phone line. "This is going to be the worst Thanksgiving ever."

Martin looked around the Hoover watch floor. The skeleton crew that covered the holiday shift seemed more dour than usual. There was still no sign of Nick, who summoned him on his God given day off; nor was there any indication of when the toxic boss would actually deign to show up and explain why he wanted Derek to come in. *He's probably doing it just to screw with me,* Marin fumed. "There's nothing

I can do, *mhboob.* I swear, I'm outta here the second they release me."

"Is something going on?"

"Nothing, *mhboob.*"

"You're waiting for something, aren't you?"

"Nothing you need to worry about," sighed. "Nothing I can talk about. You know the drill."

"If you're not here when the turkey is ready, I'm eating without you."

"I understand."

"I mean it. I hate cold turkey."

"It's good on sandwiches," Derek offered.

"I probably screwed it up anyway."

"I'm sure you did fine."

"I hate your job."

"I know," Derek clenched his free hand into a fist. "I wish I was there with you, *mhboob.*"

"Fine," Aliyah grumbled. "But you better be saving the world or something. I swear, if you're sneaking around with some *eahira,* I'll kill you in your sleep."

"Fair enough," Derek smiled. "I love you."

"You better."

"See you soon."

CHAPTER 25

SANDRA'S BLUE PRIUS glided along the D.C. Beltway. Any other weekday morning, I-495's infamous rush hour gridlock turned this very freeway into a miles-long parking lot. But this was Thanksgiving morning, so almost everyone was home, still tucked into beds or engaged in preparations for an afternoon feast. There was barely a soul on the road, save for herself.

Sandra had originally planned to spend Thanksgiving with Daniel. A few weeks ago, they had lined up a quiet, romantic holiday: just the two of them in the apartment with food, wine, and plenty of time to make memories as a couple. She knew that there was no way on Earth that Wakefield could see her anytime soon. With him as a fugitive and the apartment obviously under surveillance, there was a long road between where they were right now and any future where they could be free to see each other again - a long road laid with many obstacles.

Sandra hated everything that had happened with Daniel. She hated the idea of spending the holidays alone, too. But it was barely a four hour drive from Washington to her parents' house in New Jersey. *Thanksgiving lunch is always late,* she consulted the car's dashboard clock. *If traffic stays light, I should make it in time.*

Just then, Sandra's new mystery phone rang. She found it leaning against the door as she exited the apartment this morning. How it got there without arousing the suspicions of the agents she assumed were watching the place was a mystery, but she knew it was left there on purpose. She did not recognize the number on the screen, but was confident from the moment that she received the disposable device as to who her caller would be. The only question was when he would finally call her. Still, she chose to exercise a level of discretion - just until her suspicions could be confirmed. "Hello?"

"The woods are lovely, dark and deep," a familiar voice sounded. "But I have promises to keep, and miles before I sleep."

Reflexively, she looked down to the book that rode in her passenger seat. It was the same book that she had been reading at the apartment all month. And there was one person who knew that as well as she did. *Daniel.* "Hello, Mr. Frost." Sandra's heart was warmed by the idea that Wakefield would remember her favorite book. "Where are you?"

"Getting on a boat to a nice, anonymous island in the Caribbean."

What the - her mind raced. *He must think my phone's being monitored. He won't tell me where he really is.* "I don't think that's such a good idea right now."

"Have it your way."

"You know where I think you should go?"

"I have my suspicions," Danny snickered on the other end. "And I imagine that particular location is kind of hot right now."

Does he mean 'hot' like the police, or 'hot' like steamy? Sandra did not find the situation amusing in the least bit. *Maybe he thinks I mean he should go to Hell…*

"Besides," Daniel's Frost persona continued, "I've got a better idea. You know that place?"

"What place?"

"That place."

Sandra frowned. "You'll have to be more specific."

"C'mon, Elbee. When I say, 'that place,' what place immediately comes to mind?"

Of course. "Got it."

"Be there in an hour."

Sandra shook her head. "I can't. I'm on my way to my family's house."

"One hour."

Daniel. Just don't. "It's Thanksgiving." *Will they even be open?* "I don't think -"

"Don't think, Elbee. Just get there."

"I told you. I can't. Not today. Okay? Today I need to get my head straight. Maybe tomorrow night."

"Tomorrow night is too late," he pressed. "Tomorrow morning is too late. Fifty-nine minutes, Elbee. Be there."

"You're not the boss of me," Sandra furrowed her brow.

"When have I ever asked you for anything, Elbee?"

"Never," Sandra growled. "But you're not asking now, are you? You're telling."

"You know what else is telling?"

"No. What?"

"Today. Everything about today tells me how I can fix everything."

"How's that?"

"Because I know where he'll be today."

* * *

"Please tell me you got that," Nick Brown demanded from the anonymous cryptologist at the workstation next to him.

"Got it, sir."

"Great." Wakefield's antagonistic former supervisor glared at one of his subordinate analysts. "Martin. What do you make of it?"

Derek Martin, Danny's best friend, wore his best poker face. "It sounded kinda like Special Agent Elbee," he conceded.

"The caller said, 'Elbee,'" Nick insisted.

"Or 'El Bee.'" Derek countered. "Lover Boy, maybe? Or Lebron Brinks?"

"Get real, Martin! Now, doesn't Wakefield always call her 'Elbee?' I don't think I've ever heard him use her first name."

"And you would know this how?" Little D stabbed. "C'mon, Nick. Everyone knows that you hate Wakefield. Now you're gonna pretend to know enough about him to do voice recognition based upon his speech patterns? Other than dumping on him in the office, how much time have you ever really spent with Danny?"

"But *you* do spend time with him," Dr. Wiley countered. "By all accounts, you're his best friend. And it may not look like it from where you're sitting, but we're actually trying to help Wakefield here."

Derek heard his boss' words, but he still glared at Nick the Dick. "I want to believe you, sir. But I don't think everyone here is on Danny's side."

"Don't play games with us, son. This is too serious."

"Yes, sir." Martin stared down Nick the Dick. "Proper analysis requires us to understand our assumptions and ask critical questions. I guess you assume that this 'Mr. Frost' is Special Agent Wakefield?"

The NSA cryptologist a few seats away perked up, but his eyes remained fixed on his screen. "Just confirmed the metadata. This call used both of the phones bought yesterday with the colonel's stolen credit card and currently attributed to Wakefield."

"Well, there you go," Nick beamed.

"With all due respect," Derek objected, "you seem to be enjoying this a little too much, Nick."

"Wakefield's a hothead and a trouble maker," Nick defensively answered. "He's an embarrassment to the Department. We should've fired him a long time ago."

"We'll deal with that later," Dr. Wiley waved his unlit pipe through the air. "After we bring him in and sort this all out."

Nick's eyes narrowed into knives which tried to cut the truth from Derek's mind. "Which is also when we'll figure out whether you're an asset to this team or a liability, Martin. Tell us where he'll be."

"He didn't say."

"Sure he did, son," Jonas bit down on his pipe. "You're a bright kid, Martin. But I've been playing this game longer than you've been alive. You don't want to dance with me. You know as well as I do what he's talking about. *His* place. His favorite place." Wiley's expression remained calm, but he was deadly serious, and he was clearly not in the mood to play games. "Now, I assume that he's not talking about his apartment. Doesn't make sense in context. You're his buddy. You're also a member of this team," the older man's face grew darker, "or you're not. Either way, I know that you know what Wakefield's talking about. So, make your choice." Jonas held one hand up like an empty measuring scale. "Fill in the blanks," he weighed the other hand in midair, "or end your career."

Never before had Martin felt such conflicted loyalties. On the one hand, his duty to the Secret Service was self evident. But Derek was also Danny's friend. His *best* friend. He was Little D to Wakefield's Big D. And that kind of friendship carried its own obligations. At least, it did in Derek's mind.

You can polish a turd, he remembered hearing Danny say on several occasions, *but you can't make it taste good.* Derek swallowed hard against the lump in his throat. And then he took his bite.

*　　　*　　　*

At a workstation commandeered from some less important analyst at the J. Edgar Hoover building and festooned with oversized monitors, Michael Coffield directed a swarm of drones above and around the waterfront in midtown D.C. The swarm itself was centered on a bar called Black Sam's. And exactly fifty-two minutes after Wakefield placed the phone call that was intercepted by the Task Force, a blonde woman walked into the very nexus of Coffield's surveillance net.

Michael's hands danced over keyboards with the grace and fluidity of a practiced concert pianist as he keyed commands that moved this set of sensors *here*, that set of eyes *there*. "Not even ten in the morning," he snarked as he dragged his mouse to direct the electro-optical cameras on a set of UAVs gliding silently above anyone's notice. A collection of digital images taken simultaneously from slightly different vantages appeared in a pop-up window on his desktop. With a quick double-click, Michael compiled the pictures and fused them together into a single composite photo. "And she's already hitting the bar."

"That's Elbee alright," Nick grumbled.

"The joint's officially closed for the day," Stevenson announced from her workstation.

"She's not there to get liquored up," Dr. Wiley huffed from behind crossed herringbone sleeves. "Any sign of Wakefield?"

Agent Stevenson consulted an updated image of the entire block, courtesy of Coffield's eyes in the sky. "Nothing streetside."

"Strike teams are standing by the outer perimeter." Nick prodded. "We could move in and secure the building. See if he's inside."

"This is supposed to be a meeting between a federal fugitive and a potential collaborator," Maxine Flowers reminded him. The Assistant Director took it upon herself to sit in the seat normally reserved for the watch team leader. Nobody in the room dared to call her on the breach of protocol. Nobody felt like being unemployed for the holidays. "Wakefield's a trained intelligence operator, and we're fortunate to have good SIGINT on him at all.

We're not tipping our hand and potentially burning our best line on him by blindly kicking in the door." Flowers stroked her chin thoughtfully as she watched the operation play out on panoramic screens before her, then shook her head. "No show, no go."

"Wakefield was pretty specific about his timetable," Nick insisted. "Just wait a bit. He'll show."

"Oh, we'll wait a while," the Assistant Director of Homeland Security affirmed in her sing-song voice. "And you'd best hope he does show, Mr. Brown. If I miss a moist turkey for a Dry Hole, my Aunt Bernice's bread ain't gonna be the only thing that rolls today."

Sandra sat alone at the darkened bar while Sam polished unused glasses with a soft rag. He was here on Wakefield's request, just like her. And, like her, his face wore an expression that this was not his first choice for where to spend his Thanksgiving Day.

"Thanks for opening up the place, Sam."

"I unlocked the front door for you," Sam clarified, "I'm not taking customers."

"You look awfully nice for a guy who was up all night." Sandra's observation was more than a kind thing to say. It was the truth. Most people who closed a bar in the wee hours of the morning would look like death warmed over until some time after noon - possibly dinner. But here Sam was with a fresh shave, wrinkle-free slacks, and a clean, rust-colored shirt. "Tell me something, Sam." Elbee propped her elbows on the smooth, dark wood before her. "You're a vampire, aren't you?"

Sam's signature smile returned, as did the usual flirtatious gleam in his eye. "Now, what makes you say that, I wonder? Is it my ageless good looks? My world-wise charm and irresistible charisma?"

Sandra's eyes played across the bar's unlit lamps. "The lack of light."

Sam poured a soda from the fountain and slid it down to her. "Lights draw customers. Anybody sad enough to be out today is somebody I just don't wanna see."

"So, do you host daytime rendezvous for all of your patrons, or just your regulars?"

Sam chuckled. "Darling, I've known Wakefield a long time. We go way back. Did he ever tell you that? No? Well, after all we've seen, when he said he'd owe me one after this... You know what they say. You just can't buy that kind of debt."

"When did he call you?"

"He didn't call him," a strange young woman approached the bar from one of the rear booths. Overly high heels struck the hard wood floor as she walked, punctuating each step. "I did."

Sandra sized up the surprise attendee. She appeared to be in her early twenties and wore her dark hair in a severe ponytail. Her makeup was fresh, but her black miniskirt, striped gray blazer, and wrinkled black trench coat showed signs that they had been worn for too long. *Or maybe,* Sandra re-evaluated, *they've been taken off and put back on a few too many times since they were laundered.* "I'm sorry, but who are you?"

"I'm Devon," the younger woman held a cheap flip phone in her outstretched right hand. "Danny told me to give this to you. In exchange for the one I left at your door this morning."

Sandra looked at the new phone with all of the caution of a giant red button labelled *TRAP*. "And how exactly do you know Daniel?"

"Oh, I wouldn't say I 'know' him," Devon rolled her eyes. "At least, not like I'm guessing you do." She sighed, driven by an obvious desire to be anywhere else. "Look, Dan paid me to meet you here and trade you phones. Just take it so I can finally get some real sleep."

Sandra's glare bored into the dolled up doxy. "And where exactly is Daniel?"

"Beats me. We snuck in the back door a couple hours ago."

"I bet he did," Sam chuckled.

That better've been the only *back door action going on,* Sandra inwardly fumed. Confused, Sandra complied while Devon looked at the barkeep. She seemed less insulted than peeved at her own sloppy choice of words. "He picked the lock," she clarified. "Said you wouldn't mind. He also told me to tell you to drop dead."

"Really?" For the first time since Sandra had met him, Sam stopped polishing his glass. "Is that what he said?"

"Yep." Devon's face jerked like she suddenly remembered something that was supposed to be important to other people, but clearly had no clue as to why it was. "Oh, dead drop. That's what he said. He told me, 'Tell the nice black man and the pretty blonde lady, '*dead drop.*'"

A dead drop, Sandra knew, was a tool of spycraft by which intelligence personnel who suspected that they were under surveillance could exchange information or material without being colocated. It was historically used by operatives in the same area or between handlers and their sources. An agreed upon location and time were chosen in advance. One party would go to the prescribed location before the elected hour and discreetly deposit something - film, notes, cash, or whatnot - and then the second party would come along some time afterward and covertly collect said material. By sharing the same place but not the same time, both parties could ideally avoid suspicion altogether - or at least avoid either party from compromising the other, should one find themselves detected by an adversary.

Sandra knew all of this. Evidently, so did Sam - which made the FBI agent curious as to what else she did not know about the bartender's past. But Devon was clearly clueless. The young brunette turned to Sam. "Danny said you'd let me crash with you for a few hours."

Sam gave the tired gal a smile and a nod. "Sure thing, sweetheart. Might help me take my mind off that whole breaking-and-entering thing." Sam stowed his glass and folded his bar towel. "Lemme see those other phones for a second, would you, my dear?" Devon handed him the other burner phones. Sam pulled a roll of aluminum foil from somewhere under the bar, tore off a sheet, and wrapped the phones it in. "I'll just save these for a rainy day," he hummed. "Never know when they might be handy." Then he smiled and jerked his head toward the door. "Well, Ms. Elbee, I guess this meeting is adjourned."

A dozen pairs of eyes in the J. Edgar Hoover Building watched a trio depart Black Sam's Brewery. A black man - whose face, captured by high definition digital optics, matched the Maryland Department of Motor Vehicle's photo for one Zishawn Sampson Mitchell, aged 52, listed by D.C.'s Business Licensing Center as the sole partner in Black Sam's Brewery, LLC - walked a short distance with a caucasian female - whose face, captured with the same sensors, matched the student photo for one

Devon Birchwood, a 21 year old junior at George Washington University majoring in French Language and Literature - until they entered a silver 2010 Jaguar XK whose license plate matched the registration for Mitchell's vehicle. The NSA technician on the watch floor assessed neither individual to be of intelligence value, so the couple were dismissed to carry out whatever dalliance they had planned.

Several other drones from Coffield's UAV swarm followed the blonde caucasian female who exited the bar at the same time. Her identity was again confirmed to be FBI Special Agent Sandra Elbee, and a trio of UAVs followed her to her blue Toyota Prius - New Jersey plates and registration - while twice as many birds circled the building to scan for any other comers or goers and a few more conducted reconnaissance and security patrols over the block. With no indication of Wakefield on the scene, Assistant Director Flowers maintained her order for a tactical hold. The strike teams stayed concealed on the perimeter as Sandra pulled away in her Prius, oblivious to the amount of tax dollars being spent in her direction.

Much to Nick Brown's personal chagrin and Maxine Flowers' overall disappointment, their objective was not on target. "All stations," Flowers announced, "this is mission command. Dry Hole. Repeat: Dry Hole." The task force's leader gave Nick Brown a wicked look, then walked off the watch floor. Nick was dumbstruck as he juggled the frustration at a missed opportunity to nail his least favorite subordinate with a deep concern for his own future.

"Mr. Coffield," Dr. Wiley ordered, "maintain Icarus on standby in a parking orbit over the city and await further tasking. Return all other birds to the nest for recharge, refuel and repair."

"Aye, sir."

"We should follow Elbee," Nick stammered. "We've got a few Bureau cars on the perimeter. She's still our best link back to Wakefield."

Jonas Wiley rubbed a hand over his jowls. Even suspended, Danny was easily his best man in the Analysis Division - one of the best he had ever served with in his long career. The former Marine was like a surrogate son to him. But the mission overrode all personal preferences. It had to. "Do it," he dispassionately nodded. "One car. Surveillance only. And do remind them to be discreet." Nick relayed the order over the command network.

CHAPTER 26

"BUCK GREENLAW, sitting in for Lonnie and the crew here at the Lonnie Chase program on this day of giving thanks, and I'd like to share with you a few things for which I am thankful.

"I'm thankful to live in a country where the people value freedom. The last few weeks have been rough. The last few months, really. A serial killer - a decorated war hero, nonetheless - has rocked our nation. And a lot of people have struck out against our government, too, and the injustices that they see every day in their everyday lives." The guest host consulted his notes. "We've got another vet who was convicted of aiding him and sentenced to federal prison for what will probably be the rest of his life. Another accomplice and vet in a federal medical detention facility and at least two other alleged associates in federal custody for aiding and assisting. An old man working as a security guard who helped his own grandson stage an attack against the Vee-Aye Headquarters in Richmond in retaliation for their treatment of our veterans - in particular, his own son, who died due to the Vee-Aye's willful negligence and gross ineptitude. A mob in Texas who stormed federal buildings and killed an Eye-Are-Ess official. More riots and clashes on the streets of America in the past six weeks than I can personally recall in the last twenty years. And an order of martial law that was only lifted in the last twelve hours - which shows me that our government has finally gotten a clue and has finally realized that our people are fed up."

Buck gave a pensive sigh. It was somewhat less dramatic than the sighs that his employer was famous for, but served as a thoughtful pause in his holiday monologue. "We all know people who are thankful for all of the wrong things today. They're thankful for their house, or their job, or their bank account. And don't get me wrong. Those are all good blessings. But they pale in importance, I think, with the Blessings of Liberty our forefathers fought for. And maybe we've taken those liberties for granted for too long. Maybe - and I'm saddened to say this - maybe we're watching the sun set on the age of freedom. Maybe the American experiment has failed.

"I was reading a paper the other night in my study. It was an academic piece that, I admit, most people would find insanely boring. And I'm okay with that. It was a paper about the cycle of history and of empires - about how empires are born, grow, peak, decline, and decay. It's an inevitable cycle, the author argued. And it's one that is painfully easy to predict if you know what to look for.

"Then the author goes on about how empires basically have a shelf life. And we've all heard this before, about how an empire can last for a century or two, but that's basically it. Two hundred years or so, and the empire crumbles. And when we look at the calendar, we see that our nation has basically run the clock out. We look left and we look right and we see historians all around us saying, 'Hey, our nation has run its course. Now it's time for our inevitable decline.' And a part of me can't help but wonder if maybe what we're feeling today in America isn't too dissimilar to what people felt during the last days of the Roman Empire. You know? Right before the fall.

"But then, last night, as I put the paper down, it dawned on me: America is an empire now, but we weren't founded as an empire. We were founded as an anti-empire. This nation was conceived and constructed as a republic. Remember what Ben Franklin said, when asked. He said, 'We have given you a Republic… if you can keep it.' And the thing is, we forgot to keep it.

"Over the years, professional politicians have transformed the Republic. They twisted its principles and perverted its institutions, all in the name of democracy, until at last we were left with this broken thing. Our society didn't break this country. Our ideals didn't lead this nation into the gutter. We, the people, have been conned into handing power to corrupt individuals who have run this once bright nation into ruin.

"There's nothing wrong with being America - with being a force for good on this Earth. You know, like we used to be. A shining beacon of freedom, shining up on top of a hill and lighting the way for the rest of the world to follow. You can argue about superpower status and all of that all you want, but I firmly believe that as long as that was America's role in the world, that we served a purpose. You could even call it a divine purpose. A role of providence. I do.

"But I look at our country today, and I don't see that anymore. I don't see us leading less fortunate people to freedom. Instead, I see us following confused Socialists from failed states and morally bankrupt politicians - both here and abroad, and from both parties - down the drain. Instead of leading people out of bondage, we're just sitting blithely as more and more of our own people are oppressed until finally we're all in chains. America no longer serves our ordained purpose. And so, like every other empire before us, we shall fall.

"And what will be left behind? The late, great Ronald Reagan said that America is freedom's last defense on this Earth. So what is there when we're gone? Oh, there might be a nation sandwiched between the Atlantic and Pacific Oceans, and it might even be called America. But it won't be the land of the free or the home of the brave. It will be the land of subjects enslaved to yet another authoritarian regime. It will be a collection of people too weak, too lazy, or too afraid of upsetting their masters to stand for anything - including themselves. Or their rights. Or their families.

"I mean, at that point, what's the difference between us and China? Or North Korea? Or the former Soviet Union? Or Cuba? What's the point of having a nation of our own if we're just going to copy what all of the other losers around the globe are doing? And they are losers. By any human metric, these countries where the all-powerful government reigns supreme are absolutely horrible places to be. The only ones that are even remotely decent in any way are the ones that imitate what we used to be: a free state with a free market driven by free people.

They imitate it, but you can't have freedom and totalitarianism at the same time. Free people and authoritarian governments cannot occupy the same territory at the same time. It is an immutable law of physics.

"So this year, while you sit with your loved ones and stuff yourself like the turkey on the table, please remember freedom. Remember to be thankful for it. And remember to exercise it. Or maybe this time next year, that freedom will just be a memory."

* * *

Far enough behind the pale blue coupe that they could barely be seen, two FBI agents - junior guys whose unpopularity with their superiors got them picked for a last minute holiday detail - rode in a nondescript gray sedan. They watched Elbee drive through town, using what little traffic they could find to obscure sight lines and make themselves less visible to their quarry. They never drew attention to themselves, nor did they lose sight of their target.

It was standard operating procedure. It was what they were trained to do. And they did it marginally well.

Far enough behind the nondescript gray sedan to escape any notice, Daniel Wakefield drove an anonymous white Jeep Cherokee. He watched them leave the riverfront and followed their every move. He used what little traffic there was and the city's own terrain to obscure sight lines and make himself less visible to his quarry. He never drew attention to himself, nor did he lose sight of his target.

Sometimes, one of the sergeants at SERE - the Marine Corps' Survival, Evasion, Resistance, and Escape school - taught him, *the best way to hide from the enemy is to hunt them.* If he was right about what Phillips' next move was, Danny had to stay in the city. The only way he figured that he could do that without being detected was to let the feds lead him around town, and the best way to make sure they did exactly that was for Danny to watch as he led them on a wild goose chase. It was the perfect way to mask his presence.

Danny switched off the radio, pulled a new phone from the seat next to him and dialed the only number programmed into it. The phone on the other end barely finished its first ring before its owner activated it. "Do us both a favor," he spoke calmly, but before anything else could be said, "and don't say any names."

There was a moment's pause, then the cheap speaker carried Sandra's voice into his ear. "Where are you?"

"Not far," his eyes followed the sedan through a turn. He sped up a bit to maintain a visual, then copied the maneuver.

"You missed our date."

"No, I didn't."

"Everybody was there but you," Elbee insisted.

"I know. Big lunch. The whole family was there." Danny had to speak around his point without using any words that might tip off anyone who might be listening. The paranoid part of his mind echoed with Oscar's voice. *The NSA is probably vacuuming up every cell call and text in the country looking for you and using their supercomputers in Maryland and Nevada to query every word in every one of them, then pass those on for further analysis of content and metadata. Avoid 'dirty words' - any word that they might be searching for or that has to do with what they think might be going on.* The present circumstances made having any conversation difficult at best. Being forced to avoid any version of the words 'kill, assassin, Wakefield, Phillips, Constitution,' or any host of other terms made communicating his point nearly impossible. The solution, of course, was to talk around the subject until he circled it enough for Elbee to infer his meaning. "Including your brothers and cousins."

"Okay?" Sandra's obvious confusion reminded Danny that there was a world of difference between the FBI's training and that of *bona fide* intelligence personnel.

"You and I both know how badly your brothers wanted to meet me this morning." Wakefield tried not to put too much emphasis on his words, but just barely enough that she should know to read into them and try to follow his meaning. "Anyway, I hope the present I got you makes up for it. I'm pretty sure its your size, but if we have to return it then I'll think of something else."

"Yeah," the cheaply constructed imitation of Sandra's voice changed to an ill-humored tone. "About that present. The wrapping was a little, ah, inappropriate. Wouldn't you say?"

"Oh, yeah, that… Well, look, I had to improvise. So I borrowed something," Danny caught himself before he said *Oscar.* Even though it was only a nickname, he felt it was best to mask any reference to his misanthropic, dwarfish associate. "So I, ah, used a little something that Santa's little elf had just laying around."

Sandra was quiet for a beat. "Oh, the elf, eh?" It sounded to Danny like she understood his meaning. "And how do I know that it wasn't some piece of wrapping paper that you had tucked away in the closet this whole time?"

"You should know me well enough by now to know that's not my style." The feds' car cleared Landover Hills, but bypassed the Beltway. Danny noted their direction of travel. "Look, hon, I need you to stay in town."

"What? Why?"

"You know that project we've been working on?"

"I don't know if you noticed or not, *hon,* but I've moved on to other things at work."

"Well, I think it's gonna be finished tonight. One way or the other."

Another pause. "What do you mean?"

"It's Thanksgiving. And you know what happens on Thanksgiving."

"I know what we had planned for Thanksgiving," the cheap imitation of her voice replied pointedly, "and it wasn't work."

"Big dinner."

"Pretty big, yeah."

"At the house." Sandra's silence was telling. It told Danny that she did not quite follow his reference. "The big, *big* house."

"The big house?"

Big house. Archaic slang for jail. "Not the big house," he said more slowly. "The Big, Big, House." Inspiration struck him in the form of an old song he used to hear on the radio. "It's a big, big, house," he sang, "with lots and lots of rooms…"

"What are you talking about?"

"A big, big table," he continued, "with lots and lots of food…"

"Have you lost -"

Danny grew more insistent. "A big, big yard," *in a penny, in a pound,* "where we can play football…" *C'mon, Elbee, get a clue.*

"Oh," Sandra's voice, made weak by the disposable phone's poor speaker, was suddenly even more quiet.

"It's our father's house."

"Oh." For a moment, the only sound in Oscar's Cherokee was the *clack-thump, clack-thump* of tires as they passed over seams in the freeway.

"Look, I know things are a little, uh, chaotic at the moment -"

"No."

"What?"

"You were about to ask me to help you," Sandra dryly anticipated. "The answer is no."

"But you don't even know what I -"

"No! You know what I do know? I know that you need to throw in the towel. Just quit. Okay? All of it. This - this is insane."

"Are you telling me that as my lover," Danny stabbed, "or as a psychologist?"

"I'm telling you as someone who cares about you. Look, this only ends one way. And the last thing I'm going to do is help you destroy your life."

"I'm trying to save a life."

"You're trying to save your job."

"Not anymore. Look, I figured out the game, but I don't know how he's gonna make his play. Not exactly."

"You know who really needs to hear this."

"What, so that they can muck it up like last time? No way. We can't afford mistakes. Not at this level."

Elbee hesitated. "But why me?"

"I need someone I can trust."

"Get Oscar."

Wakefield winced at the use of his NSA accomplice's name on an open line. *It's just a nickname,* he reminded himself. *Stay calm. There's millions of phones active in this area alone. They'd have to get really lucky to get anywhere just off that.* "I need a presence. Close to the," *can't say 'target,'* "close to the finish line."

"No way. You saw what happened last time I waited by the finish line."

Danny shook his head and inwardly chastised himself. During Elbee's final operation as head of the Constitutional Killer case, she stood only a few feet away from the mayor of New York at the exact moment Phillips shot him. He knew that reminding his former partner of anything that made her focus on failure was no way to get her to cooperate with his risky plan. He tried another approach. "This started with us. It should end with us."

"I'm not sure how much of an 'us' there can be anymore," she said at length.

Wakefield shook his head. "I'm not giving up on us. This'll all work out. You'll see."

"You know," Sandra hissed, "it's amazing how the best of intentions can lead someone to screw things up so royally."

"I'm sorry. I wouldn't ask if there was any other way. I need someone close to the finish line to pull this out of the fire in case I miss him." Danny looked up at the gray sky. "You catch the forecast for tonight?"

"Chance of snow."

Snow. Harmless little white things floating and flying about at random. Blown away by forces beyond their control. "Bet on it." *C'mon, Elbee…* "Probably a big, fat, wet one." *Wet. Wet work. Get it, Elbee. Just. Get. It.*

In the distance up ahead of him, Danny saw the gray sedan exit the freeway. *Good,* he smiled. *If they got off, she got off. And if she got off…* As if summoned by his mental narration, Sandra's little blue half-a-car passed him on the other side of the highway. *Good. She's headed back to the apartment.*

"Well," the hollowed out version of Sandra's voice became more alert. "If it's gonna get nasty, we'd best get settled in. Shouldn't we?"

Danny was confident that the feds would continue to follow Elbee back to their apartment, then watch her for a while to see if anything happened. *Good. Frees me up to get into position.* "Yeah. There's something back at our place for you."

"What?"

"Santa's elf is working tonight, but he left you a gift."

"How?"

"Oh, you know him. Santa's little helper."

"When should I expect you to catch up?"

Can't go home. Can't meet up. Not until this is all sorted out. "Later. I'll be late, but I'll be at the party."

"Please be careful."

Danny wished that he could see her face. He wished that he could kiss her forehead, or to hold her hand and tell her that everything would be fine. But the closest he could safely get to the woman he had grown so close to was to hear her voice on a poorly made cell phone and imagine her car miles ahead of the proxy he followed. "I don't think I ever told you this before, babe -"

"Don't."

"I think it needs to be said."

"When you see me tonight," Sandra insisted. "If you still feel that way, tell me in person."

Danny cycled a deep breath. "You know I -"

"I know," she cut in again. "But tell me to my face. Look me in the eye and tell me in person."

Silently, Danny nodded. "I will."

CHAPTER 27

T.J. SEWED THE wheelchair's seat back together with meticulous care. Every stitch had to be perfect. The thread had to be tight. The fabric had to be smooth. This wheelchair had to be a comfortable, welcoming throne for its passenger.

He worked as only a man driven by obsession could. Absolute attention to every last detail, coupled with a growing sense of urgency. He drove the needle from his Bug Out Bag's sewing kit into a barely visible hole left by the factory-original thread, which he had pulled out earlier, and pulled the line until it held in place. Then back through another identical hole and equally tight. Poke. Pull. Poke. Pull.

T.J. did not look at the clock. He knew what time it was. It was time to finish. *One more row of stitching,* he breathed, *and then the seat pad is done.* T.J.'s handiwork retained all of the softness of the chair's original material - some form of foamy fabric - but was now far more exciting. The last seam along the seat's edge secured a wire that ran from the pad's new filler into the wheelchair's polished stainless steel frame. The hollow metal tubes concealed a set of batteries. *No transmitters to be jammed. No timers to be deactivated. No remote that relies on me to trigger it. Once the circuit is manually closed, the party's over.*

A well-meaning volunteer knocked on the doorway to T.J.'s borrowed room at the homeless shelter. "Excuse me?" the mousy female poked her head through the doorless frame. "Mr. Jefferson? We're getting ready to serve lunch."

"Thank you, ma'am." Phillips, who gave the staff the name Marcus Jefferson when he checked into the shelter, kept his frame between the doorway and his arts-and-crafts project.

"Is everything okay?" His jacket was strewn across the floor in what appeared to be laziness but actually purposefully served to discreetly cover most of his short barreled rifle. T.J.'s Bug Out Bag was unzipped, but closed to conceal the rest of the gun.

So long as nobody moves anything… "Just wrapping this up. I wanted to go grab a friend real quick."

"Well, you need to hurry," the frail church lady mewed. "The rolls tend to go fast."

"Yes, ma'am. Just a minute to finish this patch, then I've gotta run down the street and pick him up."

"We can't hold up the meal to wait for you," she warned.

"Oh, don't wait on my account, ma'am. I'll catch up."

"Do you want one of us to help you?"

"I'm fine, ma'am. Rolls or no rolls. It's all good to me."

"Okay, dear. Just let us know if you need anything."

Chow time means it's almost twelve-hundred hours, he recalled the poster taped to the shelter's door. *What I need is to get this done and get across town. Fast.*

*   *   *

Sandra did not know what to expect to find when she arrived at her apartment, except that she would know whatever Danny's surprise for her was when she saw it. A surprise that, if she understood him correctly, was delivered by Oscar while she was driving around town all morning chasing shadows and mysterious clues.

There was nothing unusual in the parking lot. No movement, no new vehicles - though she did suspect one of them might be an FBI car surveilling her and Wakefield's apartment. *As if Daniel is dumb enough to show up here,* she huffed. *That's just amateurish.* Likewise, the stairs, hallway, and door to the apartment were all perfectly normal. Everything was exactly the way it should be. Not a dust mote out of place. The sheer normalcy of it all was almost maddening. The fewer things looked like anything had happened, the more convinced she was that she had missed something.

Then she entered the abode she shared with - *What is Daniel, exactly? My friend with benefits? My boyfriend? A fling? A mistake? My lover?* - and saw it: a plain, white envelope on the floor. It appeared as though Oscar slid it into the apartment between the door and the plate. It was a tight fit, but sealed with low-end weather stripping. It was a plausible explanation.

Sandra secured the door, fetched the envelope, and extracted a folded piece of linen paper with razor sharp edges and adorned with fancy gold lettering. Words that she never imagined she would read played out in front of her as if conjured by her own fairy godmother. *Oh. My. God.*

It was an invitation to Thanksgiving Dinner at the White House.

The big, big house... she recalled. Suddenly, Daniel's rambling phone call made perfect sense. T.J. Phillips, the Soldier-turned-assassin, the serial killer with a vendetta against crooked politicians, the one-man army who waged a personal war against the United States government, the criminal who nearly derailed Elbee's career and probably ruined Wakefield's, was going to strike at the highest seat in the land. *My father's house.*

Phillips is after the president! She realized. *Tonight. And Daniel has figured it out.*

Prudence, protocol, and good civic mindedness demanded that she call this in to her superiors. She knew that she should call the watch floor in the Hoover building directly. She knew the number, and a tip like this could go a long way toward making things right between Daniel and their superiors. Or at least, she figured, talk to Derek and find out what, if anything, he knew about the situation. With the invitation in one hand and her cell phone in the other, Sandra froze in place.

The invitation told her that Daniel wanted her to be there. In person. And the clandestine delivery by Oscar - who, Wakefield had mentioned, would be working this evening - told her that the former Marine had a plan. And that that plan required assistance. *But not from the Task Force,* she reasoned.

For a moment, the choices her left Sandra paralyzed. Two alternatives, each diametrically opposed to the other, literally rested in her hands. And choosing either would compromise the other.

If she called the watch floor then they might have believed her. Or not. They might have bought into Wakefield's theory. Or not. They might have been able to leverage enough resources to stop a Special Forces trained killer from assassinating the President of the United States.

Or not.

Sandra ignored her hands. Her eyes fixated on a pile of brown leather on the couch. She placed the invitation and the phone on the glass coffee table top and picked up Wakefield's jacket - the one she brought home from the hospital. She took it up in both hands and held it tightly to herself. Her eyes closed as her fingers dug into the deceptively heavy material. The smell of worn leather mixed with the hint of gun oil and the trace of Daniel's body drifted up her nostrils. Adoration made her squeeze the leather. Frustration made her try to rend the garment. Finally, she fell onto the couch with the jacket draped across her lap.

The White House Thanksgiving was a gala of the highest order. It was the most exclusive party in town. *There's no way that an army of feds could just show up and go unnoticed*, she resigned. *But me, alone…*

"What if I'm wrong?" she asked the empty living room. "What if he's wrong?" For all of his skills, Daniel was a deeply flawed man with serious issues. "He can't be right all of the time."

But then, he never claimed to be, she mused, *did he?* Right there, in a modest apartment that she shared with a guy she had grown to trust, Sandra felt herself torn between loyalties. Duty to country fought against devotion to Daniel. The weight of her career dragged against the pull on her heartstrings. The promise and stability of safety stood at odds against her own desire to put this case to an end once and for all.

Sandra picked up the invitation again and scanned it for details. Her mind searched for an answer to her real question: *What am I supposed to do?*

CHAPTER 28

"DON'T TEAR UP my Jeep, Chumly."

Danny sat a few blocks away from the White House with the engine idling so that the heater could keep him cozy. "This old thing?" he scoffed. His latest handset rested on the dash in speaker phone mode. He took in D.C.'s night through the defrosted windshield. "Weather guesser was right. It's snowing pretty good out here tonight."

"A clean, untraceable vehicle is worth far more than its Blue Book value," Oscar insisted.

"What do you mean, untraceable?"

"Paid cash at an auction out of state. Registered it under a cat's name."

"Not a literal cat."

"You'd be amazed at the rights animals have in some states, Chumly. That's my 'Get Out of Dodge' truck."

"Your Honda will get you further on a tank of gas."

"Which would you rather have during the zombie apocalypse, Chumly - a six cylinder Ess-You-Vee or a four banger coupe? You break it, you're buying me a new one."

Daniel listened to the headset connected to the short wave radio on his vest. A radio tuned to the same UHF and VHF frequencies and loaded with the same encryption protocols used by the rest of the Secret Service. No idle passersby or looky-loos would notice that the lone man sitting inside the Cherokee's darkened cabin wore a desert tan tactical vest over his khaki colored soft shell jacket. Nobody would notice the bronzed rifle that ran up from the floorboard and rested against the empty passenger seat. But, if Daniel was right, everyone on Earth would notice when all Hell broke loose tonight.

"The rose quacks at dawn," Oscar's voice cooed from the phone.

Despite the seriousness of the situation, Danny could not help but chuckle. "That was the worst code phrase in the history of spycraft."

"Fine. Your girlfriend just walked through the front door."

Danny tensed a bit. "Any troubles with security?"

"Hey!" Oscar sounded downright offended. "Just who do you think hacked the White House server and got her on the guest list?"

"Right. Thanks for that."

"Plus, that invitation is legit."

"Really? Who'd you steal it from?"

"Okay. It's a world-class forgery."

"That's more like it."

"We've got quite the print shop at the office. We can make anything."

Danny frowned. "I thought you were just a bunch of signals geeks."

"You continuously underestimate and disappoint me." Oscar's lip practically dragged across the receiver on his end. "And that, Chumly, is why you will always lose."

"Yeah? Well, tonight we need to win. Big."

Danny checked the street in front of him for the thousandth time. Hours ago, he parked the Cherokee a few blocks away from the White House, not far from the Georgetown campus, and sat in for the long wait. Now that things were starting to happen, Oscar's truck felt cramped. Confining. Like a cage.

"I'll tell you who's winning," Oscar teased, "and that's the lucky shlum who gets to sit next to Elbee tonight. That dress she's wearing is proof that God loves me."

"You have visual?"

"Oh, I have visual, alright," Oscar chuckled. "I'm not just watching street cameras here, Chumly. I'm pulling a ghost feed off of the Secret Service's own surveillance systems in the White House."

"I thought you were just monitoring communications."

"Oh, I'm doing that, too. I'll forward you any pics anyone takes of your girlfriend on their cell phones."

Danny sat in uncomfortable silence for a moment before he caved to the pressure of his own curiosity. "So, what's she wearing?"

"Oh, well, I don't know the words, exactly." Oscar fumbled. "Because I'm not gay. It's a dress."

"Describe it," Danny insisted.

Oscar hesitated for a moment. "Okay. How do I put it? There are dresses, and then there are *dresses*. Elbee is wearing the latter."

"Use adjectives," he growled. "God, you suck at surveillance…"

"Okay. It's black. Form fitting. Full length. Oh, and I think she's wearing it backwards."

"Backwards?" Danny's face skewed. "What makes you say that?"

"Her entire back is exposed." Oscar elaborated. "I mean, the whole thing. I don't even know how that thing is staying up. She's all exposed, from the neck down. There's nothing on her shoulders -"

"Okay, Oscar. I get the point."

"You can see the whole top of her hip."

"Okay, Oscar." Daniel grew more and more uncomfortable in the Jeep's driver seat.

"She's got little dimples -"

"Seriously, Oscar!"

"Oh, hey! She's talking with Senator Evans. The new Senator Evans."

"Did you think that somehow I had forgotten that the old one is dead?" Wakefield shook his head. Duke Evans' murder in a New Orleans brothel was the launching point of this entire affair. The late senator's widow had taken up her husband's mantle after Phillips killed him, and thanks to a combination of name recognition and voter sympathy, she won Duke's seat in the mid-term.

"Well, his widow's quite the looker," Oscar leered. "A real Silver Fox."

"I thought the term was 'Cougar."

"Nah. That's for soccer moms who like to shag younger guys. A hottie over fifty is more appropriately referred to as a Silver Fox. And I'm starting to see why this particular piece of tail is so popular in D.C. right now."

"Could it have anything to do with her policies? Or the fact that her late husband was a respected member of Congress for a gazillion years?"

Oscar grumbled. "Since when does any of that matter in this town?"

As the duo continued their banter and upheld their vigil, a mid-sized limousine pulled up near one of the White House's side entrances - the one frequently used by members of the First Family. The driver, as usual, stayed in the car. And, as usual, a curbside attendant in the plain working uniform of a White House staff member opened the door to the passenger compartment.

"Good evening, Mrs. Fulbright," the black man with the kind face and the plain staff uniform smiled as he opened the door for the president's mother. "You look lovely this evening."

"Thank you, Deary," the First Mother smiled.

The attendant produced a wheelchair for the older woman. Well into her seventies, Gertrude Fulbright was plagued with a history of hip issues. And while Franklin D. Roosevelt felt the need to hide his mobility issues out of a fear of appearing weak to the public, Gertrude believed that true strength was demonstrated by letting people see you overcome your challenges rather than mask them.

The attendant held out a hand to assist the First Mother as she transitioned from the limo to her wheelchair. "And how are we doing this evening?"

A Secret Service agent quickly imposed himself between the black man and the president's mother. "Don't touch her." His left hand was outstretched, while his right reached for his hip.

"Oh, Wally," Gertrude sighed. "He's just trying to be helpful."

"Protocol, Ma'am." The agent brushed the attendant back two paces. "No contact with the First Family." The agent's face was the picture of violent intent. His expression screamed, *I want to shoot you.* The black man stood with his hands up and his eyes wide. "How many times do we have to tell you people that?"

"I'm sorry, sir." The attendant was visibly shaken. "I didn't mean nothin' by it."

The First Mother struggled to pull herself out of her seat. "Really, Wally. Would you just…"

"We'll help you, Ma'am." Wally the Secret Service gorilla scooped the little old lady up and placed her down into the wheelchair with the practiced skill and soft touch of a world class nurse. "Rules are rules, Ma'am."

Gertrude frowned at the agent like a grandmother scolding a child. "I know this may be hard for you to believe, Wally, but most people are generally good folks."

"Maybe," Wally moved behind the wheelchair and pushed the old woman inside before she could catch a chill from the snowy night air. "But it's our job to watch out for the ones that aren't."

"Sorry for the confusion," the black gentleman apologized. He lowered his hands and turned to leave, but another suited goon stopped him with another hand on his chest after barely a step.

"Hold up a second," the agent tugged at the attendant's clip-on badge, "*Chester,* is it?"

The black man froze. "Yessir."

"Look, nobody wants to make a scene in front of the ol' gal, but this'll go a lot smoother if you cooperate." The agent held his hand to his ear, nodded, then returned his attention to the black man. "Tell all of your guys to get with the program. Next time one of you tries to touch a member of the First Family, you'll be scraping him off the pavement." The younger man raised his eyebrows to drive home just how serious he was. "Granny's sensitivities be damned. Got it?"

"Yessir."

With that, the agent let the attendant go about his business. As usual, the staffer scurried out of sight just as quickly as he could. But unlike the other hundred times such an encounter occurred in the Fulbright White House, as soon as the black man was out of sight, he disappeared into a shadow outside of the service entrance. There, he dug out a backpack, swapped his plain uniform for a pair of digital camouflage pants and a black leather jacket. He quickly scurried to a lime green off-road bike that he lifted from the other side of town just a few hours prior. Even on a night with light traffic, there were enough vehicles on D.C.'s midtown streets for him to disappear. Within seconds, he was just another helmeted motorist puttering around town.

Anything?

Elbee glanced down at the cheap phone discreetly hidden within her clutch. *No,* she blindly texted into the phone. It was Daniel's sixth text since she arrived, and each of the messages contained the same infuriatingly simple word.

Sandra was many things, but naive was not one of them. Somehow, Wakefield knew she was at the White House. The impatience and frequency of his texts indicated that he probably knew that she was inside. *You'd think he'd know if something happened. Or that he'd trust me to tell him if it did.*

Sandra wore an expression of attentive neutrality as she half-listened to Chandra Lee Evans recount some trivial exchange from a subcommittee meeting earlier in the week. She knew that she should have paid more attention to the Senator, but tonight, Sandra felt that she served the widow best by finally catching her husband's killer.

"So, Special Agent Elbee, where are you sitting?"

"What? Oh," Sandra looked down at her invitation. The crisp linen paper got her past the front door, but it held no insight into what she was supposed to do once inside. "I'm sorry, I'm still trying to orient myself in here. It's my first time."

"Oh, don't you worry," the older blonde smiled and took her by the arm. "You can sit with me. I'm sure there's room at our table for one more."

Special Agent Elbee kept her face soft and swept the White House Dining room with her eyes as Senator Evans guided her to their seats. She searched for any sign that something in the room was amiss - something that the Secret Service might have overlooked during the evening's hustle and bustle. Or, perhaps it was something that they did not know to look for in the first place.

Agents in black suits, boring ties, and poorly concealed earpieces were scattered all around the room. Their eyes constantly scanned every detail as their heads moved casually about their designated areas. From their starched collars down to their polished shoes, they were as motionless as they were uniform. *They're specially trained for this. I'm not.* Sandra hid her doubts deep down within herself. *Who better to keep the place safe than the ones who know it best?*

The First Family were all at the White House to celebrate that most American of holidays. President Fulbright had decided to mark the season of peaceful celebrations with a truly American feast. Tradition, it was said, reinforced confidence - confidence in institutions; confidence in stability; confidence in security. And tonight, tradition was on full display in true White House style for the whole world to see.

President Fulbright, the First Lady, and their children - who ranged in ages from barely nineteen to thirty years of age - all sat on the same side of a long table situated next to the room's longest wall. Their seating arrangement, reminiscent of DaVinci's famous painting, prompted some members of the attending media to coin the phrase *The First Supper*. The president's various siblings, cousins, and longtime friends close enough to the leader to call themselves kin to the Fulbright family populated their own tables with their own most-favored guests. Seating around the room seemed to be based upon the nature of the relationship between the head of each table and the leader of the free world. Fulbright's most intimate friends and family were nearest to the head table, then the next closest around them, and so on until the most distant of people who merited an invitation - and, by that virtue, the ones least likely to score any real time with the president this evening - were left in the outlying areas.

Chandra Lee Evans sat herself and Special Agent Elbee at a table roughly halfway to the head table - directly next to the First Mother. *So close to The First Supper?* Sandra wondered. *Not bad for the junior senator from a troubled and obscure state.* After a quick round of introductions, Elbee did her best to not look star struck in the elite company.

As she exchanged meaningless small talk about Beltway life with Senator Evans, Elbee's eyes followed a man who looked to be in his mid-thirties - but whom Sandra knew for a fact was well into his forties - as he rose from the table nearest to the president's and wove his way through a black and white sea of silk until he came at last to the silver-haired woman who sat immediately to Elbee's right.

"Alright, Nanna," the smooth talker smiled. "Let's just slide over to the main table and say 'hi' to everyone before the night gets too late."

"Oh?" the older woman slyly smiled. "You mean you don't want me to look sleepy when the cameras film us tonight." A round of polite laughs quietly sounded from around the table.

"The cameras are digital," the man's smile never broke. "Nobody uses film anymore."

The gentlewoman clasped Sandra's elbow and giggled. "Though his oldest brother is the president, it's Jamie here who's always getting his picture taken." She gave the beautiful blonde a meaningful wink. "Can't blame them, really. He *is* the looker in the family. And single, too."

"Is that so?" Sandra returned the First Mother's smile with a snicker of her own. "Didn't I hear something on the news about him and an interpreter at the UN building just last week?"

"No, no," the youngest of the Fulbright brothers gave a quiet but dismissive chuckle. "I'm sure that was somebody else." His lighthearted expression fell just a bit, as did his voice. "Really, mother. We should go talk to Charles."

"Oh, Jamie. I think I need to freshen up first."

"Let me signal the staff -"

"Actually," the kindly older woman leaned in between her youngest son and her youngest table guest so that she could whisper to both of them, "I really don't think that's necessary."

"Is everything alright, Mrs. Fulbright?"

"Oh, yes, dear. I just need to go to the ladies' room is all."

"Special Agent Elbee," Senator Evans leaned into the delicate exchange and spoke with her voice lowered as well. "Would you be so kind as to help the First Mother to and from the powder room?"

Sandra's spine stiffened as she prepared to tell the southern debutant that in the post-antebellum world of twenty-first century America, a highly trained law enforcement professional such as herself did not excel in college and her own career just to roll a septuagenarian to the bathroom solely because they happened to be born with the same type of reproductive organs. And then Gertrude's smile - warm, but with worry hidden behind big blue eyes - evaporated Sandra's indignant feminist reply. *This was a stupid idea, Daniel.* Elbee decided to leave the heroics to the heroes - just for a moment, anyway. "It would be my pleasure," she smiled.

Escorted by a pair of Secret Service agents, Sandra wheeled the First Mother into the nearest washroom. The gorillas gladly stood outside while Sandra struggled to find a way to assist the mobility-impaired woman while preserving both of their dignities. The confined space reminded Elbee of how exactly the room earned its traditional moniker as the *water closet.*

"I'm sorry to trouble you, deary," Gertrude politely fumed. "It's just, well, I think I might have had a little accident in there."

"Oh." *Dear God in Heaven,* Elbee's inner voice implored, *If you exist, please don't let this be happening.* "Is there something you need?"

"Just some paper towels to wipe the seat," Gertrude pointed to the dispenser on the wall. "Something feels squishy."

My soon-to-be-ex-boyfriend is a Secret Service agent and I'm helping the First Grandmother wipe her own ass. Sandra suppressed a reflexive gag as she withdrew a cluster of towels and faced away as she handed them to the older woman. Gertrude did something behind Elbee's back.

"Here you go, deary." The towels slapped back against her arm. *You better pray Daniel, that they catch you and throw you in jail. Because if they don't, I'm going to kill you.* Obliged and disgusted, Sandra grabbed the slimy towels and reached for the trashcan.

Halfway into her pitch, she stopped. The towels did not feel right. They were not wet, but they were slippery with a slime other than human waste. Instinctively, she brought the bundle closer to her nose and gave a cautious sniff. The slime smelled faintly familiar, but not foul. Sandra turned toward Gertrude as her mind worked it's way through memories. The First Mother still held a few towels, which she desperately used to try to wipe her seat clean.

Sandra sniffed again, deeper. And then she noticed that the slime did not come from inside Gertrude, but from inside her seat cushion. *Nitrogen? Are those nitrates?* The FBI agent's memory flipped with grim realization as the First Mother shifted to stand up from her chair. "Gertrude! Don't -"

Daniel felt the *boom* through his feet where they touched the pedals, through his hands where they rested on the steering wheel. He heard the peal like distant thunder. He saw the slight shimmer of the rearview mirror as it shook for a fraction of a second.

Sirens screamed into the D.C. night - first one, then two, then a few more. Their cries rose and multiplied like popcorn kernels popping as they became more frequent, more common, until at last their ubiquity almost undermined their own urgency.

The radio erupted with a flurry of voices. Questions. Answers. More questions. Orders for this person to go here, or that person to do something else. Danny listened through the noise for two voices in particular. One of those voices filled the Cherokee's cockpit with urgent yet pointed updates.

"… feeds are a mess, but it definitely came from within the White House."

"Where, Oscar?"

"Looks like the bathroom over by the Red Room. That's right by the State Dining Room."

"Where's Elbee?" Wakefield threw all communications security protocols to the wind and dialed Sandra's cell. *Pick up. Pick up. Pick. Up. The. Phone!*

"She was around there last time I saw her."

"Where is she?"

"Double checking now."

Pickuppickuppickuppickupgoddammitpickup! Danny fought the tremble in his right hand while his left tried to wring Sandra's voice out of the steering wheel. Finally, his patience was rewarded with the *click* of a connection. "Elbee! Where -"

"We're sorry, but the number you have dialed has a voice mail box that has not yet been set up -"

Danny keyed the phone to disconnect the call and redial.

"We're sorry. All circuits are busy. Please hang up, and try -"

Wakefield threw the device into the passenger seat and beat the steering wheel with both hands. A visceral sound, more akin to something that should come from an animal than a man, bubbled up from his chest. *I put her in there. I put her in harm's way.* The world went silent, save for the ringing echo of blood as it flooded his ears. Time stretched beyond its normal limits. The falling snow seemed to hang in midair -

And as that exact moment burned its way into Wakefield's memory, a light green motorbike crossed his headlights from right to left. The rider wore a helmet with the visor down, a black jacket, backpack… and the exact same digital gray camouflage pants that Phillips wore during his assault on DHS Headquarters.

Acting on instincts born from years of training and experience rather than conscious thought, Danny dropped the Jeep into gear, turned out of his alley, and followed the bike. His mind struggled to catch up with what his senses told him when Danny saw the motorbike's front wheel rise up and the rider launch himself into the night. Wakefield stomped on the accelerator and cued the radio on his tactical vest.

"All stations, Six Lima Niner. In pursuit of suspect vehicle…"

CHAPTER 29

AROUND THE FBI crisis watch floor, heads popped up and looked around like so many lemurs. "Six Lima Niner?" Agent Stevenson announced from the big chair with realization, "That's Wakefield."

Derek, halted halfway to the door, sprang to the nearest unoccupied workstation and logged into the terminal. Somewhere, someone ordered up a live video feed from the city's traffic camera network, cross referenced to locations described as Danny narrated his pursuit. In accordance with standard operating procedures, phone calls were made to the higher-ups.

Stevenson quickly donned a headset and patched her terminal into DHS tactical operations' radio channel. "Six Lima Niner, this is Hoover Command. Please acknowledge."

Wakefield powered through a left turn and sped down K Street. The little bike was more nimble than the bigger sport utility vehicle, but it was also less stable and its smaller motor, while great for acceleration, had a much lower top speed than the Jeep. The long stretch of road allowed Danny to quickly close with his target.

"Making our way to Georgetown," Danny called into his radio.

"Units from Foggy Bottom are waiting," Stevenson's voice answered. Wakefield closed to within a few yards of the green dirtbike's tail light. Foggy Bottom was the unfortunately-named district that was home to two distinct features: George Washington University and a particularly nasty traffic circle where K Street and a half dozen other major avenues all came together into one snarl. It was the perfect choke point to stop a vehicle pursuit in midtown D.C.

A block short of the Foggy Bottom roundabout, the motorbike's rear wheel kicked out to the right. The little green dirt racer shot to Danny's left like a laser.

Wakefield slid sideways and willed the Cherokee into a turn on the slick city street. "Headed south on twenty-first," he barked. Flashing lights blinked red and blue behind him as he followed the rider across Pennsylvania Avenue.

The bike barreled down the campus road at breakneck speeds. GWU's streets were lined with parked cars, which made the already narrow roads even more difficult to manage. With another turn, the green bike leapt up G Street the wrong way. Danny drove right after him, as did a few police officers who were more interested in catching murderers than obeying road signs.

A Metro squad car flew at the motorbike as it crossed 19th. The policeman failed to stop the quick little off-roader, but his maneuver forced everyone else in the pursuit to turn to the south to avoid a collision.

The Cherokee fishtailed to the left, but Danny corrected the skid and drove the accelerator down so hard that it threatened to punch through the floorboard. The Jeep's famous in-line six cylinder engine roared to life as he barreled down 19th Street.

Ahead, the dirt bike's lone crimson taillight flashed. The little motorcycle pivoted to the left once more. Wakefield raced toward the green profile, which paused curiously just before it reached Constitution Avenue.

White-yellow flashes strobed from just above the green motorcycle's chassis. Spiderwebs burst across the Cherokee's windshield with a *crack-crack-crack*. Sparks leapt up from the pavement.

Danny slammed on the brake, ducked behind the dashboard, and tried not to swerve as bullets ripped through the Jeep, but he lost control and the truck spun sideways to the right as it slid through the intersection. The Cherokee lurched as the driver's side jumped the curb on the far side of the t-shaped junction. Wakefield's head popped up and gifted him with a view of three Metro police cars, hastily pulled to either side of the street immediately to his north to avoid incoming fire - and a single red tail light that grew smaller as it sped away behind him.

Wakefield whipped the Cherokee back around and sped after the bike. "It's Phillips alright," he called into his radio. "Eastbound on Constitution from 19th."

"How's my truck, Chumly?" Oscar's disembodied voice demanded from the phone's speaker.

"Find Elbee!"

"I'm working on it, Chumly. There's a lot of faces moving around in there. Just stay calm and don't frack up my truck."

Danny swept the phone off the dash and followed Phillips as the assassin jumped the curb just before the German-American Friendship Garden and cut through the Washington Monument park. "You know, Oscar," he announced as he plowed through the snow-encrusted grass, "I just don't think you're getting this one back." A flurry of vindictive profanity sounded from the phone as Wakefield dropped it and willed more acceleration from the Jeep's engine.

"Lima Six Niner," Stevenson's voice sounded from the radio, "be advised. Units have completely blocked off fourteenth street."

"Roger that, Command." Danny chased Phillips up to the famous obelisk, which rose from a small artificial hill that obscured their view of the street on the other side. *Time to drive this fish into the net.*

Phillips' bike cleared the artificial mound and revealed the leeward side to be awash in a sea of flashing red and blue lights. The bike rolled hard to the right, dug deep into the frozen lawn, and spat a rooster tail of grassy mud as the driver cut a hard orbit around the memorial and sped back to the west.

Wakefield echoed the maneuver. The Cherokee dug a set of wicked furrows into the previously well-manicured national park and raced back to 17th Street.

Red and blue lights danced and wove all around them as Phillips darted between a pair of cruisers that were still jockeying into containment positions and bolted down Independence Avenue. Danny's larger turning radius forced him to clip a cop car as he continued after the fleeing assassin. A significant portion of the Cherokee's rear end stayed behind with the Capitol Police car.

"Lima Six Niner," another voice sounded on the radio. This voice was fresh, sober, calmed with maturity - and decidedly masculine. "Acknowledge."

Gripped with indignant rage, Wakefield's mind barely registered the speaker's familiarity. "Father?"

"Lima Six Niner," the voice calmly persisted. "Disengage your pursuit. The area is locked down tight. There's nowhere for him to go."

Driven by commitment to see the deed through, Wakefield followed the bike up to Ohio Drive.

"Back off, Danny boy," Wiley's voice continued over the radio.

At the base of the Arlington Memorial Bridge, Danny saw the bike stopped in front of a quartet of D.C. Metro Police Department vehicles with blazing lights and their officers, all with guns drawn down on the suspect and fingers on triggers. Azure and crimson flashes lit the night sky as DHS, FBI, and Capitol Police vehicles flooded every road, alleyway, and sidewalk. Helicopters circled overhead and bathed the scene in blinding white light.

The bike's rider dropped his carbine to the street, shut off his engine, and spread his arms like wings. There, in front of God and everybody, the motorcyclist dismounted and removed his helmet. Danny stepped out of the Cherokee, pulled Vera out of the passenger seat, and shouldered the bronze carbine. He walked forward with controlled steps.

"Homeland Security!" Wakefield yelled over the noise of engines, radios, and other voices that called out from behind gunsights and badges. *It's over,* he breathed. *It's finally over.* "Keep your hands where I can see them and get down on your knees!"

"All units, standby," Wiley's voice echoed over a thousand radios. "Lima Six Niner, this is Lima Six Zero. Secure your weapon and stand down."

Confused, Danny halted his advance a dozen paces from his target, but he did not lower his rifle. There he was: Thomas J. Phillips, the infamous Constitutional Killer himself. Unarmed, outnumbered, and immobilized. His face was clear. There was no mistaking the killer's identity. This was not a trick. The word 'suspect' really did not apply. There was no doubt - not for Danny, not for anyone, that this was the man who had brought him and the nation so much grief.

"Six Zero," Danny queried his radio. *That* is *Father's radio handle. What's the deal?* "Send your traffic."

"Six Niner," Wiley called back, "we have eyes on and the scene is secure. You are ordered to stand down and await updated information."

Wakefield shook his head in disbelief. *Every cop in the world is here,* Danny wondered. *What the Hell is Wiley up to?* "I have visual confirmation of the target as our suspect. Request clarification of instruction."

"I'm sorry Danny," Jonas' voice answered plainly, "Elbee is dead."

CHAPTER 30

IF YOU COMBINED enough light, the colors eventually washed each other out and the world became white. And if you exposed a human mind to enough white, that mind eventually treated it like a void and tried to fill it with something. A freshly painted wall begged for graffiti. A blank page elicited stories to be written. A new canvas demanded to be painted.

Red and blue and white lights bled into a blinding swirl that filled Danny's sight with a white curtain. And against that hazy background, his mind conjured an image: Sandra. Her head rested on a white fluffy pillow. Her blonde hair lazily swept back just enough to expose her still sleepy smile. Her soft skin glowed in morning's delight as she gently reached for him through filtered sunlight.

The light grew brighter and brighter until it burned Danny's eyes. Then it grew brighter still, until it washed the vision of Sandra out with cruel, white-hot pain. And then the light faded through red-grays into the black of night, the cold of winter's air, and the sight of a killer surrounded by policemen.

In the midst of all of the chaos and confusion, all of the people and parts that tried to synchronize with each other even while they moved about, Phillips sensed a change in the agent who had chased him. It was something subtle - a shift in his body language, perhaps, or the expression on his face. T.J. knew in his heart that his race was run. His time was up. *God, if today is my day, let me die worthy.*

With his hands already outstretched and half-raised in surrender, Phillips became a whirlwind. He backhanded the nearest officer across the carbine, followed the move with a left elbow to the cop's jaw, then spun under the gun and came out of the turn shooting.

The nearby officers all went down. Phillips slid across one of the cars' hood and took off running across the Arlington Memorial Bridge. Every step came faster than the one before it as he poured all of his strength into a vain hope of escape.

Danny snapped out of his moment of shock. He steeled his jaw and thew himself into the night. With every step, he drank from a fountain of fury that sprang up from somewhere inside himself.

Across the nation and around the world, people sat in rapt attention as they watched the Constitutional Killer flee from authorities once more. This time, though, they were treated to a new sight. A lone warrior chased after the killer. At first glance they looked to be equally matched. Both men carried scary looking guns as they ran. Both men were obviously motivated - even, it was argued by some, moved by the same love of their country.

And so the nightly news feed carried the main event, in real time and high definition color suitable for screens both large and small. Killer vs. Cop. The Revolution vs. The Republic. Black vs. White. At least, that was what the media commentators told their audience. And the whole world watched.

It was the gasp heard round the world.

In a display of raw black athleticism, the lead runner opened the distance between himself and his white pursuer as he made his way across the historical bridge and opened the distance between himself and his would-be captors like a running back peeling away from his tackles as he sped toward the end zone. Rooms everywhere were filled equally with frustrated screams and delighted cheers as fans watched the game.

Danny's legs screamed as they pushed against the pavement. His thighs threatened to rip the seams in his pants as his muscles drove harder and harder. Phillips was getting away. Again. Danny's chest pounded. Each beat of is heart was a thunderclap. His Marine training overrode his body.

The thought that Elbee's killer might once more escape tore at the edge of his mind. Danny's rifle married his shoulder. He piled rage after rage into each Herculean step. He sighted in on the murderer. A shot rang out; asphalt exploded just short of the target. Faces flashed across his vision and cried out in voices that hung in his ears with maddening echoes. Jenkins. Brown. Yvette - their mockery and constant jibes tormented him. A second shot struck Phillips in the shoulder and spun him around as he fell to his knees. Evans. Rogers. Ramierez. Biltmore. Dagenhart. Jefferson. Shibaaz. Elbee. They all demanded justice from beyond the grave.

Wakefield exhaled and smoothly pressed the trigger again. Adrenaline and focused rage blinded him to the rifle's recoil as another massive round struck Phillips squarely in the chest. His body fell backward and slumped in a half-sitting position against the wall. His arms splayed out and the gun fell from his hand. A last few spasms made his lip and torso twitch. Dark red blood poured from the black man's gaping wounds and flowed freely across the white marble like a blood sacrifice to some insatiable pagan god.

CHAPTER 31

SILVERY GRAY CLOUDS covered the sky over Washington like a blanket. A haze hung in misty, frozen droplets that could not decide whether they were snow, rain or fog. The atmosphere was still, as if the air itself could not be bothered to muster up the slightest breeze.

Special Agent Wakefield stood before a field of sleeping grass. In between patches of snow that lingered here and there, smooth marble markers stood upright. The fallen did not rest. They laid in perfect rank and file - waiting, watching, asking those who were given with another day if they deserved such a gift.

Danny stared at the newest white stone perched at the head of the newest grave. Sunglasses hid his bloodshot eyes. A lambswool scarf in Irish tartan almost kept the stinging cold off of his neck. His black suit and trench coat did nothing to insulate him from either the chilly weather or the cruel world as he searched the engraved letters for the answer to that very question.

"It was a lovely service," Jonas Wiley offered from behind Danny's right shoulder.

"Yeah, it was." Danny sniffed drily against the frozen air. "Nice of them to put her here."

"Elbee's family seemed like nice folks."

Danny thought back on the grieving family who lined the gravesite earlier and nodded. "They said that you helped cut through some of the red tape. Got this done."

Jonas' tan trench coat shuffled with a dismissive shrug. "Aye-Dee Flowers and I talked about it over the weekend, then I reached out to some people I know and made some phone calls."

"Thanks for that."

"She deserved it."

Danny choked back his initial reply and shook his head. Then he found his voice again. "She deserved better."

"Speaking of things people don't deserve," Jonas placed the stem of his unlit pipe into his mouth and bit down. "You know you're not supposed to shoot a fleeing felon, right? Oh, don't even start with me, son. Not today. That's another thing I talked to Flowers about. Reminded her the guy was armed, that he was a threat to public safety. Mentioned that you were probably *non compos mentis* anyway due to the news of your partner being killed by the suspect." He patted the younger man on the shoulder. "Plus, I reminded her that it was more than a bit hypocritical to try to punish you for not shooting the guy, then again when you actually *did*. Consider this your formal counseling. Case closed."

"Thanks," Wakefield sniffed. A part of him understood that Wiley did his best - for both

Danny's career and his spirits. And that part of him appreciated the effort, even though it paled in comparison to the parts that were too raw with pain to be consoled or uplifted.

The older man gave Danny's shoulder another pair of pats. "*Axios*," he offered. "It means 'deserving' in Greek. It's also a proclamation. When Greek Orthodox clergymen are ordained, they are presented to the people of their parish, who shout *Axios!*, 'You are worthy!' to show their support to the candidate."

As Dr. Wiley explained, Wakefield watched volunteers move about the grounds. They pushed carts along the national cemetery's pathways, each laden with evergreen wreaths. Silently, somberly, the workers laid a wreath on each grave. The holiday halos leaned up against each headstone, bright green rings with blood red bows that brought a subtle bit of Christmas spirit to a sacred resting ground.

"You know, Danny boy, Elbee took the same oath that you and I did. The same one that Phillips and everyone he targeted did. And she was a good cop. But she was a better person." That remark drew Wakefield's attention away from his partner's grave. "You knew her better than I did, so toss it if I'm off target here, but it seems to me that it wasn't some slavish adherence to a grand idea that drove her. It was her dedication to people. Elbee didn't try to change the world, Danny. She just tried to help the people around her a little bit. And in this time we live in, where it seems like everybody is just looking out for themselves, maybe that selfishness, that service to others, is what made her so special. Maybe that's what made her sacrifice so worthy."

"She shouldn't've even been there." Tears welled up in Wakefield's eyes behind darkened glasses. His lip quivered. "I'm the one who arranged for her to be there. She didn't even want to go. She was on her way to New Jersey. If I hadn't convinced her to help..." He sniffed. "She's dead because of me."

"She's dead because somebody tried to kill President Fulbright," Jonas corrected him. "And she died saving him. And a lot more people, too. I saw the video, Danny. She wheeled the chair with the IED out of the room before it blew. The White House is built like a fortress, son. Inside and out. That bathroom contained enough of the blast that the damage was minimized. You put her into play, son, and in the process she saved a lot of lives."

"Yeah, by accident."

"Maybe," Jonas hedged, "maybe not. Doesn't matter. Even if it was by accident, she did good. And even though it's not everything we all wanted, at the end of the day, you did, too." Dr. Wiley pulled a piece of folded leather out of his pocket and handed it to Wakefield. You got the job done."

Danny opened the black bifold to see his badge. *I got the job done,* his thoughts returned to the casket in the ground, *but at too high a price.* "*Axios,*" he repeated. *You were worthy, Elbee. I'm not sure I am.*

"Did you get to spend some time with the family?"

"Just a few minutes to share my condolences."

"Might wanna think about taking the time," Wiley advised. "And for now, keep that part of the story about her coming up to them to yourself. You have to carry that, but there's no sense adding to their grief." Jonas looked at the sea of fallen comrades before him. "History is paved with the sacrifices of those who came before us. The living owe the dead a debt. We owe it to them to live. It's alright to grieve, Danny boy. When we lose someone we care about, it should hurt. It's only natural. But you can honor her by taking a minute to appreciate what she lived for. Celebrate who and what she loved." Danny's mentor pointed out to the memorialized host who stood at immortal attention all around them. "All of them. Our hollowed dead. That's the only way that we can be worthy of their sacrifice."

A fresh wave of emotion washed over Wakefield. The weight of Wiley's wise words and the challenge that they presented almost brought Danny to his knees. But as he stood and gazed upon generation after generation who paid so high a price for the promise of a better tomorrow, Danny heard a chorus echo across time.

Axios! Such a supreme sacrifice as that which they paid had to be sufficient, for the nation and for himself.

Axios! The hollowed dead demanded to be heard by those they left behind.

Axios! He would carry and honor the memory of the men and women - those who were familiar and strangers alike - who made his tomorrows possible. Forever.

Danny closed his burning eyes. *Eternal Father,* he silently prayed, *may Your angels speed her to everlasting peace. And may Your Grace fall upon us, though we are unworthy. Do not let the cause of liberty die simply because her champions are mere men.*

As he opened his eyes and turned to leave, Danny saw the great flag at the cemetery's heart stir just a little under the most faint of breezes. The sadness of loss still hung on his shoulders, but it was a burden he could carry into the future. One step at a time, he walked into a future that was paid for with the greatest of loves. And somewhere along the path, he swore he heard a familiar voice whisper, *Axios.*

EPILOGUE

"WHY AM I HERE?"

"I would have thought that was obvious, Mr. Coffield. Your Icarus program is of great importance to this office."

"I understand that," the spectacled technician replied, "but why am I *here*? I was only at the Hoover building for a few days."

Garrett Ambercrombie Lehman, confirmed just two days ago as the new Secretary of Homeland Security, gestured to the tech's workspace. "You don't like your new office?"

'Office' was an understatement. In his years working for DARPA and the NRO, Coffield had grown accustomed to working in plain, government-issued cubicles. For years, he quietly dreamed that he might one day have an office to call his own.

He never imagined that he would have a 1200 square foot building all to himself.

The hollow steel structure was dimmed to near-blackness on the inside. A single glass and steel workstation sat under a pool of subdued light cast by colored LEDs installed in the rafters. The idea was that his eyes would not grow fatigued from the massive multiscreen desktop that wrapped around his high-backed chair. A few feet away, on the blind side of the main monitor, a touchscreen desk that Coffield knew cost as much as a new car slept, waiting for him to design his next prototype or deliver his next brief. The space just inside the overhead door was completely cleared to accommodate the sedan which drove them from the airfield.

"When you said that my new office came with a parking space," Michael laughed, "I had no idea I'd be parking *in* my office."

"All in the name of security, son." Lehman gestured widely to take in the whole interior. "Doesn't look like much on the outside, but it's completely shielded. During the Cold War, this was a remote telemetry station for tracking missiles."

"In case the launch sites got hit," Coffield nodded his understanding. "So, it'd have to be Eee-Em-Pee and Are-Eff resistant." He looked at the cables that ran into and out of junction boxes against one of the long, dark gray walls. Michael pointed to a set of lines that sprang from the concrete slab foundation, "Hardline connections to all of the Dee-oh-Dee and En-Ess-Aye networks," then to another line that ran up to a connection in the ceiling, "satellite uplink." He nodded. "I should be able to run Icarus from here. But you never answered my question. Why not keep me in D.C?"

Secretary Lehman put his hands on his hips. While he was not obese, he clearly never missed a meal. "A more remote location keeps you away from prying eyes and possible security threats."

I wonder if it also makes me easier to snuff out if you need to cover your own ass, Coffield could not help but wonder. "Yessir."

"Secretary James assured me that relocation wasn't a problem."

"No, sir. Not a problem at all. It's just, well, I was under the impression that I'd be working for Dee-oh-Dee. Not that it matters, sir."

"You're still getting paid by the Army," Lehman clarified, "but you'll take your tasking from my office. Specifically, from me. Your chain-of-command starts and ends at my desk. You'll have no staff under you, no other authorities over you," the Secretary cast a meaningful look at his newest minion, "and no social interactions. With anyone. So long as you're here."

One of the few things that anyone said to him before Michael got on a private plane out of Washington with the Secretary was, *Your new promotion includes isolation pay.* Coffield had always been a social outcast. He was the class nerd growing up in school; his wife left him years ago because she thought he was more interested in planes and circuits than being a husband; even the supergeeks at NRO made no effort to include him in their circles. *If I'm gonna be alone anyway,* he figured, *I might as well get paid for it.* "That's not a problem, sir."

"See that it isn't." Lehman consulted the Rolex on his wrist. "I've got appointments to keep back in Washington. Unless you've got any questions, best get to it."

Coffield shook his head as he settled into his new chair. "What're your orders, Sir?"

Secretary Lehman slowly paced next to the drone king. "There are threats out there that we just can't afford to be blind to." He pursed his lips and shook his head. "Not anymore. We need a singular asset, one brain with a thousand eyes, all looking out for us. Watching what we want to see."

"And what is that, exactly?"

"Everything." The head of Homeland Security laced his fingers together. "Anything. From bases and battlefields to homes and offices. Auto traffic and cellular traffic. Nigerian uprisings, Russian officials, and even domestic operatives working against us right here in the States. We need to be able to track ships crossing the ocean, trucks moving weapons through the desert, or find a single face in any mall or bazaar on Earth. Armies. Insurgents. Terrorists. Lone wolves. Criminals, Anyone or anything that might be a threat. A source that can act discretely, without leaks or contamination from other parties compromising it. And if time-sensitive action is required, a compressed kill chain so that we can sort it out."

"I'm here for you and the mission, Sir," Michael steepled his fingertips under his chin. "But I don't want to wast time by duplicating effort, so I have to ask: isn't that what the whole intelligence community is for?"

"Don't worry about duplicating effort," Lehman assured him. "The agencies can sometimes be cumbersome. Different masters, different jurisdictions, different resources…" his eyes grew more accusing, "different agendas. You're free to access the community as a source for information, but you're an independent program with a separate mission. We need to eliminate the red tape. We need a one stop shop for answers and actions."

"Yessir." Coffield was more than a little overwhelmed by the daunting task. And it showed. "But, one guy? For all of Homeland Security?"

"One guy," the Secretary held up a single pre-diabetic digit, "for *us*. Not the Department."

"And who exactly is 'us?'"

"For now, me. That's all you need to know."

Startup screens cycled through status updates as various information systems came online around Coffield's workstation. The technician had just been given a career boost, a cozy salary, and the elimination of all of the bureaucracy and office politics that made government work so mind numbingly painful. It was the opportunity to see his brainchild come to its full fruition, the perfect work center, and an important mission for an engaging customer.

Michael dared not pinch himself, lest it all be a dream. "Roger that, Sir. I'll put my birds in the air and await specific tasking."

"You'll have it." He turned to the reinforced and heavily monitored personnel door. "That's it, then. Submit your budget through Special Projects.""

"As you wish." Michael logged into his command suite and fired up the satellite. *Wake up, little birdie,* he smiled. *Let's go find who's up to something.*

Recommended Playlist

I find music in everything. It is my escape, my inspiration, and when words fail me, my voice. The following songs capture the mood within some of the various scenes in this book. Think of them as a soundtrack to enhance your reading experience.

"X Gon Give it to Ya" - DMX. *The Best of DMX.*

"Rebel Yell" - Billy Idol. *Billy Idol - Greatest Hits.*

"Power of Consequence" - Immediate Music. *Gates of Valhalla.*

"Angel" - Sinead O'Conner. *Bones (Original Television Soundtrack).*

"Oil Rig" - Hans Zimmer. *Man of Steel (Original Motion Picture Soundtrack).*

"Does She Love That Man" - Breathe. *Peace of Mind.*

"When We Dance" - Tony Guerro. *Ballads.*

"They Don't Care About Us" - Michael Jackson. *Michael Jackson's This is It (The Music That Inspired the Movie).*

"The Burden of War" - Immediate Music. *Gates of Valhalla.*

"Gravity" - Sarah Bareilles. *Little Voice.*

"Another Way to Die" - Jack White & Alicia Keys. *007: Quantum of Solace (Original Motion Picture Soundtrack).*

"Nobody Praying for Me" - Seether. *Isolate and Medicate.*

"Mad World" - Seal. *The Passion: New Orleans (Original Television Soundtrack.*

"I Don't Care Anymore" - Tweaker. *Call the Time Eternity.*

"History of the Greeks" - Junkie XL. *300: Rise of an Empire (Original Motion Picture Soundtrack).*

"Greeks are Winning" - Junkie XL. *300: Rise of an Empire (Original Motion Picture Soundtrack.)*

"Elegy" - Lisa Gerrard & Patrick Cassidy. *Immortal Memory.*

- DEJS

ABOUT THE AUTHOR…

DARYL E.J. SIMMONS is a distinguished former naval intelligence analyst and decorated veteran whose career includes multiple combat deployments embedded with Special Operations elements as well as serving as an advisor to senior executive leaders. Mr. Simmons has hunted terrorists and drug traffickers on five continents. He is an esteemed expert on international relations. He has served as the policy advisor to American and Allied leaders on matters of global security, counterterrorism, counternarcotics, and counter-human trafficking.

A graduate of the University of Tulsa (B.A. Philosophy, *cum laude*, with a minor in Psychology), this 5th degree black belt (Hapkido) serves as a trainer and consultant for various agencies and organizations. When he is not writing, Mr. Simmons counsels with other vets in his personally adopted crusade to reduce the number of veteran suicides from 22 per day to zero.

You can read more from Daryl on his blog, www.SmartestGuy.me

Made in the USA
Columbia, SC
20 August 2017